KT-387-253

THE TWISTROSE KEY

WINTERWOODS
SYLVEROS
Observatory
Sylver Lake
Observatory Hill
Burning Bird
Red Cat
Falcon Road
Teodor's House
Dr. Kott's House
CLAW
WISHBOXES
Sylver Bridge
WINDERSIDE BY THE LAKE
Great Square
Lake Road
HEARTWORTH
Main Road
Machine Vault
Waffleheart
BERGROOST
FIDDLEBRICK
Winter Road
Eversnow Square
WARRENS
Sylver River
Caravan Road
Paw Bridge
Ursa Minor's Cottage
Rimedeer Stables
PAWFIELDS
Hall of Winter
Sylver Fang
WINTERWOODS

THE TWISTROSE KEY

TONE ALMHJELL

ILLUSTRATED BY
IAN SCHOENHERR

LITTLE, BROWN BOOKS FOR YOUNG READERS
www.lbkids.co.uk

LITTLE, BROWN BOOKS FOR YOUNG READERS

First published in the United States in 2013 by Dial Books for Young Readers,
a division of the Penguin Group
First published in Great Britain in 2013 by Little, Brown Books
for Young Readers

Text copyright © 2013 by Tone Almhjell
Illustrations copyright © 2013 by Ian Schoenherr
"The Margrave's Song" lyrics copyright © 2013 by Tone Almhjell
"The Margrave's Song" music copyright © 2013 by Eivind Almhjell

The moral right of Tone Almhjell and Ian Schoenherr to be identified
as author and illustrator respectively has been asserted.

*All characters and events in this publication, other than those
clearly in the public domain, are fictitious and any resemblance
to real persons, living or dead, is purely coincidental.*

All rights reserved.
No part of this publication may be reproduced, stored in a
retrieval system, or transmitted, in any form or by any means, without
the prior permission in writing of the publisher, nor be otherwise circulated
in any form of binding or cover other than that in which it is published
and without a similar condition including this condition being
imposed on the subsequent purchaser.

A CIP catalogue record for this book
is available from the British Library.

ISBN 978-0-349-00166-1

Printed and bound in Great Britain by
Clays Ltd, St Ives plc

Papers used by LBYR are from well-managed forests
and other responsible sources.

MIX
Paper from
responsible sources
FSC
www.fsc.org FSC® C104740

Little, Brown Books for Young Readers
An imprint of
Little, Brown Book Group
100 Victoria Embankment
London EC4Y 0DY

An Hachette UK Company
www.hachette.co.uk

www.lbkids.co.uk

For my beloved sister, Line

With blood on her thorns she must creep through the wall.
When the last hope is lost, a Twistrose is called.

CHAPTER ONE

The grave that Lin had made for her friend could not be touched by wind. Above, the dripping rose-bush flailed, scratching its thorns at the wall. But the whittled cross of twigs and string did not so much as shiver. Instead a lick of rime had crept up to cover the wood with white. Later, Lin Rosenquist would remember this as a sign, the first.

Perhaps she might have caught it then, if she hadn't been too busy watching the storm. It came from the north and roared up the river, wrenching through the cobbled streets of Oldtown, pulling dusk down between the wooden houses in the early afternoon. Lin stood by Mrs. Ichalar's flower bed, with her hand in her pocket, grinning to herself. At last, a storm that showed some promise! She crouched down to whisper to the cross, "See you later, little one."

The front door groaned when she opened it. The house her parents rented from Mrs. Ichalar leaned out over the river, supported by tarred poles on one side. Like the other narrow houses crammed together along the bank, the whole building had been warped by centuries in the bitter mist. It smelled crooked, too. Whiffs of rotten wood and chemicals drifted from floor to floor to hide behind the curtains.

Lin hung her coat next to the grandfather clock in the hallway. A husky recording of gnarled voices and violins seeped out from the kitchen. Her mother was working in there.

"Lindelin, is that you at last?" The music stopped and Anne Rosenquist appeared in the doorway. At the sight of Lin's drenched coat, her face clouded over with concern. "Have you been standing by the rosebush again? In this weather?"

"I'm not that wet," Lin lied as she squelched out of her boots. "I just need to go upstairs and . . ."

"Don't go up just yet," her mother said quickly. "I've made rice pudding, your favourite."

Dessert before dinner. That was ominous.

Lin followed her into the kitchen that also doubled as a study. Her mother collected old songs that would otherwise have died with the last people who knew them. In August, she had unexpectedly been offered a teaching position at the university. It meant that she could pass them on, all those theories on broken knights and bergfolk. But it also meant that the Rosenquists had to leave Summerhill, the farm where Lin had lived for all her eleven years, where the fields smelled of freshly turned soil and the mountains hugged the stars between their peaks.

"What a nasty squall." Her mother shoved aside some notebooks to make room for the fluffy pudding and raspberry sauce. The rice cream recipe was ancient, too, a Summerhill tradition with chopped sugared almonds sprinkled on top. "There could be snow at the end of it, though," her mother added. "Wouldn't you like that?"

Lin did like snow, though she wasn't sure what good it would do here. At home, she and her best friend, Niklas, would have snowball fights until their fingers were numb and blue, and they would have to warm them on Grandma Alma's giant cups of hot chocolate. And when dusk crept down the mountain slopes, they would make snow lights, little igloos with candles inside, that sent flickering beams up the frozen stream. "The better to ward off the enemy," Niklas would laugh, and Lin would laugh as well, scanning the forest edge for eyes.

"I'm afraid there'll be no snow for you just yet, Miss Rosenquist." Her father came sauntering into the kitchen, sat down at the table, and dug the serving spoon into the rice cream. "It will rain for another week at least."

"Surely not a whole week," her mother said, but of course she knew better. Harald Rosenquist owned a rain gauge, four thermometres, and no less than three barometres in well-polished frames. He kept temperature records and checked the forecast several times a day. So if he said it would rain for another week, it would.

"I heard one of your songs today, Lin," her mother said, and hummed brightly as she heaped pudding into a bowl.

Lin knew the tune, it was the one with the hair. She was named for her mother's greatest discovery, the ballads of fair Lindelin, who grew enchanted apples, and rescued princes, and spun her locks into gold. *My daughter deserves to be the hero of a song,* her mother liked to say. But her mother didn't have to spend the first weeks at a new school explaining why her name was so strange. Picking up her spoon, Lin said, "It's not exactly my song, Mum. And my hair is the opposite of gold."

"Remember what I told you about reading songs? Gold doesn't always mean gold." Her mother's mouth twitched into a smile. "Your father and I have some exciting news to share. My class is full for next term already. They want me to stay, at least until next summer." She saw Lin's face and amended it to, "*Only* until next summer. Another year at the most."

Another year in Mrs. Ichalar's skeleton-legged house. Lin put her spoon down. It clattered against the table.

After a brief silence, her father cleared his throat. "You know what? I think it's time for a riddle." It was their little ritual, one Lin used to love when she was younger. Every night, over tea and sweet buns in the Morello House kitchen, she would decipher badly worded poems and pore over treasure maps or quizzes until she came up with the right answer. "Are you ready?" He winked at her. "How do you spell deadly mousetrap with only three letters?"

"Harald!" Her mother's face went white. "Don't . . ."

"What? It's too easy?"

Lin's hand went to the left pocket of her cardigan. With one half of his head filled with novel writing and the other half with pudding, her father had forgotten about Rufus. But she didn't feel like talking about it, so she answered, "C—A—T."

"Perfect," her father laughed. "One point to Miss Rosenquist!"

"If you'd like, we could go to the museum again on Saturday," her mother said. "Or the library? Or the cathedral? And I could make you peppernut cookies! They're your favourite, right? You know, they match your . . ."

"My eyes, I know." Lin pushed her chair back. "Actually, I am soaked through. I'll go change." Her parents began to speak in soft voices as soon as she left the room.

On her way up the stairs, she skipped the squeaky steps. She liked to move silently in this house, so the grandfather clocks and hulking furniture wouldn't hear her coming. The bureau on the second-floor landing seemed especially malevolent. Lin always stopped in front of it, to prove she wasn't scared. Her mother had noticed and dressed it up with a lace runner and two of Lin's favourite photos.

The first photo, Summerhill viewed from the mountains. It seemed so small from afar, just a patchwork of meadows and potato fields stitched around a barn, an ancient elm tree, and the two houses. Niklas lived with his grandmother and uncle in the long, white main house with many shadowy rooms in a row, too many for such a small family, Grandma Alma always said. Therefore she had invited the Rosenquists to live in the red house in the morello garden, so Anne could work on her song collection, and Harald could work on his novels, and Lin could climb straight from her bedroom window into the sweet cherry tree, to work on her pit spitting with Niklas.

The second photo, Lin and her father sitting on the slopes of Buttertop. He was smiling, completely unaware that he was being tricked, and Lin was frowning, keeping both her lips and her left pocket pressed tight around her secret.

Rufus.

She had just found him when that photo was taken. He had been lying in the heather, not far from the entrance to a burrow. His left leg had been bleeding, and he was panting so hard his rust-coloured back and grey flanks trembled. A mouse pup, Lin had thought, and though she knew she should call to her father so he could put the little thing out of its misery, she had instead lifted the mouse gently and put him in her pocket. Back in her room, she had fed him bread crumbs and cheese rinds and watched his wound heal. But it hadn't taken Harald Rosenquist long to sniff out the secret.

"You do *realise*, Miss Rosenquist," he had said in his most serious lecturing tone, "this mouse is not a pet. In fact, it's not even a mouse, but a *Myodes rufocanus*, a red-back vole. It belongs in the wild, not in a child's room. You cannot possibly keep it."

In the end it was her parents who had to *realise* that Lin would not give up Rufus. They had insisted on a cage, and Lin had agreed, and even kept the cage by her bed. But Rufus had never lived there. He lived in her cardigan, her favourite blue one that Grandma Alma had knitted, where he nestled in the left pocket and chewed the tassels of the drawstring in the collar. Out in the woods, he rode on her shoulder, whiskers wide and claws dug deep. On the farm, he kept out of view from everyone except Niklas, and he had a special knack for scrambling into her sleeve two seconds before her father crossed the yard. In the city, Rufus had been her only friend, her only tie to home. He had slept curled up on her pillow, and when she scratched him, he had leaned against her fingers to say he understood.

But as the trees shed their leaves and the afternoons grew dim, Rufus had changed. He stopped sneaking off on nightly expeditions, and he no longer raided Lin's plate for cheese. Once, he had tumbled from her shoulder and fallen hard to the floor, and after that he kept to her pocket, even when they were alone. One crisp Tuesday five weeks ago, there was no brush of whiskers on her cheek in the morning. Rufus had quietly crept into his cage to sleep, and there was nothing Lin could do to wake him.

She had buried the shoe box under the rosebush because that happened to be the sole patch of uncobbled ground on the street, and she had spent so many afternoons there that her parents had taken to hovering like moons in the kitchen window. "Would you like to have someone over?" they had asked, all chipper and hopeful, as if it were that simple. "Someone from school, perhaps?"

Lin shut the door to her attic room. She went straight to her closet, which she kept so messy no one else would bother to go near it. Her trap, the paper clip on the handle, had not been sprung. Under her worn hiking trousers, she found the thing that had lured her away from Rufus's grave.

The troll-hunting casket.

She pulled the carved box out on the floor and checked the contents: A magnifying glass, to make sunbeams strong enough to cut through bark-and-sap armour. A roll of maps that she had drawn, with marks for all three precious oak trees. And a small jar of carefully gathered acorns, the only weapon that would kill a troll outright.

It had all begun with a jar like this, the one she and

Niklas had found among Grandma Alma's old fishing gear in the Summerhill loft. The faded label had said TROLL'S BANE. From that seed, the troll hunt had grown, game by delicious game, into the Summerhill woods and all the way up to the Trollheim Mountains.

Lin unscrewed the lid, letting out an acrid puff of air. It was her special concoction. Since bright sunlight turned trolls to stone, and since sunburns and nettle welts were much the same, curing the acorns in a brew of nettles and sour leaf made them even more lethal. But she didn't take any. The acorns were for Summerhill trolls, wood trolls who slept under rock and sniffed under trees. Oldtown trolls lived in sewers and slime, so the acorns would not work on them. Their bane would be different, something that could be found naturally in the area, something very rare. She just hadn't figured out what it was yet.

She riffled through the map rolls. There were six of them, all drawn after her father had sent Lin and Niklas out to add details to a map of the Summerhill woods. He had needed it as research for his novel. But ever since, Lin had created her own maps for the troll hunt, with legends for sightings and lairs. She picked out her work in progress – a map of Oldtown – and put the casket back into the wardrobe.

Her cardigan had damp stripes along the shoulders, but she pulled it back on over dry pyjamas, tied the drawstring, and climbed onto the windowsill. Lin rolled out the map, turning it so it fit her view. She had pencilled in a few potential lairs, but there were no marks for sightings, because in the three months since they had moved to the city, she had not seen a single troll. But now there was a storm, a terrific one. That always brought the enemy out, to roar back at the wind.

Lin leaned close to the window, peering through the sharp raindrops that pelted the glass.

"Come on," she whispered. "I'm ready."

At the end of the street, by the foot of the bridge, there were two flashes.

Lin sat up hard, squinting toward the red pillars. It must have been a coincidence, a bicycle light cut in half by the bridge post or reflected in a sign. But no. There it was again, two blinks in quick succession, this time in the window of the closed coffee shop across the street.

In the troll hunt, this was the fastest and easiest of signals, because it was also the most desperate: Danger. Trolls nearby.

She pressed her brow to the pane, holding her breath so it wouldn't cloud the glass. Did something stir in the violent sheets of rain, a billow of cloth, a flitting shape against the cobblestones? The third signal appeared where Lin could only see its halo. Right below her, on Mrs. Icha-lar's steps.

Lin pushed herself off the windowsill, stuck her feet in her slippers, and raced for the stairs. Summerhill was a long and expensive bus ride away, and in his last letter, Niklas had written nothing about coming here. Yet he must have, because only he knew that signal.

She hadn't reached further than the second-floor bureau when she heard the mail slot creak and clack. And as she rushed down the remaining steps, she got her first glimpse of it, a small, flat parcel, lying facedown on Mrs. Ichalar's musty doormat.

The slap of wet wind met her when she tore the door open. She looked up the street and down the street. It was deserted. "Niklas!" she called. "I know you're there!" But he was not done with his game, it seemed, because he didn't emerge from the murk. A square of wan light illuminated Rufus's grave, making it glitter. The thin layer of frost covered almost the whole flower bed now. It must be getting colder after all.

Shivering, Lin retreated into the hallway to examine the parcel. The rough paper was the colour of a broken mountainside, and bound in sodden string. She turned it over, and a chill hand caught her heart.

Niklas could not have sent her this parcel. No one could.

On the front, there was no stamp and no address. Only a single word, written not by pen or pencil, but scratched into the wet paper with the sharp tip of a knife.

"Twistrose."

CHAPTER TWO

The grandfather clocks struck the half hour, one by one and out of rhythm. The third-floor bedroom one first, the upstairs bathroom one second, and the hallway one last as always, after a grudging effort of whispers and clicks.

Lin's hands trembled as she held the parcel under the brown silk lampshade. She had thought the letters would shift in the light, that her eyes would adjust and the mistake would be corrected. Yet no matter how hard she stared at the scratched word, it did not change.

The parcel felt heavier than it looked. When she shook it, something jangly slid from side to side within. She paused to listen. In the kitchen, the violins had resumed their yammering, and from the second floor came the faint din of a TV audience that meant her father had stopped writing to call out the answers to a quiz show.

She ripped the paper and emptied the parcel into her hand.

Out tumbled two keys. One was grimy and had an orange plastic tag that said CELLAR. The other was large, as large as the length of her hand, and blackened, as if it had grown from ashes and dirt. Its head was fashioned as a petal, and the stem was that of a rose, with three curved, sharp thorns. Engraved across the petal, there it was again: TWISTROSE.

In the troll hunt, they always used code names. For years Niklas had been Summerknight and Lin had been Nettle, because of her special nettle brew. But for the Oldtown hunt, she had taken a new one, inspired by the rosebush over Rufus's grave.

One day, she had noticed how it hooked its thorns into the paint of the facade, stretching its branches toward the sky. It reminded her of the junipers that clung to the Trollheim Mountains with their twisted roots; they never let go no matter how cruel the wind blew. And that's when she had thought of it – the perfect code name for a troll hunter who was exiled for the moment, but not forever: Twistrose.

Lin had wanted to wait till their next game to share it with Niklas, so she hadn't said a thing about it. Not to Niklas, not to anyone.

"So, Miss Rosenquist, what have you got there?"

Lin whipped around, shoving both the folded paper and the keys in her pockets. How very like her father to know about the squeaky steps. He had his quizzy face on, the lifted-chin one he wore when his curiosity had set in, and she knew she wouldn't get away with lying. "A parcel," she said. "But it's for me."

He tilted his head. "From a friend?"

Which was of course an excellent question. With the troll-hunter signal, whoever had delivered the parcel had made sure Lin would be the one to find it. And the name Twistrose could only mean that it was for her, and her alone. But for what purpose? Shrugging as casually as she could, Lin said, "I don't know yet."

The quizzy face softened. "A little mystery. I see. Miss Rosenquist, you may carry on." He patted the arm of her still-dripping coat before he started back up the stairs. "But if your mystery takes you out into the storm, I know I can trust you to dress for the part."

Only when she heard him shout "What is the Arctic Circle!" from the living room, dared Lin bring the keys out from hiding. Moving deeper into the hallway, she ignored her coat, because she had no intention of going outside of the house. She was going *under* it.

The cellar door at the end of the hallway had remained locked since they moved in, despite her father's attempts at wringing the key out of Mrs. Ichalar. All sorts of trouble could be brewing down there, he had argued, fires and floods and rodent invasions. Mrs. Ichalar had claimed that she couldn't find the key, and that she needed the storage space for her little hobby, now that she lived in a retirement home. "What sort of hobby?" her father had asked, but for once, his questions got him nowhere. Lin smiled. If Harald Rosenquist knew that his daughter's "little mystery" involved the cellar key, there would be no stopping him. But he didn't know.

She turned the cellar key in its lock and opened the door slowly. Dank air oozed up from below, thick with rot and chemicals. All she could make out was a dented flashlight on the wall, and three tapering steps dissolving into black. She picked the flashlight off its peg, turned it on, and closed the door behind her, muffling the violins.

Below, she could hear the river mumbling by, gusting chilly air up the stairwell. The draft was so cold that Lin's breath made frost clouds. With a shudder she followed the dust-speckled beam down the stairs. At the landing, the light fell on an animal skull on the banister. It had cracked teeth and large, tilted eye sockets. Lin hesitated for a moment. What sort of old lady would nail skulls to her banisters? But she pressed on, and when she reached the final step and learned the truth about their landlady's "little hobby", it all made sense.

She was watched by a hundred eyes.

Among the usual clutter of boxes and crates, there were animals everywhere. Cats curled up on barrels, ferrets peeking out between mildewed coats, and falcons strung up under the crossbeams of the ceiling. They were all positioned to glower at Lin with their glass bead eyes, and they were all dead.

Mrs. Ichalar was a taxidermist.

The old woman's workbench stood right next to the stairs, cluttered with hooks and scoops and bone cutters, and several bottles of a clear liquid that might explain the chemical smell. Lin took a deep, icy breath, annoyed at how hard she was shivering. A troll hunter did not back away at a little creepiness! Taxidermied animals looked grisly, but they couldn't hurt her. "Calm down," she whispered to herself. "And bring your brain to the party!" That's what her father always said if she got impatient with a riddle, and he was right. She would not solve the mystery if she didn't keep her head clear.

With both hands on the flashlight, she looked again, more carefully, letting the beam rove around the room. There had to be a reason why the two keys had arrived together. One to unlock the cellar door, and the other . . .

The flashlight beam found the back of the cellar. It was overgrown with pale, wet, ghostly roots. They had broken through near the ceiling and crawled down the wall in a tangled mass, crumbling the mortar and splitting the bricks. In the centre of the wall, the roots shied away to make an open circle, and in that naked patch, two fissures met and formed an oddly shaped crack. Lin could swear it resembled a keyhole.

She had of course expected to find the keyhole in a door, or a cupboard, or a painted chest. But gold didn't always mean gold. At least the strange crack deserved a closer look. She crossed the rough floorboards, where the river showed through between the gaps. All the boxes that had been stacked in the back lay toppled on the floor, pushed away by the roots. Lin shoved them aside so she could see the entire shrub.

The roots were not pale and wet after all, they were coated in rime. Lin frowned up at the holes, to where the roots had broken through the bricks. If her mapping skills did not deceive her, this wall lay directly beneath the front door—and the rosebush outside. For the first time that evening, it occurred to Lin to wonder why Mrs. Ichalar's flower bed was covered with frost.

The cold seemed to radiate from the bare, circular patch. Lin leaned forward to study it. Yes. Her first impression had been right: The oddly shaped crack definitely looked like a large, ragged keyhole. One point to Miss Rosenquist! She lifted the Twistrose key for measure.

The roots stirred.

Lin gave a cry and lurched backward, stumbling over a crate, pricking her finger on the thorns of the key. A single bead of blood pushed out. She sucked at it, staring hard at the wall. Roots couldn't stir, could they? It may have seemed like they had reached for her, but there had to be some other explanation. Maybe the storm? Maybe it rattled the rosebush hard enough for the tremors to reach all the way below ground? She got to her feet and raised the key again, waving it back and forth in front of the shrub from a safe distance. Nothing.

She cast a look behind her, toward the mounted animals and the banister with its sad skull. If she wanted, she could walk back up the stairs. She could tell her father about the cellar key and Mrs. Ichalar's hobby and the curious rose infestation. But then the key would be confiscated and the mystery – the whole adventure – would be over.

A faint snatch of music murmured in her ear. It must have come from the kitchen above, except it wasn't the usual hoarse violins, but a sweet, soft humming that made her think of Summerhill, and deep woods, and secret maps. Lin's throat clenched. She did not want the adventure to end, not yet. Before she had time to reconsider, she pressed her lips together, stepped forward, and thrust the Twistrose key into the wall.

It fit perfectly in the crack. As she turned it, there was no click, but she felt something slide into place in there. No. Dislocate was a better word, like something had been pried apart that was never meant to be separated.

Freezing air poured against her fingers, along with a flicker of blue, shimmering light.

Whatever lay on the other side of this wall, it was not the riverbank.

Fear came crashing into her body with painful thumps. She wanted to turn and run, but all of a sudden, the spindly roots shot out and grasped her, winding hard around her arms, wresting the flashlight from her hand. The bricks split apart with a tremendous crack. A torrent of icy air rushed out to meet her. The roots tightened, pulling her toward the opening, but Lin was too astounded by the sight beyond the wall to put up much of a fight.

There was no cellar, and no riverbank, either. Instead she looked out on a desolate, frozen mountain valley, where winter twilight painted the snow blue, and stern peaks rose into the sky. A creature crouched in the snow before her, facing away, but so close that she could smell it: a musky scent. Now it turned toward her. Lin watched helplessly as an elongated face came into view. Two needlelike teeth glinted in its mouth, and a pair of liquid, black eyes stared back at her.

Then the creature darted forward. With a fast, clawed grip it pulled Lin free of the roots and into its pungent embrace.

CHAPTER THREE

The wind died down, and a creaking cold took its place. Lin's face was buried in thick, silky fur. She couldn't move, for the creature was strong, and it squeezed her so tight that her slippers dangled in the air. Nevertheless, Lin felt the panic that had gripped her flowing out of her limbs, breath by breath. It was the smell, so strange, and yet so very familiar. Now that she was wrapped in it, she found that the musk was laced with other scents: nutmeg and sweet hay and woodsmoke. But she flinched again when the creature suddenly spoke.

"You're here," it breathed into her cardigan, sounding half-choked. "I was beginning to fear you weren't coming!"

The embrace unravelled and Lin was dropped into knee-deep snow. She tried to step back, but the creature grabbed her shoulders. It was a rodent, five feet tall, with whiskers that brushed against her cheeks. The creature studied her so intently, it felt like she was about to plunge into its inky eyes. They sat high up on a tapering face that ended in a brown snout.

It was a face she had seen a thousand times.

Rufus.

Apart from the size and the long, green scarf around his neck, it looked exactly like him: the rusty stripe along the back and the soft, grey flanks; the round ears, so thin and delicate the twilight shone through them. A gigantic redback vole.

With trembling hands Lin reached up and touched the scruff under his chin. It was dense and glossy, the coat of a young, healthy animal. She buried her fingers deep, and he leaned gently against her hand.

"Little one?" she whispered.

"Hardly," he replied, drawing his cleft upper lip outward so it revealed the long front teeth in a smile. "I'm as tall as you now. Taller, if you count this!" He swished his tail forward in a dashing arch and held it up for Lin to see. It was as thick as her wrist.

"You should be glad I still have this," Rufus continued. "I've been waiting for hours. Do you have any idea how *long* that is here? I could have frozen my tail . . ."

Lin interrupted him with another hug. She felt so light-headed her thoughts were all jumbled. "Rufus! How? I mean, you're so . . . You're so . . ."

"Handsome?" He grinned. "Eloquent? Alive?"

"Yes!" Lin laughed. "All of those! And where . . . ?" She turned in a circle. There was nothing left of the wind but a wavy ridge in the snow. Rufus's footprints led to the entrance of a small burrow, where the last embers of a campfire were winking out next to a little backpack. Lin's own footprints appeared out of nowhere, and the wall and the grasping roots were gone. "Where's Mrs. Ichalar's cellar?"

"Gone, and good riddance. I went down there once, you know. A cellar full of skinned and mounted animals! No wonder the place smells cruel!" Quickly, Rufus got down on all fours and kicked a flurry of snow over the sputtering campfire. Then he grabbed his backpack and rose up on his hind legs. "Come on. I cannot wait to show you this."

He guided her up a short slope, appearing perfectly comfortable to be walking on two legs. Lin trudged through the snow as best she could, struggling to keep her slippers on. She nearly lost her footing altogether when the crest of the slope fell away before their feet.

They were standing on the lip of a deep valley of hillocks and forest-clad slopes. Snow lay draped on the hillsides like a glittering mantle. A naked, frozen river ran along the bottom like a steel ribbon, and at the end of the ribbon twinkled the lights of a town enclosed by snow-laden trees on three sides and a lake of blue ice on the fourth.

The town was surrounded in a warm glow. Lin could make out a host of small spires, a soaring, slender tower in the middle of the town, and a white palace with a single dome. No snowy valley Lin had ever seen had boasted towers and domes like that.

Yet it was the sky that truly confounded her. Its colours were that of winter dusk, soft blue with golden, bleeding edges that told of a sunset beyond the mountains. Above the towering peaks at the end of the vale hung a most extraordinary light, streaking across the sky like a comet or a suspended shooting star. A halo of curved blades churned around its head, and its tail danced like northern lights.

Lin put her hand on Rufus's arm, quite lost for words.

"The Sylver Valley. Quite something, isn't it?" Rufus flashed his cleft smile again. "I watched the star rise from my camp. It's a rare phenomenon called the Wanderer, and there's this grand feast to celebrate it tonight. The bells tolled the third hour right before you arrived, so we need to hurry, or . . ."

In the distance sounded a long, shivering wail. Lin felt Rufus's fur rise under her fingers, and she gripped it hard. She could only think of one creature that would howl like that. "Wolves!"

"*Not* wolves." There was a new note in Rufus's voice, hushed and tense. "I've been hearing them ever since the Wanderer rose. They're somewhere deep in the mountains, but they're coming closer. And I can't help but wonder if it's got something to do with your coming here." He scanned the peaks behind them, whiskers wide. Abruptly, he pulled his backpack on and turned sharply to the right. "We have to go."

He set off along the ridge at a brisk near-run, and Lin stumbled after him. Her slippers were starting to freeze around her toes, and her pyjamas were weighed down by chunks of snow that clung to the fabric. She glanced back at the remains of the campsite. How was she supposed to go home? And what could be worse than wolves? "Rufus!" she called after him. "What do you mean, it has something to do with me?"

Rufus didn't slow down. Though he dragged his bad leg slightly, he moved fast enough for the air to sting in Lin's lungs. "I'm not sure," he said over his shoulder. "I don't know any details, because they never let me in on secrets like that. But I've seen the statues and heard the stories, so I know it's something big." He leaped smoothly over a shallow depression in the snow. Dips like that looked innocent, but Lin knew from skiing trips with her father that they sometimes hid cracks in the mountainside. If you weren't careful, you could break your leg, or worse. She slowed down to measure her jump. Rufus turned back to catch her. "Watch that. I almost fell in the last time. This is where I arrived, too. I never had a key or a fancy gate, though. One moment I was lying in the cage, listening to your breathing. The next I was standing here on this ridge."

Now Lin's throat really hurt. "I'm so sorry . . ."

Rufus gave a little shrug as he tugged her along, leading her toward a small, dark rumple in the landscape. "It wasn't so frightening, really. I felt light afterward, like a strap had loosened around my chest, and lucid, like a fog had cleared in my head. I had awakened. I didn't know what to call it then, but I had changed into a Petling."

"Pet . . . ling?" Lin panted. This fast wading through knee-deep snow wore her out quickly.

"That's right. Nearly everyone who lives here in Sylver was once the favourite pet of a human child, so we call ourselves Petlings. Except the Wilders. Their ways are a little different. You'll see for yourself when we get into town."

Lin's head spun with questions, but she was too winded to ask any more, so she just squeezed Rufus's hand to let him know she had missed him, too. Rufus gave her a sideways look, and finally eased his pace a little. "I know that face," he said. "I promise you'll have more answers soon. But we really have to get back to Sylveros before darkness falls. It's not just those howls. Teodor has been expecting us for hours, and he doesn't like waiting. Which is why I brought you here."

He let go of her hand. They had reached the dark rumple, which turned out to be a juniper thicket clinging to the ridge under a snowdrift. Lin leaned on her knees to catch her breath while Rufus searched around beneath the prickly branches.

"Ow, this stuff gets into your fur." Soon he emerged again with a coil of dark blue rope in his mouth. "I found this the last time I was here. Help me get it out."

He dug his legs in and pulled. Rodents were strong; Lin's father had taught her. It was mostly their size that had them at a disadvantage from natural enemies such as foxes, owls, and lynxes. So Lin was not surprised when Rufus didn't need her help at all. In a shower of broken twigs and juniper needles, he pulled it free: the biggest sled Lin had ever seen.

Rufus walked around the sled, whistling between his teeth. "Well, aren't you a beauty!" And it was. It had a low seat of flawless, burnished wood and cast-iron runners that curled up into extravagant spirals at both ends. The blue rope was fastened to a silvered crossbar at the front of the sled, and there was even a little lantern. Beautiful, yes, but Lin knew at once they would never be able to use it. The left runner was broken, snapped off at the front.

"Too bad," she said. "We won't make it down the hill with a runner like that."

"True." Rufus opened his backpack. "But I've come prepared. I had actually planned on coming back here anyway. I couldn't bear the thought of this wonderful thing being left to rust just because it's a little damaged. So I had this crafted."

He lifted out a piece of metal, curled into a spiral at one end, and hollow at the other end. A spare tip. "Come on, my friend." Rufus hunched down to wiggle the tip into place. "It's not as lovely as the original, but take it from an expert: any leg is better than no leg."

The spare part slid on as if it had been made to measure. Rufus gave a little cry of triumph. But his enthusiasm paled some as they hauled the sled to the edge of the hill.

"It's a little steep," he muttered, chewing the tassels on his scarf. "But it took me ages to get down from this hill on foot, and Teodor did say 'with all possible speed'. Besides, you've done this plenty of times, right?"

Lin peered down into the valley. It was true that she had done a lot of sledding, and that the slopes behind Summerhill were not for the faint of heart. But this was no slope. It was an almost sheer drop that levelled out only as it disappeared under the eaves of the forest far below. Even Niklas wouldn't be so reckless.

And yet Lin found herself climbing up behind Rufus, locking her arms around his waist, holding on to the reins. Snow creaked like fiddle bows under the runners as they hung over the lip of the cliff, but Lin wasn't afraid. She even leaned out to see better, because she had this calming notion that they wouldn't race down the hill at all, but float serenely off toward the suspended shooting star until she woke up from this strange and wonderful dream. And if not, the fall would surely do the job.

Rufus shivered in front of her, but if he was scared, he pretended not to be. "All right," he said, leaning forward. "Let's go find Teodor!"

They plunged into a wild, rattling stoop that kicked Lin's guts up into her chest. She squeezed her eyes shut and waited for the jolt to shake her awake. But it didn't. Instead the jolts kept coming. The hillside rushed at them so fast and the sled bucked so violently that it was impossible to know up from down. Spurts of snow whirled into Lin's face.

She withdrew behind Rufus and opened her eyes. A wide, blurry shadow grew before them. They were going to hit the tree line at full speed.

When the forest swallowed them, branches whipped at their backs and twigs caught in Lin's hair. Yet the sled lurched between the trunks in a series of miraculous escapes, until they slipped past a great oak tree and into a clearing in the forest.

The sled headed straight for a giant tree stump that stuck up from the snow. No, not a tree stump, but a well of dark stones, with a broken lid that had slid off to one side. There was no bucket, just a frayed rope, which dangled from the tarred crossbeam like a gallows rope. Lin bunched her fists in Rufus's fur, waiting for the crash, hoping that she wouldn't break any fingers or legs.

But right before they slammed into the well, the sled must have jumped a ramp of snow, because suddenly they were in the air. Lin lost her grip on the reins and flew off the sled. She landed face-first in a small drift that cushioned her fall. Her head rang with a weird humming, but otherwise she was unhurt.

"Rufus!" she said, getting up on her knees. "Are you all right?"

Rufus didn't answer. He was already standing upright, mouth slack and whiskers spread, turned toward the cottage in the middle of the clearing. It was no larger than the old woodshed at the bottom of the Summerhill fields, with a sagging turf roof under a white blanket.

"The Winnower," Rufus said. "But Sylver is protected. It's safe. It just can't be true!"

"What?" Lin searched the cottage for signs of danger. The timber logs glittered with rime, and so did the ramshackle porch that jutted out from the left corner. No smoke rose from the chimney, and the crude windows were dark. And yet she felt someone was in there, whispering to them.

A door grated around the corner.

Rufus turned toward her. Thin sickles of white showed at the edges of his eyes, and his voice was a broken squeak.

"Run!"

CHAPTER FOUR

Rufus threw himself down on all fours and bolted for the trees across the clearing. Creaking footsteps sounded on the porch. They were coming closer.

But Lin's legs wouldn't move. The joints seemed to have frozen, and her feet were much too cold to lift. Before she could run anywhere, she stumbled and fell. Lying flat out in the snow, she looked over her shoulder and back at the cottage.

On the porch stood a crooked and hooded shape, black against the sparkling snow. It lifted its arm. Deep within the hood there was a high-pitched crowing.

Lin wanted to get up, but all strength had abandoned her. Why couldn't she just wake up? She lowered her face into the snow.

The cold dunk didn't wake her, but it brought Lin's legs back to life. She gathered them under her and tore into a run, making her way across the clearing to Rufus, who waited for her at the edge of the woods. Under the shelter of the trees, the snow was shallower. Soon they were galloping like spooked horses, dodging branches and trunks, racing across cone scatterings and animal tracks until they struck a path.

Only then did Lin realise that one of her feet was bare. At some point during the frantic escape, she had lost a slipper, and now she was bleeding from a cut on the sole. She hobbled over to a tree stump and sat down.

Rufus doubled back to sniff her foot.

"A bad cut," he said, wrinkling his snout. "We'll get someone to fix it, but we have to get into town first. I think this is the old path to Tinklegrove. If I remember the maps correctly, the road should be just across this ridge. Can you make it?"

Lin stood up again and put her weight on the injured foot. The cut didn't smart. Rather, it felt like standing on a lump of ice. "I think so."

"Come on." Rufus offered her his arm. "Lean on me."

They left the path and headed up a rough little hill. It was slow and painful going. The mountains were hidden by a dense latticework of boughs, and only a faint blue light trickled through to twinkle in Rufus's eyes as he urged her on. Behind them, the woods were silent. No creaking snow, no snapping twigs, and most importantly: no eerie, high-pitched crowing.

"Who was that? Did you see him?" Lin's voice came out very small.

"I saw him," Rufus said, bending back a rowan branch. "Or rather, *it*. I still can't fathom that it was actually there, though. The Winnower's Well is a tall tale, a legend they scare freshers with at the Burning Bird when they're all new and skittish. It's not supposed to be true."

He lifted Lin over a fallen branch, and as he continued, he lowered his voice.

"The legend of the Winnower's Well says that a long time ago, before the guard runes were carved and before the hedge had grown tall and dense, a Nightmare from the mountains came creeping through and settled in the Sylver Valley. Nightmares are monsters, vile creatures with bleak and hungry souls. And there are none hungrier than the Winnower, so named because it reaps its victims from unwitting Sylverings who walk the woods.

"Of course I thought it was just a story. But now it strikes me that everything was there, exactly as the legend says. The sagging roof, the creaky porch, the broken well . . . and the hooded Winnower." Rufus's voice was a whisper now. "It twists the paths near its cottage so they all lead back to the clearing, no matter which way you try to flee. And when it has caught its victims and eaten them, it throws their bones in the well."

Lin felt numb. The cold was leaking into her, weighing down her mind as well as her arms and legs. Around her, the forest sighed and whispered, and for a moment, the ground really did feel like it was shifting under her feet. She shook her head to clear it.

"That's what I thought, too, back in the cosy warmth of the mead house," Rufus said, mistaking her reaction for disbelief. "It's just that there aren't any other wells in Sylver. Why would there be? The ground is always frozen."

Lin didn't answer. She didn't want to think of the well and the hooded figure, but it was as if invisible hooks pulled her thoughts back to the clearing. So she tried not to think at all, concentrating instead on putting one foot in front of the other, past bushes and boulders, until they made it to the other side of the ridge. There the forest gave way to a cleared road that wound along the darkly gleaming river between tall shoulders of snow. Rufus helped Lin climb over the plough bank.

"The Caravan Road," he said. "We should be safe now."

Lin's breath escaped into the evening as wispy clouds. She was quite exhausted. What warmth had come from running through the forest had long since drained into the snow. At the nape of her neck, sweaty curls were freezing into a crackly tangle. She lifted her left foot again to examine it. It was blue, and the cut looked ragged and inky.

Rufus stared at her, whiskers wide.

"You're a little pale. But Sylveros isn't far now. A mile or three along the road, and we're there." He tried to smile, but his eyes were brimming. "I'll take you straight to the

Burning Bird. Get you some starmead. And you can have my scarf . . ."

"Thank you," Lin said. "I just need to rest a little bit first."

She sat down with her back against the snowbank and hugged her knees tight inside the cardigan. Funny. The ground was pleasantly warm all of a sudden. She felt sleepy.

"Lin!" Rufus cried. "You can't sit down! Get up!"

But Lin's head was full of churning stars and a sweet chiming.

"I hear bells," she mumbled. "We're already there, I think."

The snow grew black around her.

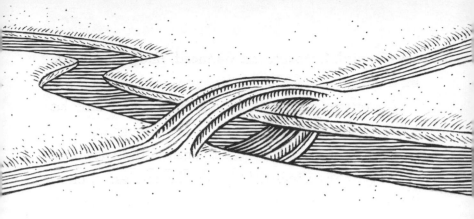

CHAPTER FIVE

When she came to, the delicious chiming was all around, accompanied by the dull thump of hooves on hard-packed snow. Lin peered out through her lashes. She was lying beneath a pile of blankets and furs in a deep, wooden sleigh, pulled by a little horse whose belled harness sang and creaked as it cantered along the road. Lin's hands were snug inside a pair of big mittens, and a musty, fur-trimmed hat threatened to fall into her face.

She turned her head and drew a sharp breath. Then it was no dream. *Rufus* lay next to her, staring up at the sky. When he noticed that Lin was awake, he got up on one elbow with mingled shame and worry on his face.

"How are you feeling?" he whispered.

Lin thought about it. She still felt tired, but her limbs tingled, a sign that the cold was letting go. Her injured foot felt weird, though. It itched and buzzed, and waves of heat surged through it. A quick peek under the blankets told her that it was bandaged and smeared with some sort of sharp-smelling ointment that oozed through the gauze.

"He dressed your wound with one of his special salves. It reeks like nine kinds of dung, but if *he* uses it, you can bet your tail it works."

Lin followed Rufus's glance to the sleigh's driver on the seat in front of them. His head and neck were covered in orange-red fur speckled with grey, and his triangular ears were tall and black. The tail that hung limp through the vent of his tweed coat was tipped in pure white.

"A fox!" she whispered.

"A Wilder. Not any Wilder, either. It's Teodor," Rufus whispered back.

Teodor reached behind himself with one skinny arm. He groped around until he found the worn briefcase that lay on the floor between the driver's seat and the blankets. Gruffly, he tugged the lid and checked the locks on the metal clasps before he withdrew his hand and harrumphed.

"I do not know what you were thinking, Rodent. Dragging a half-naked human through the Winterwoods!"

Rufus winced. "I'm so sorry, Lin. It never occurred to me that you would show up in your pyjamas. I should have prepared better, brought a coat or a blanket at the very least, but I left in such a rush. Still, I hoped that if we just kept moving, you'd be fine, but then you turned all blue, and . . . I don't think I've ever been so relieved to hear a sleigh approaching."

He took her hand.

"Are you angry with me?"

Lin squeezed his fingers. "No. I'm not even cold anymore."

She sounded more confident than she felt. No, she wasn't cold anymore, but her prickling legs and woollen head told her that her temperature had dropped dangerously low. After all those lectures on respect for nature and "I know I can trust you to dress for the part", she had attempted to trek down a frozen mountainside dressed in slippers, pyjamas, and a wet cardigan. Not worthy of a troll hunter at all.

"But it's not supposed to be like this," Rufus said. "You're supposed to have a wonderful time. You're supposed to love Sylver. Instead you're hurt and half-frozen."

He was right, Lin thought. These woods were dangerous. And if neither snow nor shock nor fainting could transport her away from them, she would have to watch herself. But she didn't say that to Rufus. He was searching her face with such guilt and hope that Lin felt sorry for him.

"I'm fine. I promise."

"And that's where you were both exceedingly and undeservedly lucky, Rufocanus," Teodor said.

"People call you *Rufocanus* here?" Lin whispered. Rufocanus was the name Harald Rosenquist had come up with that day when they were discovered, after the Latin name for redback vole, and somehow, it had stuck. Lin had never used the whole thing, though. It reminded her too much of her own real name, clever and smug and far too fancy to be of any good to the one who had to wear it. "Only Teodor," Rufus mouthed with a hard frown at the tweed coat. "But let's not talk about it now."

Lin settled back into the furs and blankets. Above, the first stars were coming out. They seemed too close and bright and formed none of the patterns she knew from her father's lessons. The frozen shooting star shimmered on its field of darkening blue. "The Wanderer," she whispered.

"Beautiful, isn't it?" Teodor still spoke without turning, but his voice had softened. "Some say it is a slice of star, trapped by gravity. Others say it is a giant crystal lens created by mirror magic. But whatever it is, the Wanderer travels the border between this world and yours. It visits our sky every four-and-ninety years, on Wanderer's Eve." Teodor lifted his arm in a slow arch. "At twilight, the star enters our sky in the east, and nine minutes past midnight, it dips behind the Sylver Fang, not to return for nearly another century."

"A century," Lin whispered. "That's rare."

"Yes. There are few now who remember its last coming. They know it only from stories and songs."

The little horse shook his mane, causing his bell to chime, and Teodor broke into a dulcet song.

> *The Margrave wandered in woods winter-wild.*
> *Stole through a gate for the heart of a child.*
> *The boy gave to them his heart to devour.*
> *A Winter Prince lost in the Wanderer's hour.*
> *Roses will wilt as the eve grows old.*
> *Silenced and caught in the secret cold.*

The words were eerie, but the melody melted into Lin's ears and soothed her. Now that she felt safe, she even found the woods lovely. Tall, snow-laden spruces flowed by. Old tracks crossed in the snow. Winter dusk painted the icy river blue. She leaned closer to Rufus and whispered, "I am glad to be here with you, little one."

But Rufus had tucked his nose under his tail and fallen asleep. Lin studied her friend for a moment. His dense eyelashes twitched, and his delicate ears were folded tightly against the head. He looked so much like the Rufus who had spent his life in her pocket that it seemed impossible that he had changed into this person who could speak and get into trouble and read maps and worry about her. Yet he had.

Sighing, Lin pulled the blankets up under her chin, enjoying the heat that was spreading through her body. And all the while the sleigh carried her closer to the town of spires and domes.

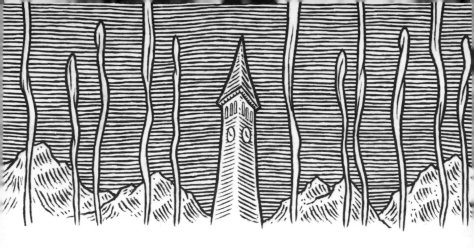

CHAPTER SIX

S he must have drifted off again, because suddenly Rufus's whiskers scratched at her cheek.

"Lin. Wake up. You have to get down on the floor."

Lin sat up in alarm. The woods were still quiet, but a muted, golden glow tinted the treetops and Rufus's eyes, which were serious. "What's going on?" she asked as she slid down to the cold floor of the sleigh. "Why do I have to hide?"

"Teodor doesn't want anyone to see you as we enter Sylveros."

They were driving down a long slope rimmed at the bottom by the river, picking up speed with every step. A lofty bridge of white stone curved over the frozen water, and beyond it, a large town spread out on the shore of the lake like a rumpled quilt of light and wooden houses.

Teodor offered no explanation for his request. He just hunched his back against the wind and harrumphed, impatiently, Lin thought. She pulled the covers down from the seat and huddled beneath them. Rufus leaned over her, pretending to tuck the blanket into place. "The masks," he breathed into her ear. "You can use them to see through."

The sides of the sleigh were carved with fox faces that all had holes for eyes. From the inside they also doubled as masks. Lin shifted so her face pressed against the polished grain of the wood, squinting against the wind as the landscape rushed by outside.

The horse galloped up the arch of the bridge, bringing the sleigh over the top and down again in one smooth pull. On the other side, the road widened into a broad street lined with small, snug houses painted in reds and blues and purples. A lush pile of snow lay on every roof and turret and on top of the wrought-iron lampposts that shed a warm light onto the streets. Frost roses obscured the many-paned windows. Some of the houses had a carved sign of lacquered wood mounted on a rod beneath the gable. Lin saw signs shaped like a curled bun, a ski, a winter apple, a stunted shoe.

Petlings appeared in great numbers as they moved along the street, and soon they were teeming about the sleigh. Teodor climbed off the driver's seat to guide the little horse through the crowd, and Rufus took the opportunity to whisper down to Lin beneath the covers, pointing out members of all the five Petling clans. She soon grasped that cats were Felines, dogs were Canines, all birds were Beaks, and the horses were Hoofs.

"And I," Rufus added, "am a Rodent. We're not the most powerful of clans, but I like to think that we're the cleverest."

Some of the Petlings wore coats and breeches over their feathers and furs, others carried leather satchels or clumped along in heavy boots. But all except for the Hoofs were roughly the same size and carried themselves like people, whether they were peddling sweets or playing flutes for coins or ambling at leisure with their muzzles in steaming cups of hot drinks.

"See that ermine?" Rufus said as they approached a sleek, white weasel who sold smoked fish from a cart. "See how twitchy she looks? That's one way Wilders differ from Petlings. They have never lived among humans, so the city makes them nervous. Most of them like to keep to their old ways – in the woods." The weasel scanned the street, head whipping back and forth. "Hello, Mikula!" Rufus called, pointing to one of the many posters of the Wanderer surrounded by streaky fireworks. "See you in the Square tonight!"

The weasel inclined her head, but her nostrils flared as the sleigh passed, as if she'd caught a most interesting scent.

"She's here for Wanderer's Eve," Rufus added for

Lin's ears only. "That's why the streets are so crowded. The preparations for the feast have been going on for weeks, and there will be music and food in the Great Square, maybe fireworks, too, or so the rumours say. No one knows exactly what to expect, save the House elders. They are the only ones who were here the last time the Wanderer visited."

Sylveros was hilly, and as they moved deeper into the town, the street rose and fell a dozen times. Teodor clicked his tongue and led the horse into a quiet side street where the panelled houses leaned so close that Lin saw nothing but walls from her hiding place. Rufus scampered onto the driver's seat.

"But this is Peppersnap Nook! Aren't we going to the House?"

"No. You would draw far too much attention to your-selves. We will talk at my place."

They pulled up in front of a red house. It was larger than the other buildings on the street and had a hand-some front door, a double gate that led on to a backyard, and even a little turret. But the paint was peeling and the windows were thick and smoky. From a rod under the eaves hung a sign shaped like a quill. Lin thought the nib had once been gilded.

Teodor walked over to the gate to unlatch it. His gait seemed stiff and cramped, and his tail hung slack from his coat.

"What does the quill mean?" Lin whispered up to Rufus on the driver's seat.

"The signs are an old Sylveros tradition. They used to show what every house owner did for a living. These days they're mostly used by shops and artisans, and by Sylverings that have been here a very long time. Teodor is chief chronicler at the House. He keeps records of Sylver events and history, and his work is highly respected. Hence the golden pen."

Lin's saviour turned toward her so she could see his face for the first time. Grey had replaced almost all the red on his muzzle, his eyes were wet and rimmed in pink, and when he spoke, his teeth showed yellow and cracked. No fox that old would survive a winter in the woods, she knew. But Teodor's irises shone golden and clear inside their black rings. They reminded her of glass beads in the skull of one of Mrs. Ichalar's mounted beasts.

"Come here, Rufocanus!" he said. "I require a word."

Rufus jumped out of the sleigh and trudged over to the gate. Teodor spoke to him, too quietly for Lin to catch the words. She could tell that Rufus was unhappy, though. His brow was furrowed, and he was scraping snow into a little pile with his feet. Teodor held out his paw. Rufus muttered a reply and shrugged.

"You've *lost* it?" Teodor's voice rose to a growl. "Are you utterly useless? Have you any idea what this means?"

"I'm sorry," Rufus said. "I'll try to find it."

"You had better!" Teodor threw his hands up and stalked toward the sleigh, old boots creaking. "Attend the horse!" he barked over his shoulder to Rufus, and then said to Lin under the covers: "Come with me, *fresher*. We've precious little time as it is. But make sure you keep the hat on and your head down."

He fished a key out of his briefcase and unlocked the front door. Lin caught Rufus's eyes over the rim of the sleigh. The vole nodded. "You should go with him. I'll be in as soon as I can." Nudging the gate open, he sighed, "Come along, Fabian. I imagine you're rather cold and tired as well."

To Lin's surprise, Fabian answered in a very refined voice. "Am I ever! I could certainly do with some caramel oats and a rubdown." The horse continued listing his various needs and cravings as they disappeared into the backyard. "A hot blanket wouldn't go amiss. And if you could change my book, that would be perfect. I keep telling Teodor that Hoofs need assistance with such things, but you know how distracted he can get . . ."

Lin climbed out of the sleigh in her makeshift disguise. Her pyjamas were wet and her bandaged foot unhappy to be plunged into the snow again. She still didn't know why she couldn't show her face, but it had her nerves on edge. Shivering, she pulled the hat down and her cardigan tight and hobbled up the steps. Teodor had left the front door ajar. As Lin slipped through it, she noticed it had a stained-glass window depicting three leaping tongues of fire.

The long and narrow hallway immediately felt familiar to her. The rickety stairs to the upper floors reminded her of Morello House on Summerhill, and the air smelled faintly of dung and hay like Uncle Anders's barn clothes. In the red and violet light that poured through the stained glass, Lin could see that the panelled walls were covered by photographs of Petlings, buildings, and winter landscapes in dusty frames.

"Girl!"

Teodor glared at her from the end of the hallway. "This way."

Lin followed him into a dim room that smelled of dry paper and leather. The old fox got down on his knees to kindle a fire in a blackened soapstone fireplace. Soon a wavering, reddish glow pushed the darkness into the corners, and Lin saw that this must be Teodor's library. But it did not at all resemble the prim rows of plastic-covered and labelled titles she was used to from the public library in the city. In fact, even her father's sprawling hoard of meteorological books and clippings seemed neat compared to this.

Bookcases filled the walls from ceiling to floor and threatened to close the small gap where the room's only window held its own. There were more books in stacks on the floor and desk, buckled old tomes bound in leather with specks of gold on their spines. On a three-legged table flanked by two worn armchairs sat an inkwell, a sand pot, and a quill. Teodor's briefcase with its clasps of stained silver stood next to the table.

The old fox pushed the chairs closer to the fire and swung a sooty teakettle over the flames. "Sit here. You must get your strength back after that barefoot trek through the woods. I really don't know what Rufus was thinking."

He shuffled out of the room and returned with a knitted blanket, a robe that stank of mothballs, and a small jug of milk. Lin took off the hat and hung her cardigan to dry before the fire, then wrapped herself in the robe and blanket and climbed into an armchair. There she sank into the dark brown plush seat, toasting her feet. She wanted to ask why Teodor was so gruff with Rufus, but she was afraid he'd transfer his anger to her.

"I'm glad you showed up when you did," she said cautiously.

"You should be," said Teodor as he eased into the other chair, tugging his coat straight and draping his tail over the farthest armrest. "I don't often go sleighing at dusk."

He regarded her closely, and for a much longer time than any human would find polite. To avoid his gaze, Lin let her own eyes wander to the doorway, where Rufus made no sign of appearing, and the parchment rolls that stuck out of clay pots, and the clutter on Teodor's desk. They fastened on a table clock of gleaming wood. She squinted. Was she mistaken, or did it show nine minutes to four? Up on the ridge, Rufus had said that it was just after three o'clock. Surely they must have spent more time than a short hour in the woods? Suddenly she remembered something else he had said, too. *I've been waiting for hours. Do you have any idea how long that is here?* Was there something wrong with time in this place?

Teodor nodded with a lopsided smile that reminded her oddly of her father. "That's right, girl. Time flows differently in Sylver."

"Rufus mentioned something about that. It goes more slowly?"

"An hour here can be a day in your world, or a day can be a week, we never know. And it's all because of you."

"Me?" Lin shifted in her seat. It made her uneasy that Teodor had known what she was thinking about the table clock. Now he grinned with his cracked teeth as if he knew that, too.

"Not you in particular, but your kind. Let me ask you this: Have you ever sat in your room, finding the afternoon impossibly dull and long? Or spent a day playing some game and been surprised by nightfall?" He shuffled over to the desk and brought back the clock with its ivory dial behind black roman numerals, placing it on the table between them. "When you are young, you perceive time in a way that has little to do with mechanics and measured units. And what the young people of Earth perceive, or experience, or feel has consequences here. Go on. Touch it. What do your fingers tell you?"

The clock felt warm against Lin's skin. In the wood, there was a sign engraved, three leaves filled with unfamiliar letters. The clockwork buzzed, not in the tick-tock rhythm of Mrs. Ichalar's grandfather clocks, but speeding up and skipping beats under Lin's fingertips.

"It's like a heart."

"Just so." Teodor smiled again. "The passage of time is not the only thing that is affected. Nearly every creature who lives here was once loved by a child of Earth, and loved the child in return. That bond was so strong that when the animals died, they woke up here in Sylver to live a second life."

"When they died," Lin repeated. "Does that mean that I am . . . ?"

Teodor shook his head. "No. You are responsible for the presence in this world of Rufocanus of Rosenquist, because of the love you two share. But you yourself are here by different means. By invitation, as it were. We have a task for you. A puzzle."

Lin felt her cheeks flush with relief. A puzzle. Now, that was something she could do. Compared to the idea of possibly being dead, it seemed rather comforting.

"What sort of puzzle?"

Teodor bent down and picked up his briefcase. At his

touch, the silver clasps sprang open and the lid flew up, but the old fox tilted the opening away from Lin so the contents remained hidden. He took out a photograph and placed it next to the clock.

A dark-haired human boy of Lin's age stared up at her with sapphire eyes. He sat in a window seat, clutching an orb of glass that glowed silver milk and golden white like a captured star. Though he smiled faintly for the camera, there was something about the pull of his mouth that made Lin think this boy was very sad.

"This is Isvan Winterfyrst. He has been missing for five weeks. Disappeared from his home without a trace, without so much as a scent for an old fox to catch."

Lin waited for more, but Teodor lapsed into another silence, caught by the sad boy's gaze. "I see," she said at last. "And my task is to find him?"

"Your task is to find him *tonight*. While the Wanderer still shines on our valley."

Teodor gave Lin a sideways look as he closed the lid on his briefcase. "I see the word 'why' on your face. Good. If you are to succeed, you will need to ask questions, and the right ones. This . . ." His paw hovered over the gold and silver orb in Isvan's photo. ". . . is Isvan's snow globe. It is the source of all his life and magic. His soul."

"Then he's not human?"

"No. The Winterfyrsts are glacial kin. Their flesh is shaped of ice, not born like ours. Of all the creatures in

Sylver, they are the most strange and powerful, but also the most rare. Their numbers have quietly dwindled over the years, until only Isvan remained, the last of his people. And this is why we need you to find him tonight. At the celebration of Wanderer's Eve, Isvan must be there. He must perform the most important of all Winterfyrst magic: the Wandersnow."

From her father's books, Lin knew the basic principles of snow: low pressure and cold fronts and freezing temperatures so it would settle. But what sort of snow would come from magic? Teodor clicked his tongue. "The Wandersnow is not a thing of science. It is unexpected, the kind that baffles meteorologists, a massive snowfall that grows and grows, sweeping over borders and continents, until it covers all the lands of the world." He hooked his golden eyes in Lin's. "But not this world. Your world."

Lin couldn't help but draw a breath of surprise. Snow in every country in the world! That would definitely confuse her father. Teodor nodded, pleased with this reaction.

"Millions of children see the crystals swirl out of the sky," he continued. "Some watch from their windows; others run outside to play. But all of them are possessed by glee, for while grown-ups worry about shovelling and frozen pipes and slippery roads, children know only wild joy when there is sudden snow."

It was true, Lin thought. Every year for as long as she could remember, she and Niklas had raced outside to greet the first snow as it fell on Summerhill, making wishes for every flake they caught on their tongues. And every year, Uncle Anders would watch from the kitchen window of the main house, grim of face.

"Now I told you, what children feel has consequences here in Sylver. Every thought and every dream drifts through to us in tiny flecks and flakes. But the wild glee of millions of children is like a worldwide storm of raw power. It is *magic*." He pointed to the little window, from which the flickering tail of the shooting star could be glimpsed. "Tonight, the Wanderer travels the border between our worlds, like a fleeting doorway. It only takes a powerful knock from the other side – such as a storm of raw magic from gleeful children – to blast the door open. Make a gate – the Wandergate – between Sylver and Earth." Teodor tapped the table clock. "At nine minutes past midnight, Isvan must have conjured the Wandersnow and the gate must have opened. I say must, for the safety of our realm and everyone who lives in it depends on this."

"Why?" Lin asked.

The kettle whistled mournfully. Teodor busied himself, pulling it out of the heat with a poker and sprinkling a handful of exotic-smelling leaves into the water. He did not meet Lin's eyes. "I will not burden you with this, not yet. But there is one more thing you should know about the Wandergate, Lindelin Rosenquist. *You* need it to open, too."

"Why?" Lin said again, too absorbed to even care he had called her Lindelin.

"Because it is the gate – the only gate – that can take you home."

Lin stared at him as he shuffled over to a cabinet to fetch two cups along with a pot of honey. "What about the gate on the hilltop?"

"You came here through a scargate, torn open by great longing and sorrow." Teodor's hand trembled ever so slightly as he poured the tea, and the honey spoon clinked against the delicate china. "The one in your cellar had been preparing for you for some time now. You may have noticed a chill in Mrs. Ichalar's house, or that the clocks ticked too slowly? But that's all gone now. Once a Twist-rose passes through a scargate, it is like the purging of a festering wound. It closes up forever. You cannot go back that way."

The fire blazed as hot as before, but Lin felt like she had been doused in cold water. "You are telling me I need to solve your puzzle or I'll never see my home again."

Teodor held out a cup for her. "I began my life on Earth in England," he said. "There it is widely known that a good cup of tea cures every ailment, particularly if there is milk in it."

Lin sipped the spicy drink, but it had a bitter undertone. Teodor seemed to enjoy his, though, because he drank deeply from his cup. "We know it is no easy burden," he said. "We thank you for volunteering."

"Volunteering?" Lin's voice sounded brittle in the book-lined hush of the room. "What do you mean volunteering?"

"Oh, you chose yourself for this. The name of Twistrose never lies."

Lin put her tea down on the table with a loud clink. "I invented that name because of Mrs. Ichalar's climbing rose. For the troll hunt. It was only a game!"

"Tonight, young Rosenquist," Teodor said, flashing his crooked smirk, "you will find that some games are real."

Somewhere in the house, there was a scratch and a hiss, like a match being lit. Teodor sat up, flicking his ears toward the hallway, lifting his upper lip to taste the air.

With a low growl, he stalked out of the room. Lin followed him out into the hallway in time to catch his shadow melting up the stairwell toward a cold, blue radiance in the turret. Now she smelled it, too: the acrid tang of something burning. "Stay there," Teodor barked from above.

And she did, until she noticed the painting on the wall of the first landing. It represented a dark mass of roots that clung to a stone wall, cracking the stones and crumbling the mortar, exactly like the roots in Mrs. Ichalar's cellar.

Lin sidled up the first flight of stairs, wincing whenever she hit a squeaky step. She thought she heard Teodor mumbling to himself, snatches of strange words. Though the blue light from above was fading, it was enough for her to read the painting's brass plaque.

With blood on her thorns she must creep through the wall.

When the last hope is lost, a Twistrose is called.

She tilted her head. The dark colours of the background bled into one another, and she had missed it at first. But now she saw that the wall had tumbled in the middle, so a hole opened into unknown shadows. On the edge stood a girl with her back turned, with tangled hair and a scruffy-looking sweater. She held in her hand a key with dripping thorns.

"Rosa torquata."

Teodor had descended from the turret like a wraith and watched her now from the landing above. His eyes were cold mirrors that reflected every trace of light, the way feral pupils do at night. Lin held her breath.

"The Latin name for Twistrose, a very old plant whose roots reach from this world to the other." Teodor came toward her, step by slow step, and now the stairs creaked like old bones. "But it is also the name of the handful of children who can travel between our worlds. When true danger rises, when the last hope is lost, it is said in Sylver that only a child of Earth can help. In such times a key is sent through the *Rosa torquata* with hopes that it will bring back aid. This time it brought us you."

He stopped not a foot from her face.

Lin swallowed. The *rosebush* had brought her the key. The parcel had been scratched by thorns, not a knife. She turned away from the grasping roots of the painting, up toward the turret. "Is everything all right up there?"

"No," Teodor said. "It is not. Not in the slightest. But that is for me to worry about. You must concentrate on *your* task. Find the boy, Lindelin. Find him while the Wanderer is in the sky."

"It's *Lin,*" Lin said, to buy herself more time. Teodor seemed shaken. Afraid, even. And if he was scared, should she not be doubly so? If the safety of Sylver and everyone who lived there depended on the finding of Isvan Winterfyrst, why did they leave it to her, who knew nothing about this world?

"Twistrose, then," he said quietly. "Take heart. The *Rosa torquata* has deemed you suitable for this task. We trust in your skills, and so should you." His black ears flipped backward once more, toward the hallway. "And perhaps you might take some comfort in this: Only those who truly long for someone on the other side of the wall grow into Twistroses. Well. Now you and the one you longed for are both here in Sylver. I can only hope young Rufocanus proves a boon and not a burden to your work."

His eyes slanted to the figure that was standing in the library doorway, arms crossed and whiskers wide. Rufus! Out of old, sweet habit, Lin's hand went to her left pocket. Whatever happened, she would not be alone in this.

She lifted her chin. Twistrose or no, she was here in this frozen world. And unless she managed to find this Winterfyrst boy, she appeared to be trapped. There really was no choice to speak of. She looked the old fox right in his cold mirror eyes.

"I will try."

Chapter Seven

Rufus slammed the front door with a rebellious flick of his heel. "So. All we have to do is find a boy who Teodor hasn't been able to locate in weeks. In a few hours. Without letting the Sylverings know they have a human girl in their midst. That'll be easy, won't it?"

He turned and marched up Peppersnap Nook, favouring his left leg again, leaving Lin to hurry after as quickly as her bandaged foot allowed. Behind them, a streak of orange fur could be seen at the round window below Teodor's spire. After his visit to the turret, he had been terse and impatient, eager to shoo them off.

"But you have been looking for Isvan for weeks," Rufus had protested. "There must be something more you can tell us about his case?"

In reply Teodor had given them a piece of paper, upon

which he had written down the song he had sung for them in the woods.

"I have always thought of 'The Margrave's Song' as an old ditty," he had said. "Beloved by penny singers, but mostly nonsense. But in my research into Winterfyrst lore, I discovered that it was originally a Telthic Soothsong. A prophecy if you will. And the words of a Soothsinger have a way of drifting into place." He had shoved the paper into Lin's hand. "The Wanderer's hour is tonight, of course, and the Winter Prince can be none other than Isvan. But I do not know what to make of this Margrave. It means 'lord of the border', and my best guess is that it is simply another name for the wandering star. Perhaps you will make more sense of it as the night unfolds."

After all the songs her mother had played and picked apart for her, Lin did have a little training making sense of lyrics. *Take the words out,* her mother would say, *look at them from a different angle. Gold doesn't always mean gold.* But Lin had to admit that "The Margrave's Song" made little sense to her, save perhaps for the ominous line Teodor thought referred to Isvan.

A Winter Prince lost in the Wanderer's hour.

Was he silenced and caught in the secret cold, too? Lin pulled her cardigan close, trying to stay as hidden as possible inside the smelly hat. Teodor had insisted she keep it, and keep her presence secret. The Sylverings didn't know that a Twistrose had been called to their aid, and even Rufus had agreed that Lin's presence was a telltale sign of great danger. "And fear is a destructive force," Teodor had told them; "even among the most peaceful of people."

Rufus chewed the tassels of his scarf, muttering to himself. "A boon and not a burden. That crafty old grump! He knew I was standing there!"

Even the most peaceful of people could bicker, it seemed. "What is going on between you two?" Lin asked. "You're like two firecrackers in a pot. Is it because foxes and voles are natural enemies?"

"No, no." Rufus spat out the tassels. "Sylver's not like that. The different clans all have their preferences and quirks, that's true. Hoofs like rose-painted wood; Beaks like shiny things. Canines like open squares; Felines stick to alleys. And we Rodents have this really annoying urge to, well, chew stuff." He frowned at the frayed ends of the scarf. "But though we may have been enemies on the other side, we've put all that behind us. We call it the Sylver Pact. It's the first thing they teach us when we arrive: We're all just people here. Still," he added darkly, "there are always some who just don't like each other."

They were moving through a neighbourhood called Wishboxes, named for its lavish window displays. On the opposite side of the street, a black cat was scrutinising his reflection among pies and chocolate loaves in a bakery window. He kept getting up on his hind legs, dropping down on all fours, and rising back up again, tail shaking with confusion.

"Fresher," Rufus said. "Probably his first day."

Presently a smiling dog with a sixpence on his head approached the fresher, patted him gently on the back, and pointed down the street toward the centre of the town. "That's the direction of the House," Rufus explained. "They'll sort him out there, help him find somewhere to stay and something to do."

"What is the House exactly?" Lin asked.

"The House is where all decisions concerning Sylver life are made. If anyone has a problem, they bring it before the House elders. All records and maps are kept there, and the important guilds like the snow clearers and the gatherers have offices there, too. I suppose you could say it's the heart of the realm. A big, complicated heart with a lot of chambers. I work there, actually."

"You do?" Lin said, impressed. Rufus had only been here for a month.

"It's a bit of an honour, for someone as fresh as me." He gave a mock-humble bow, and Lin could see the bad mood sliding off him like puddle water. "Granted, I spend my days copying letters, or hovering about trying to find out what everyone else is up to. As chief chronicler, Teodor is my superior. He keeps telling me to do the letters over, that my handwriting is sloppy. I do believe he thinks I'm rather incompetent." Rufus shrugged, but Lin thought she detected a smug curve to his whiskers. "But I've made a few friends here and there, dug up a secret or two. Teodor doesn't need to know everything."

"What was that thing he wanted you to find?"

"Oh, don't worry about that." Rufus winked at her. "I've got it covered."

They rounded a corner into a stump of a street where the windows were crowded with clothes and hats. Rufus stopped in front of a blue door under a sign fashioned as a threaded needle. "Here we are! Stitch Lane is the best street for tailoring in all of Sylver, and Sofie is the best on Stitch Lane."

"You think Isvan came here?" asked Lin.

"No," Rufus said. "But you can't very well traipse around in your pyjamas all night."

Behind the blue door there was indeed a little tailor shop. A grey rabbit in a red brocade coat sat at a desk in the middle of the room, cutting patterns from grease-proof paper. When they stepped under the tinkling bell, she muttered without looking up, "Will it be pockets or tassels today, Rufus dear?"

"Neither," Rufus said, peering quickly around the shop to make sure they were alone. The racks that lined the walls were full of mismatched garments: coats and vests and hats, and quite a few pairs of knitted socks. "I need a full set of warm clothes. Wool if you have it."

"A full set? I should think your fur is perfectly good

enough to . . . Oh." The rabbit gawked at them. "It's not for you. A new friend?"

"Uh, yes. Just arrived. I'm showing her around."

"Welcome to Sylveros." Sofie put her scissors down and came plodding over to inspect Lin's clothes. "This won't do! A wet cardigan and ditto slipper!" She pulled out a measuring tape and held it up to Lin's arm. But when she reached around to measure Lin's waist, her pink nose suddenly twitched. Lin took a step back, but it was too late.

"You smell like morellos!" Sofie peered into Lin's hat. "Can it be that you are . . ."

"She's a little wary still," Rufus interrupted with a too-bright smile.

Sofie lowered her hands. "I understand. Don't worry, dear, I won't touch you." She returned to the desk for a parcel with blue ribbons. "I think I have something that may fit. I made it because it would suit my human girl, but she has changed her style. She smelled nice, too, like peppermint." Sofie gave Rufus a glance. "Isn't it sad, Rufus? One moment, everything is as it used to be, and the next . . ."

Rufus tightened his scarf. "Right."

The rabbit held out the parcel. "Go on, dear. It's a gift."

Lin opened it and found a tunic of soft white wool. There were also mittens, socks, and thick trousers, all in icy colours. "Let me see if I can find you a parka," Sofie said. "So you can get rid of that grubby, old cardigan."

"She may want to hang onto that for now," Rufus said. "It's nice to have something lived-in when you're far away from home."

Sofie raised her eyebrows, but she didn't argue. Instead she rustled up a strange garment called a chaperon, a pointed hood with shoulders that covered the top third of Lin's cardigan. "Take these, too," the rabbit said, and placed a pair of white lace-up boots on top of the pile. "Colbear made them, so they're good quality. Now, try everything on so we can see if it needs adjusting."

Lin stepped behind a folding screen and rubbed her skin dry with a towel that Rufus handed to her. The bandage on her injured foot was soaked, and she unwound it. The cut had grown a brown scab already. It still twinged, and it reeked from Teodor's ointment, but there was no need for a bandage.

Quickly she dressed in her new outfit. The boots were a little oddly shaped, wider at the toes, but the supple leather moulded to her feet. The chaperon fit perfectly, and as she pulled on the mittens, she felt warm at last. Somewhat self-consciously, she walked over to the mirror, peeking out from the deep shadow of the hood. A smile spread on her face. At last she was dressed for the part. She could be the hero of a polar expedition, or a master troll hunter ready for a blizzard. If only everyone at Summerhill could see her now!

"Not another stitch needed, I think," Rufus said, scooping up Lin's discarded hat from behind the screen.

"Leave me the pyjamas," Sofie said. "I'll mend them for you."

Rufus bowed again, but this time sincerely. "Thank you so much for your help. And we'd appreciate it if you'd keep from mentioning our fresher to anyone. Just for tonight."

"I won't tell. I only ask . . ." Sofie nibbled at her paw. "I only ask that you enjoy your time together while it lasts."

As Rufus pulled Lin out the door, she thought the rabbit's eyes were watering. "What was that about?"

"Ah, that's just Sofie," Rufus mumbled. "She misses her girl a lot, and she's a little mushy. But trustworthy, or I wouldn't have brought you here."

Lin lowered her voice, too. "We're going to need a better plan next time."

"You're right," Rufus said. He didn't steer her back out on the street, but down some steps to Sofie's cellar.

"Where are we going?" Lin asked as Rufus opened the door for her. She had to stoop so she wouldn't bump her head on the lintel.

"To make a better plan," Rufus said. "This is the safest place in all of Sylver." He ushered her into a little den with crisscrossing rugs on the uneven floor and small windows under the ceiling. The furniture was simple – a stove, a bed, and a table – but still the room seemed crowded, for the table and the walls were covered with maps. "It's not much, but it's comfortable."

"This is your place!" Lin said. "Look at all these maps!"

"I copied them from originals I've borrowed from the Cartography Chamber. It's forbidden, of course, but I borrowed Teodor's key and had that copied as well."

"You *stole* Teodor's key?" Lin grinned. It didn't surprise her at all that Rufus had a light-fingered streak. In Grandma Alma's kitchen, he used to climb down her leg to help himself from the food bowl of Summerhill's fat cat.

"Borrowed. And copied. It's not the same." He shrugged. "No one ever goes in there anyway. The Sylverings aren't interested. They have a whole world to explore, and most of them have never even visited the Palisade." Rufus ran his hand over a map titled "The Realms of Dream and Thorn", a great almond-shaped island of cities, fjords, and mountain ranges, where Sylveros made a tiny speck to the far north. "When I go, I won't be stopping at the border. I'm going across the Nightmare Mountains to the other Realms. I'm going to see everything."

He turned back to face her, and his eyes were shining. "But back to our plan. Secrecy first. Your disguise looks great, but your scent gives you away."

It was true. Up close, Sofie had no problem smelling that Lin was no ordinary fresher. In the wild, Lin knew how to avoid being detected by animals: stay upwind and stay away. But that wouldn't get them far in a town. "Do I really smell all that different from a Petling?"

"Yes. But luckily, most Sylverings find that their senses have dulled since they came here." With his teeth, Rufus tore the earflaps off Teodor's hat and gave them to Lin. "This won't fool those who still have keen noses, like Sofie, but the old fur will mask the morellos a bit. Put them somewhere they won't be conspicuous. Your boots maybe?"

Lin sat down on the bed to tie the fur pieces to her laces. For some reason, Rufus turned away, twirling his tassels quickly while he studied the maps. "The bed's a little lumpy," he muttered. "But you get used to it."

The bedding was hay, covered with a knitted sleeping bag that was too wide at the top. "Wait a minute," Lin said. "This looks just like my cardigan pocket!"

"Sofie knitted it for me when I first got here." Rufus cleared his throat. "It helped me get through the awakening. I guess it comforted me."

Lin put her hand under the dark blue yarn. "Does it feel strange? Being a Petling?"

"It did at first. But memories from before are fading, and the new me, the Petling me, is bleeding in. As if I've always loved mead houses and old legends and the colour green."

"Oh," Lin said. While she had been grieving by the

rosebush, Rufus had slowly been forgetting his old life. She did want him to be happy, but it stung a little. Bending down to adjust the earflaps, she said, "All right, stink pads secured to boots. And I think your showing around a skittish fresher is a good cover. It would explain why I keep my distance, plus it gives us freedom to search around for Isvan. Where should we begin?"

Rufus flung the scarf ends over his shoulder. "My first thought was to seek out places Isvan usually goes and speak to his friends. But the funny thing is, in all my time here, his name has never once come up. It's like no one knows him."

With a coldness in her chest, Lin remembered the sad tug of Isvan's smile. The last Winterfyrst in all of Sylver. "Well, Teodor said he vanished from his home. Do you have any idea where it is?"

"I think I might!" Rufus began riffling through his maps. "I can't remember seeing the Winterfyrst name anywhere, but . . . Ha! This is the one we want." He smoothed out a roll on his desk, pinning the corners down with a pocket-knife and two coffee mugs. Unlike the rest of his collection, this map was made of creamy, weaved paper. But the details and names had been scribbled with light, uncertain pencil strokes, erased and done anew. The only part written in ink was the title: "The Comprehensive Chart of Sylveros and All Its Lands." "I couldn't find a detailed map of the entire town, so I've been piecing together some smaller ones." Rufus scratched his head. "But the proportions seem off somehow."

"Well, it's hard if you can't use your eyes for measure. Remember when Niklas and I made that Summerhill map? We climbed up to Buttertop to get it right." Lin traced the line of the long, straight Main Road, which ended in the Great Square and a minuscule drawing for the House. "These symbols are beautiful!"

"I just tried to make them look like yours." Rufus's whiskers perked up. He pointed to the south end of Sylveros, which was severed from the rest of the town by the looping river. On the very edge of the street grid, all but surrounded by the woods, nestled one of his symbols. "I added this one from an old map of magical sites in Sylveros. Doesn't it strike you as somewhere a Winterfyrst could live?"

It was a snow crystal marked as the Hall of Winter.

Lin smiled. "For the first time in history, I think I can say: one point to Rufus of Rosenquist!"

CHAPTER EIGHT

The streets of Pawfields were quiet and broad and the houses less embellished. Most of them had no paint, but lay watchfully in the snow with tarred timber walls and a glower in their foggy glass.

"This way." Rufus glanced at the map, which he had decided to bring so Lin could help him improve it. "Pawfields is one of the few areas where I'm pretty sure this thing is correct. Canines like their surroundings to be open and straightforward."

As they walked past a barn with a huge gate, a nasal and haunting bellow sounded inside the building.

"Rimedeer," Rufus explained. "They send their young down into the Sylver Valley when the winds blow especially cruel or the Nightmares grow restless. I hear the stables are full of calves this year."

"Nightmares?" Lin said. "Like the Winnower?"

"The Winnower is one, but the mountains outside Sylver are haunted by many kinds of horror. I've never seen one of the creatures myself, though. Nightmares can't cross our borders."

"But the Winnower did."

"Well, yes." Rufus shrugged. "According to the legend. But the more I think about it, the more I wonder if we didn't spook ourselves in that clearing. Anyone could have been hiding inside that hood. One of the gatherers who forage in the woods, or a Wilder."

A rimedeer cried again and, for a moment, Lin was put in mind of the howl they had heard up on the scargate hill. Except that voice had sounded darker. Less sorrowful, more cold.

"It could be the star that spooks them," Rufus said, frowning back at the barn. "Wanderer's Eve stirs up all souls, good and evil, or so I heard at the Burning Bird. That's my favourite mead house over in Winderside by the Lake. All the storytellers come there to test their mettle."

They followed the map south. Soon the ground began to rise, and the houses gave way to woods. Halfway up the hill, the street ended in a tall stone wall that stretched out to either side, far enough for shadows to swallow it at both ends. In the middle, there was a wrought-iron gate. The black bars were shaped like a thorny hedge with a silver snow crystal caught between the branches.

"I think we're in the right place," Rufus said. Behind the gate they could see a sleeping garden of frozen bushes and trees. It sloped upward with the hill, and at the top a grand house loomed against the rosy sky. At first, Lin thought the house was painted blue, but the colour shifted with the flickering light from the shooting star, and she realised the whole mansion was built from hewn ice.

Rufus tried to open the gate. It didn't budge.

"It's locked! How odd. There aren't very many locked gates in Sylver."

"Teodor's door was locked," Lin said.

"Teodor is an old, suspicious grump. Most Sylverings keep their doors open."

The iron bars of the gate were much too closely spaced for them to slip through, and when Rufus poked his hand in among the branches, he withdrew it with a yelp. "These thorns are sharp! We can't climb up this thing. The wall, then. Maybe we can get over there."

They both tried, but the stones were frosty and slick. Even with the mittens off, it was impossible to get a decent grip. Rufus sucked his finger. "Wait here. I'll run along the wall and find out if there's another way in."

"But what if someone comes?" Lin said. The street was deserted and the forest still, but in the tarred houses down on the field, the lights were on. Rufus guided her into the shadows by the gatepost. "It's not likely up here, I think. But keep your hood up and stay hidden. If someone approaches you, stick to the plan. I'll be back in no time at all."

He set off along the wall, and his fur quickly blended into the dusk. Lin chewed her thumb and tried to be patient and calm. With Rufus by her side, it was easier to forget that she was far, far from home. But now, when all she could hear was her own breathing, she felt lost. She kept her attention to the ground, away from the bright smear of the wandering star, and pretended she was standing in an ordinary street, somewhere in the outskirts of the city, on a day with very few cars about.

Down in Pawfields, a rimedeer bellowed again, piercing the silence like a foghorn.

Lin shuddered. She didn't just feel lost, she felt as if she should hide better. Along the wall there was no sign of Rufus.

Something creaked loudly up on the hill.

Could Isvan have returned? She leaned out from the shadows to spy through the iron thorns. The mansion had two tall floors under winged gargoyles of ice. All the windows were shut and blinded by lacy curtains. But the silver front door was ajar, and a creature oozed out through the crack, like a shadow spilled into the air. Lin watched, mesmerised, as the shadow became a grey striped cat clad in pointed boots and a three-cornered hat. Furtively, he glanced over his shoulder toward the town. Then he whirled about. He had seen her.

Two eyes gleamed at Lin like molten coins as the cat came gliding down the slope. Ten steps away from the gate, he faltered.

"You're *not* him. But who are you, hmmm?"

While the cat dragged his "hmmm" out and up like a crooked grin, he slunk closer to the bars until he was only an arm's length away. Lin shifted her weight and said nothing. The plan to stay silent if spoken to seemed pitiful now.

"Fresher. I see," he purred. "But why are you hiding your face, hmmm?"

Lin hesitated. It would look suspicious if she suddenly turned and ran. But she did not trust this Feline. His tail was curled up in a placid loop and he smiled encouragingly, yet there was something about him that made her pulse race.

"Come, you needn't be afraid. I am Figenskar, and I know everyone in this town. We'll soon become fast friends, you'll see."

He took another step toward her. His black pupils eclipsed the irises. That was it, Lin realised. She had seen enough of the Summerhill cat to know that this was the gaze of a hunter about to pounce. She stepped backward, but her stupid knees had weakened again. The cat darted his paws through the gate and caught her as she stumbled.

"Careful there! We would not want you to get hurt. But I must insist you tell me now: Who are you?"

Finally, Lin tried to flee, but Figenskar had slid his claws into her chaperon. They didn't pierce the layers of wool, but she couldn't get away. Blood pounded in her ears. "Let me go!" she cried. She braced her boots against the gate and tried to push free, but his grip was too strong. Instead, her hood slipped back.

When he saw her face, the cat let out a hiss of surprise. "A child! A Twistrose!" The thorns of the gate had nicked his arms in several places. Drops of blood fell on the snow below the wrought iron. But he didn't let go, and his eyes were all dark, all hungry. "Well now. This changes the game! Tell me your name, Twistrose!"

Lin kicked and struggled, pressing her lips together, and Figenskar growled deep in his chest. "Name!"

Suddenly she heard fast footsteps approaching. Relief sparkled through her veins when she saw that it was Rufus who came bounding along the wall toward the gate.

"Figenskar!" he yelled. "What are you doing?"

Figenskar snarled so softly it was almost inaudible. Then he retracted his claws from Lin's clothes and let her go.

"Why, Rufus," the Feline said, and at once his voice was bright and silken. "How good to see you! I was merely asking this young miss a question. How extraordinary to encounter a human child here. Is she your responsibility?"

Rufus drew himself up, curling his hands into fists.

"Step away from her! You're scaring her half to death! And what's this blood on the ground? Lin, are you hurt?"

Lin shook her head. "No. It's not mine."

Figenskar pulled his paws gingerly back through the gate. "Please forgive me. I meant no harm. It's just that no Twistrose has set foot here in my time. Sylver must be in great danger."

"There's nothing to worry about," Rufus said. "We're doing some work for Teodor, that's all."

"Teodor." A glint of distaste muddled Figenskar's expression, but it was quickly dispelled. He nodded pleasantly. "Then I won't keep you. I only stopped by to speak with our young Winterfyrst. You don't happen to know his whereabouts, hmmm?"

"No," Rufus said.

"A pity." The cat's tail flicked. He tried to hide it by shifting his feet, but Lin noticed.

"It shall have to keep. Thank you, Rufus. And thank you, young *Lin*. I'm afraid I didn't catch your last name . . ."

"Summerhill," Rufus said quickly. "Her last name is Summerhill."

"Summerhill," Figenskar repeated with all his needle-teeth showing, and Lin knew he wasn't fooled. For a moment he stood there, waiting. But when Lin and Rufus didn't leave, the cat fished a black key out of his heavy, pointed boot, and opened the gate. He tipped his hat to Rufus and headed down the street. Before he reached the bottom of the hill, he glanced over his shoulder twice.

"Why does *he* have the key to Isvan's house?" Rufus narrowed his eyes.

"Thank goodness he left," Lin breathed, pulling her hood back up. Her pulse had calmed a little, but the notion that she should hide immediately remained. Uneasily she watched the dark blotch of Figenskar disappear among the houses. "I guess we're not the only ones who are out to find Isvan tonight."

"No, and I don't like it," Rufus muttered. "Figenskar is a regular at the Burning Bird, too, so I know him. He's the worst sort of slick. On the day I arrived he told me the Winnower legend, just to watch me go all quiver-tailed." Rufus rubbed his neck. "I wish I hadn't slipped your name. I'm still not used to how fast my pesky tongue is. At least he doesn't have the whole of it, he . . ."

"Rufus!"

Lin was staring up at the ice mansion. "Do you see it? On the second floor, to the right?"

Rufus whistled softly through his front teeth.

Behind one of the tall windows, the lacy curtains were swaying as if in a gentle breeze. Only the window was shut, and there was no wind. Three heartbeats ago, someone had been standing in that window, watching them.

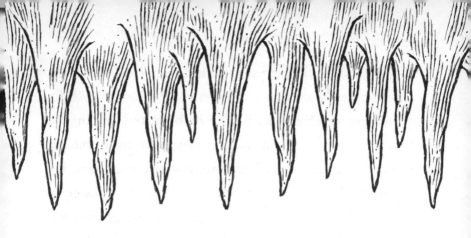

CHAPTER NINE

U p the hill they went, following the pathway where nobody had cleared the snow, but several had walked since the last snowfall. The Hall of Winter loomed over them, block upon block of opaque, blue ice, shrouded in silence. The gargoyles watched them from the roof. Lin couldn't stop eyeing their brooding shapes and scythes for arms, but Rufus was more preoccupied with the footprints.

"Figenskar has been here more than once," he said. "His boot prints are easy to recognise, even for an amateur like me. It's hard to read the rest, though, they're too jumbled. One set of small, dainty feet, I think. And over here are some really big paws. . . . You're certain you didn't see a face?"

"I only saw a shape moving behind the curtain," said Lin.

The entrance door was adorned with a stained-glass window; three light blue icicles set in a purple panel. Rufus peered through the glass before he opened the door. The hinges groaned, and freezing air gusted out. It smelled fresh enough, but there was something unpleasant about it even so, like discordant fiddle strings.

"Isvan!" he called across the threshold. "Are you there?"

There was no reply. Rufus tiptoed into the hall, claws scratching against the ice floor. Lin joined him, closing the creaking door behind her. The floor was tinted indigo where light fell through the stained glass, and the walls were diamond blue, carved with white swirly patterns. Under the ceiling soared a cloud of icicle pendants. Rufus sniffed quickly along the walls.

"What an odd smell," he said. "Like sweets and table polish. Well, there are no candles anywhere, but the twilight through the ice walls will be enough to see by. Which way is the room with the shape?"

Somewhere above them there was a faint thud. Lin laid one finger over her lips and pointed up the slender flight of stairs that curved up toward the upper floor. "To the right," she mouthed.

They crept up the stairs and passed through one ghostly quiet room after another. It was like sneaking through a glowing museum after hours. The furniture was covered by white sheets. Frost obscured the paintings on the walls. Delicate ice sculptures perched blindly on pedestals, their features worn away. Lin still had a feeling that someone was watching them. Twice, she flinched at a pale, wide-eyed face in the ice, only to find that it was her own reflection.

When they reached the final room on the second floor, they found the door open, and through the crack, they glimpsed a nursery. They paused to listen. Silence.

"Isvan!" Rufus called again. He stepped through the doorway and walked to the middle of the floor, whiskers spread wide. "Come out, Isvan, or whoever you are!"

But nobody sprang from the corners.

"Rats," he said, bending down to check under the bed. "I was so sure I could flush him out. But there's no one here."

That, Lin thought as they quickly searched the room, was not quite true. Isvan may be gone, but he still lingered here. The clothes in the wardrobe were too small for a boy her age, and the toys on the shelf were those of a young child, but Lin felt certain that he still used this room. The flattened, faded pillow in the windowsill told of many hours whiled away.

Beneath the windowsill lay a telescope. She picked it up. The lens was cracked, and the floor was chipped where it had fallen. "The thud we heard."

Rufus wrinkled his snout at it, as if it reeked. "Yes. But if someone dropped it, I don't understand how he got away."

Lin set the telescope gently down. Her hand shook only a little. "Maybe he didn't," she whispered. "I haven't heard the front door open."

Without another word they raced through the mansion, peeking under sheets and behind doors. At last Lin discovered a back stairway that led from the gallery above the hall to the downstairs winter garden.

"This explains the mysterious escape." Rufus jumped through an open window to sniff a clearly defined set of very small footprints on the porch. "Same smell, but stronger. These are fresh, and they aren't Figenskar's." The tracks led to the front of the building. There they were lost among the other prints on the pathway.

"Oh, mould." Rufus kicked a spray of snow toward the patchwork of houses and yards below. "He could be anywhere in Pawfields by now."

"Do you think it was Isvan?" said Lin.

"I doubt it. Somehow, I imagine a Winterfyrst to smell . . . cold. Like frost roses or something. Not table polish."

They had no choice but to go back inside to do what they had come for, and they quickly narrowed their search down to Isvan's room. Rufus breathed on a framed photograph on the nightstand, rubbing the glass with the tip of his tail. Out of the rime appeared two smiling persons, a lady and a young boy of about four. They both had inky hair, pale blue skin, and eyes that shone like sapphires, and they each cradled a shimmering orb in their arms.

"I think this must be Isvan's mother," Lin said.

"I've never heard anyone mention a woman Winter-fyrst about town," Rufus said. "And this lady definitely wouldn't slip your mind."

Lin agreed. She was too beautiful. And all that covered furniture . . . "I don't think she's here anymore. The house feels too empty. And Teodor said Isvan was the last of his people."

"Where did you go, Isvan?" Rufus leafed through a stack of drawings, all done in charcoal. "Who were you with? We're trying to help you. You can tell us your secrets."

Lin thought of her troll-hunting casket concealed in her wardrobe. Everyone, even those with an entire mansion to themselves, had secret hiding places. And the best hiding places were the ones you could keep an eye on. Or even better: keep under guard.

She frowned at the lumpy pillow in the window seat. The pattern was of silver snow crystals, so faded it all but bled into grey. Two letters were embroidered in the centre: C W. Not Isvan's initials, but perhaps his mother's? Lin took off her mitten and traced her fingers along the stitches.

The pillow crackled.

"There's something inside!" She extracted a piece of paper that had first been crumpled, then smoothed out and folded carefully. It was a letter dated July 19. Or rather, it was the draft to a letter, because several words

and the entire last part were crossed out, and there was
no signature.

My dear ~~XXXXXXXXXXXXXXX~~ colleagues,

Nearly seven years have passed since
Clariselyn Winterfyrst disappeared, and
all our efforts to find her ~~XXXXXX~~ have
failed. We must accept the grim truth: Isvan
Winterfyrst is now our only hope.

The boy continues to grow into a bright
young man. But, though I have taken every
precaution to protect him from undue heat
and influence, the Winterfyrst magic we
hoped would surface has not manifested.
Before Wanderer's Eve, Isvan must learn how
to conjure the snow, or I do not know what
will become of ~~XXXXXXX~~ us.

I implore you. If you have any solution to
the Winterfyrst plight, now is the moment
to speak. For every day that goes by, Isvan
becomes more restless. I fear I may not be
able to control . . .

Rufus scratched his ear. "The letter is in Teodor's hand.
I know that much from all my copy work at the House.
What does he mean by the Winterfyrst plight?"

"I'm not sure," Lin said. "But we were right about Isvan's mother. She went missing as well. A whole family, just gone."

The Winterfyrsts smiled after them as they left the room.

"I have to say I think it's cruel to leave him here all alone," Rufus said as they walked down the stairs. "I wouldn't put it past Teodor, but the rest of the town?"

Lin ached in sympathy, too. Or perhaps it was the unpleasant sense of discord she had felt as they first arrived. It was more pronounced in the purple-tinged hall than in the rest of the mansion, and as she stopped in the middle of the room, it grew to a low-pitched whine that clenched at her temples.

"Rufus! Do you hear that?"

"Hear what?"

"I don't know. There's this weird noise. Maybe it's some sort of echo."

Under the ceiling, the cloud of dangling icicles pointed directly toward Lin's face. She took a quick step to the left. And then she saw what she had been standing on.

There was an image carved into the floor.

It was the size of her palm and shaped like three narrow leaves covered in tiny symbols of spiralling curls and spiked dots. Lin recognised the mark. It was the same as the engraving on the table clock in Teodor's library. There was a difference, though, one that made Lin's hairs stand on end. A crack ran through the carving, tearing the symbols apart, and surrounding the three leaves was a jagged circle of deep, triangular cuts.

Someone had bitten into the ice with impossibly long and sharp teeth.

CHAPTER TEN

Rufus closed the thorny gate behind them.

"That was interesting," he said as they wandered down the hill. "But we're no closer to figuring out where Isvan has disappeared to."

"The neighbours might know something." Lin glanced back at the forbidding wall that surrounded the frozen garden. It didn't exactly encourage visitors. "If they've even been inside the gate. I thought you said the Sylver Pact makes sure everyone here lives in peace and tolerance. Why would the Winterfyrsts need a wall?"

"Here." Rufus rolled out his map, pointing to the snow crystal. "On the old map where I found this, the Hall of Winter was the only thing on the Pawfields side of the river. No streets, no bridges. If the mansion was built before the border was closed, they would have needed some extra protection." He twirled his whiskers. "But you're right.

The Pawfielders might know something. And remember those big tracks we saw on the pathway? I have a theory on who made those." He rolled the map back up. "Come on. Let's go for a visit."

He took Lin to a Pawfields street of ramshackle sheds and big yards near the river. "I've actually been here before," Rufus said. "On House business. And come to think of it, it makes sense for Isvan to know Ursa Minor. They're both outsiders, and they're both . . ."

A gigantic crash like an avalanche of dinner plates shattered the rest of the sentence. The noise rolled toward them from a timber cottage with a broad door under the sign of a crude china pot. Inside the cottage a voice roared, so deep and savage that Lin fought the urge to run.

"Oh, no," Rufus said. "Not again. Not now!"

"What was that?"

"The Ursa. Let me put it this way: not all Sylverings are as lucky as me. See these?" He wriggled his fingers, big-knuckled and nimble. "They're even more useful than they were before. Rodents have them. Beaks and Felines, too. But not all of us are as lucky. Some, Canines mostly, have rather clumsy paws. And the Ursa is more challenged than most." He gave the cottage a worried look. "Well, his timing is predictably horrible. Poor man. I think you had better wait outside."

Lin took up position by a window, through which she could see a warmly lit room with a terrific mess on the

floor – a big, knocked-over shelf and heaps of broken porcelain.

Rufus breathed in her ear. "And stay upwind! Minor
has a sharp nose."

With a wink, he skipped to the door and tore it open.
"Ursa Minor! What the rats is going on?"

Something moved between two shelves, something big
and brown. A paw.

"I'm fine," grunted the owner of the paw as he emerged
from under the debris. It was a bear, a huge bear, with a
large snout and small, close-set eyes.

Lin had never seen a bear before. There had been
the occasional sighting in the Summerhill mountains,
and once a cub and his mother had broken into Uncle
Andero's hunting cabin and drunk all the beer. But they
always stayed as far away from people as they could, and
all hikers and farmers returned the favour. What manner
of weird happenstance had let a child form a bond with an
actual bear? Lin would have been terrified if there weren't
a teapot spout perched between Minor's ears.

"Are any of the teapots unbroken?" he rumbled.

Rufus bent down to peep under the shelf.

"No such luck, I'm afraid."

The Wilder hung his head. The spout fell to the floor
and broke in half.

"I guess I wasn't meant to be a teapot painter."

"I guess not," Rufus said.

"Just like I wasn't meant to be a jewellery maker or a cake decorator."

"I'm sorry, Minor."

"I wonder what they will say at the House. They've been so kind and I just keep breaking things. Rufus, do you think they'll be mad?"

Rufus shook his head. "They'll understand. But Minor, you don't have to live in town if you don't want to. Many Wilders prefer the woods."

"My Sarah always said I was just as civilised as any dog," said Minor, pushing his muzzle up.

"Of course you are, but . . ."

Minor's nostrils flared, and he reared his head stiffly toward Lin's window. She stepped to the side, pressing against the timber wall and holding her breath so the frozen puffs wouldn't give her away. Heavy, crunching footsteps approached behind the wall.

"I thought I saw . . ." The Ursa pressed his snout to the pane, fogging the glass with huge snorts. When he spoke, Lin felt the tremors in the wall. "I thought I saw Isvan. But he wouldn't lurk around outside and not show his face. Not after all this time."

Lin heard Rufus trying very hard, and not quite managing to sound casual. "Isvan, did you say? I was just up on the hill to visit him."

The Wilder rumbled softly and moved away. Lin risked peeking back in.

"No point in that," Minor said. "He's gone. Has been for a while. I've been up to his house several times, but no one answers the door. I even asked around Pawfields. None of the locals have seen him either." He brought out a gigantic knapsack and began sweeping armfuls of crockery into its mouth. "I'm not surprised, mind you. They don't know him very well. They don't understand what he says."

"What do you mean?" Rufus asked.

"Isvan can't speak properly," Minor said. "Not like people, with words and stuff. It's all peep-this, swoosh-that, and whistlewind-here. It doesn't bother me, but it's not for everyone."

Lin bit her lip. Isvan couldn't speak!

"Doesn't he have any other friends?" Rufus asked.

"He spends a lot of time at the Waffleheart. Or outside the Waffleheart, I should say. It's too hot for him inside. Anyway, he probably knows some of the regulars there, those that have thick enough fur to stand being near him. And there's old Teodor. He used to visit often, but he must have been busy these past few months."

"Must have been," Rufus muttered.

Minor swept the last heap of broken pots into the sack and lifted it over to the door. "There we go!" He straightened a curtain that had been thrown over the rod and lifted up the last, dented chair. "A nice, clean den, just right for a nap. Can I offer you some honey, Rufus, straight from the tin and no nonsense?"

"Maybe later," Rufus said, eyeing the encrusted wooden spoons on the counter. "I should run along."

"Good! You young kids should be out playing in the snow. I'm always telling Isvan that he should get his hair messy and wipe his snot on his sleeve, like my human girl always did. Bears or no bears, my Sarah was the true terror of the reserve." He snorted repeatedly, and Lin realised it was a fond laugh. "But Isvan is a different sort. When he isn't over at the Waffleheart, he just mopes about in his house. Telescopes are all well and good, but they only show things that are far away, if you know what I mean."

"I know exactly what you mean," Rufus said.

"There's nothing wrong with drawing, either, but it won't bring roses to your cheeks. He's good at it, though. Want to see?"

"You have one of his drawings?"

"Right here on the door."

Lin heard them moving closer to the doorway. There was a faint whisper that might be Rufus's tail sweeping over the floorboards. Minor grunted. "It's a little melancholy, but I like it anyway. That lad can draw a face."

"It's very pretty," Rufus said, but there was a strained note in his voice.

"He tried giving me a letter first, but I can't read. He blew and wailed, but I didn't understand that either. After a while he came back with this. That's the last time I saw him." Minor cleared his throat. "I'd better get rid of the broken pots. Please have some honey, Rufus! You can stay as long as you like."

Lin pressed herself against the wall once more, but there was no need. The Wilder hoisted the sack up on his shoulder, and with a "See you in the Square tonight," he walked right past Lin and down the street.

"Lin," Rufus breathed when the bear had passed out of hearing range. "Come here. You have to see this for yourself."

The drawing on Minor's door was a portrait of a messy-haired girl with wide, dark eyes. She resembled Isvan a little, but she looked even more like Lin.

"Maybe it's a Winterfyrst relative," Rufus suggested.

"Maybe," Lin said, but she didn't think so.

And the portrait girl looked nothing short of terrified.

CHAPTER ELEVEN

They didn't speak much as they made their way to the Waffleheart, Isvan's favourite café. Upon crossing the bridge to the centre of Sylveros, the street became too busy for them to talk without being overheard. It became impossible to avoid close contact with the Sylverings, too. Twice a Canine stopped and sniffed the air as if he'd caught an unexpected scent. Lin hunched her shoulders, nervously searching the faces in the crowd from inside her hood. Rufus clicked his tongue and consulted his map again.

"Let's take a shortcut. There's something I want you to see."

He led Lin away from Main Road and up a steep alley lined with colourful, narrow houses, all with triangular foundations and crooked steps. At the top of the hill, they turned into a small square lit up by flickering snow lights.

Despite the many snowballs that must have been rolled there, the snow was perfect and untouched, and as they walked through the square, their tracks filled in, leaving the surface unblemished.

"This is Eversnow Square," Rufus said. "In my opinion the most beautiful spot in all of Sylveros. Come on. I want you to meet the family." He steered Lin toward a group of tall, unmoving figures in the middle.

They were statues of human children, seven of them, on bases wreathed in vines of stone, all bearing thorned keys.

Twistroses.

Rufus stopped in front of two girls who shared a base, holding hands. "Tiril and Aurora Helland. They were here together."

Lin stared up at the girls. They each carried a sword. "Did they solve their task?"

"Yes. If you don't, you don't get a statue." He grinned at her expression. "Never fear. You'll have yours. I'm convinced of it."

Lin snorted. "Well, I'm glad one of us is."

Rufus gave her a careful, almost nervous look. "Lin. I have to talk to you about something. I've watched you. I know you're not happy in Oldtown. All those hours by the rosebush . . ."

"How do you know about that?"

Rufus swished his tail, annoyed with hir
I'm not saying this right. Here." He took h

dragged her over to the next Twistrose, a skinny boy of Lin's age. Someone had removed the snow from his frail form, and from the plaque, which said "Balthasar Lucke. 1935." At his feet, a single rose lay withering. "He gets a new one every week."

"They still remember him," Lin whispered.

"You don't understand," Rufus said. "They remember all of them. The seven Twistrose legends are told most nights at the Burning Bird. Like this one." He tugged her over to a statue of a tall, cleft-jawed girl. "Julia Wallin. She arrived in the middle of the Fimbulstorm of 1867, and even though all the paths were closed, she got word across the mountains that Sylver was in need. The snow clearers' honour badge is named for her. She is still beloved."

"What about their Petlings?" Lin asked. "Didn't they get statues?"

"Their Petlings didn't need statues. They had already had their greatest wish fulfilled." Rufus took a deep breath. "Lin. When your Twistrose task is completed, I was kind of hoping that you could maybe stay."

Lin turned to him, confused. "You mean not go through the Wandergate?"

"Just for a little while." Rufus clutched his scarf. "You will be a hero here. And we could see the Realms together! Find out if those maps are any good."

Lin Rosenquist, a living legend, travelling with her best friend! She couldn't help but smile at the thought of it.

And time moved so slowly in Sylver. If she could just stay for a month or two . . .

She shook her head. "Nothing could be more wonderful, but Teodor said the Wandergate was my only chance at getting home."

"There is another way back," Rufus said. "Look at the plaques. Some Twistroses were here in years when there was no Wanderer. The legends don't say how they got back, but they must have."

"I don't know," Lin said. "What if the other way is closed or lost?"

"It isn't. I'm convinced of that, too." He looked up and smiled bravely. "We don't have to decide right away. We have a Winterfyrst to save first anyway. But please think about it?"

As they turned to cross the magical snow in the square, Lin thought he limped more than usual, though he sounded chipper. "Now," he said. "How would you like to sample a special Sylveros delight? Just smell that!"

Lin sniffed the air. A sweet, buttery scent wafted through the air, and she was suddenly very aware that she never did get something to eat before she sneaked into Mrs. Ichalar's cellar. They chased the scent eagerly until they reached a small park with naked trees. On the other side of the park there was a green house with large, frosty windows, and as they drew close, they saw the golden letters on the panes: THE WAFFLEHEART.

"This time, I think it's safe for you to come inside," Rufus said. "The waffle scent should drown out yours. And freshers really do act weird right after they've arrived, so I think you can get away with keeping your hood up in there. Besides, I don't want you to miss out on *every* good thing that Sylveros has to offer."

They hardly had time to climb the stairs before the white door flew open and the doorway was filled by the fattest hamster Lin had ever seen. Below his short, chubby arms there were great rolls of flesh covered in creamy fur. Between the fourth and the fifth roll a red apron stuck out like a besieged handkerchief. When he spied Lin, his round chin dropped.

"Oh!" he exclaimed after a moment, peering at Lin with unmistakable disappointment. "I thought you were someone I knew."

"Not possible," Rufus laughed, loud enough for his voice to carry into the café. "Unless you know the freshest of freshers. We haven't even got a name out of her yet. I'm showing her around to help her settle, and I thought your waffles might do the trick!"

The hamster recovered his smile and put out his paw, which was pink and very small compared to the rest of him. Lin shook it, but she kept her mittens on to conceal her hand.

"Welcome, dear! Welcome to the Waffleheart. Pomeroy is my name, and waffles are my art form. Would you like your hearts with jam? Hard cheese, brown cheese, no cheese? Honey, cream, or lemon? I've got everything you can think of!"

He stepped aside, quite daintily for a fellow his size, and ushered them into the warm café, where a mouth-watering fog thickened the air. A counter ran along the back, heaped with jars of fresh strawberries, raspberry jam, golden treacle, and sugar. Behind it, waffle irons were heating up in the embers of a long, slim hearth. As Lin and Rufus entered, the other guests stared at them curiously, particularly a blue-eyed Feline with white fur and very long whiskers. She gave her napkin to the Saint Bernard at her table. He had slobbered on his plate.

"Ready for your next round, Bonso?" Pomeroy said to the Canine. "That appetite of yours is admirable." He nipped over to pick up the wet plate even as he waved Lin and Rufus over to a free table. "What may I get you tonight?"

"What is the Wanderer's Eve special?" Rufus asked, nodding at the chalkboard menu.

"Oh, excellent choice! Au flambé with a tail of chocolate-dipped strawberries and whipped cream. Mulled cider on the side. I guarantee you'll love it!"

The hamster skipped behind the counter and poured spluttering batter into the irons. Rufus leaned forward and spoke in a low voice.

"I bet my tail Pomeroy thought you were Isvan, and

that he knows something. We'd better ask when the other customers aren't listening."

The door opened again, and in came a grey dog with big, pricked-up ears and a frayed shoulder bag. More than anything, she resembled a wolf.

"Why, there you are, brave gatherer!" cried Pomeroy. "I was beginning to wonder if the woods had eaten you!"

The Canine put her paw up. "No chatter, Rodent. I just want some waffles."

Pomeroy laughed, undaunted. "The usual?"

The dog squinted around the room, daring anyone to speak to her. When she saw Lin, her hackles rose.

"Everything all right there, Lass?" Rufus said.

After a moment, Lass relaxed her stance. "My apologies. I mistook your friend for someone else. I thought it was Isvan, that cold little mongrel."

"Now we're getting somewhere," Rufus muttered under his breath. He pulled out a chair. "No, she's just a fresher. Come sit with us. What do you mean, cold mongrel? Isvan's a sweet lad, isn't he?"

"That's easy for you to say," the dog grumbled as Pomeroy placed their drinks on the table. "You haven't been robbed blind! I caught him in my own barn, riffling through my gatherer's gear. When he saw me, he hurtled himself over the fence. No one with a clear conscience climbs like that."

She squinted into Lin's hood. Lin ducked and sipped her cider.

"I disturbed him before he could steal anything," Lass continued. "But the next morning, I couldn't find my ice axe. I just know that he came back and took it. It was a special axe, too, carved and engraved like nothing you've ever seen. Almost cost me my life." She lifted her right paw. Half the toes were gone, as if they had been chewed off, leaving only knobby scars. "Nightmares."

Lin spluttered cider on the table. There were Nightmares in Sylver after all? Rufus had said they couldn't cross the border.

"You haven't told her about our neighbours yet?" Lass smirked as Rufus patted Lin's back. "I don't think gathering will be for you, little fresher. The Winterwoods have many treasures to offer, but it's not a job for quiver-tails."

"Nightmares attacked you? Here in Sylver?" Rufus raised his eyebrows.

"Of course not," Lass said. "Don't worry, little fresher. As long as you're inside the Palisade of Thorns, the Nightmares can't touch you. No, this happened *outside* the Palisade, on the Cracklemoor. I found the axe stuck in the carcass of a rimedeer on the slopes of the Towerhorns, near the Crackle Creek Spring. And a good thing, too, because moments later, the monsters jumped me. They chased me all the way back to the Palisade. I would never have made it without that axe. It was so sharp and well balanced, it almost fought them on its own."

"You've been outside the Palisade?" Rufus twirled his whiskers. "I thought the gatherers didn't go there."

"We don't. But the woods have been unusually stingy this year. Either that or someone is picking all my trees clean right under my snout. I haven't been able to deliver half my orders of silvercones, so I wanted to see what I could find out on the moor. The Nightmares are worse than they sound, though. I don't reckon I'm going out there again. Not without my ice axe, anyway."

"And you're certain Isvan took it?"

"Sure as bone. I made the mistake of showing it to him last summer, and he almost wouldn't give it back. He has been trying to get his hands on it ever since, hooting and wailing like a fresh puppy."

"It's not his fault he can't talk," Rufus said. "Maybe he just wanted to compliment it."

Lass scoffed. "Oh, no. I heard that he's been sneaking around a lot, climbing into attics and stealing into back-yards. Young Nit at the Machine Vault says Isvan caused a scene there, too." She nodded darkly to herself. "I suppose that's how it is, when you don't have a soul, just a frozen ball."

Lin had no idea what Isvan had been up to, but she had been in Isvan's room, and she knew he had a soul.

Besides, with Niklas she had done a fair share of sneaking around in old barns herself, not to mention apple stealing.

Pomeroy came over with their waffles. They were warm and soft on the inside and perfectly crisp on the outside, and the berries tasted just as sweet as the ones Grandma Alma grew in the garden. Lin chewed slowly so they would last as long as possible. Rufus turned his waffles around and around in his hands, nibbling at the edge until there was nothing left and his whiskers were full of whipped cream. Pomeroy watched them smugly.

"Good, aren't they? It's the vanilla, a secret I picked up from my dear Dorret. Never was there a child who loved waffles more. But listen! Here comes another patron!"

He sprang over to the door and opened it. A cold gust blew into the café as the new guest stepped over the threshold. Lin stopped chewing in the middle of a mouthful.

"Figenskar!" Pomeroy said. "The chief observer himself! What a delightful surprise! Do come in!"

The cat ignored him and slid through the door. As he removed his triangular hat, Figenskar swept the room with his yellow eyes. They snagged slightly on Lin. He ordered lemon waffles, sat down at the table closest to the door, and put his boots up.

Lass received and finished her waffles. The cider dregs dried in the bottom of their mugs. One by one, the guests left, except Lin, Rufus, and Figenskar. Under her chaperon, Lin sweated in the steamy room, and her hands were damp inside the mittens.

At last Pomeroy spoke up. "You must excuse me, dear guests," he said. "I have to go set up my waffle stand for the feast tonight."

Figenskar stretched and pushed away his untouched plate. As Lin and Rufus got to their feet, he stood up slowly. Pomeroy gave a little squeal.

"Great cheek pouch," he said. "I plum forgot your to-go order, Rufus. If you'll stay behind a moment, I'll just wrap it up for you."

Figenskar put his hat on and floated toward the door. Before he left, he cast a glance over his shoulder, pupils glowing in the shadow of his brim. Rufus waited until the door was firmly shut before he whistled between his teeth.

"I thought he would never leave."

"So did I," Pomeroy said. His bubbly demeanour was gone. "You're here because of Isvan, I presume. About time. It's been forever since I left a message at the House that he was gone."

"Uh, of course," Rufus said. "The message. Right. When did you see Isvan last?"

"Five weeks ago. October third. I already said so in the message."

"You know how the House is, they don't let everybody

read the documents," Rufus said. "October third was the day before I came here."

"It's just so unlike him," the hamster said, wiping his hands on his apron. "Isvan is the only person I know who loves waffles more than I do. Since I opened the Waffleheart three years ago, he's been here every single day. I even set up a special table for him outside so the heat wouldn't hurt him. He always has at least two rounds of cold waffles heaped with sugar. I think the sugar crystals remind him of his mother's cooking, you understand. So sad. But what boy could get over losing his mother?"

"Where did she go?" Rufus asked. "Did she die?"

Pomeroy puffed his cheeks out. "No one knows. There was a terrible storm around the time she went missing, and many thought the weather caught her. I was a fresher myself back then, and I can still remember how the snow clearers struggled to keep the streets open. But I also remember Clariselyn. People said she was the most powerful Winterfyrst Sylver had seen in ages. That lady wouldn't have got herself lost in a blizzard, no matter how furious. So I think something else must have happened to her. Isvan was only four."

"Poor lad," Rufus said.

"And to make things worse, he didn't have his Ice Mask yet. When they're born, Winterfyrsts can neither speak our tongue nor tolerate warm temperatures, and they can't control their cold so they're safe to be around. They must wait to be a part of the warm-blooded world until they're old enough for an Ice Mask, a magical shield that keeps the cold in and the heat out. Clariselyn was supposed to create Isvan's mask the week after she went missing. I remember this, too, because it was my first ever waffle order. One hundred hearts for the Ice Mask feast." Pomeroy sighed. "Cancelled, of course. No one knew how to make the mask except Clariselyn. And without it, Isvan had to stay out in the cold, alone most of the time."

"I'm sure he had someone," Rufus said. "Teodor, or . . ."

"Teodor, certainly. He is Isvan's guardian, and guard him he does, as if the boy would melt at a kind word. They visit my café together sometimes, but I have the feeling Teodor doesn't like it much. I think they had a bit of a falling out last summer, because these past few months, Isvan always came without him."

"Did you ask him about it?" Rufus said. "I know he couldn't talk, but he could read and write."

Pomeroy shook his head sadly, and all his chins wobbled. "I was always too busy to sit down and chat. The last time I saw him, I think he did want to tell me something. But it was October third, the gatherers' annual waffle tea, and I had a stack of orders, and Isvan just kept ordering more and more. Fifteen rounds! I'm afraid it rather frazzled me. I hope I didn't scare him away with my rash words . . ."

The hamster untied his apron and used it to dab his cheeks. "I can't bear the thought of him all alone and hungry. . . ."

Rufus patted him on the arm. The creamy fur billowed softly.

"I'm pretty sure you're not to blame for this, Pomeroy. But do you think Isvan felt threatened by something? Or someone?"

Pomeroy blinked. "Threatened? No, I . . . He did leave as soon as he saw the gatherers on the other side of the park that day, but . . . Who would threaten a Winterfyrst?"

"That's what we're trying to find out," Rufus said. "One more thing, Pomeroy. When you went to the House, whom did you see? Sometimes messages get lost."

"I talked to Teodor himself. He said he would handle it personally." Pomeroy's tears welled up again. "It's Wanderer's Eve. Isvan should be here for the feast. He would if he could. Wouldn't he?"

As the hamster closed the door behind them, Rufus muttered, "Handle it personally. I wonder if he even told anyone else."

Lin opened her cardigan, letting the blissfully cold air in. "Teodor did say that he's tried to keep things quiet so the Sylverings wouldn't be upset."

Rufus made a rough sound in his throat. "Pomeroy is

already upset, and he's a Sylvering. No. The old fox is up to something here."

"Maybe this has something to do with that letter we found in Isvan's pillow," Lin said. "Pomeroy thought Isvan and Teodor had quarrelled last summer, and Teodor wrote the letter in July. We should ask him about it."

"No." Rufus kicked a lump of ice along the street. "Let's not reveal that we found that just yet. Let's follow our other leads first."

"All right. There is that place where Isvan had caused a scene."

"The Machine Vault," Rufus said, cocking his head. "Yes! I've wanted to inspect that thing for a long time now."

"What thing?"

"The Machine. You know those strawberries we just had? And remember those sacks of china shards that Ursa Minor carried off? If something gets broken or left over, you can deliver it to the vault, where it's fed to the Machine and rebuilt into new things. Cardamom or silk or fresh berries – just about anything."

"That sounds incredible," Lin said. "Too incredible. How can a machine make fresh berries out of china pots?"

"I don't know. But I do know that Teodor doesn't care for it. I overheard him complaining that it's too dangerous."

Lin nodded. If Isvan had visited the Machine Vault

to get something, it might be a valuable clue. And if the quiet, careful Winterfyrst had caused a scene, they should try to find out why. "Let's go there."

"This way," Rufus said, rustling his map. "Hey, this park is all wrong. Remind me to fix that, will you?" Lin was about to follow when she stumbled against a small, snow-covered table by the steps. There was only one chair next to it. It must be Isvan's.

She hesitated. It worried her that Isvan had run away at the sight of the gatherers. Had he really stolen the ice axe? And why had he ordered so many waffles?

"Come on!" Rufus called. He was already halfway through the park.

Lin hurried after him.

None of them noticed the fresh tracks that led from the Waffleheart's steps and stopped beneath the golden writing on the window. There, someone had rubbed the frost off the pane in a small, eye-sized circle, before continuing into the darkness of the backyard.

The tracks were pointy, with hard, heavy heels.

CHAPTER TWELVE

The Machine Vault lay deep beneath one of the storage barns in the central and straight-lined neighbourhood of Heartworth. Above the barn roof in the distance rose the slender, white tower that Rufus called the belfry, and Lin could hear the hum of many voices coming from the glow of the Great Square. But they weren't headed for the light and music. Instead they passed under a big, black cogwheel and down into a clanging stairwell of metal and echoes. The rusty wall had vents that oozed out a sickly sweet stench.

"Ugh! That's disgusting," she said, hiding her nose in her mitten.

"It smells like scorched caramel," Rufus said.

"Not to me." Lin's belly churned. Maybe she just felt queasy after the heat of the Waffleheart, but she definitely did not like this place.

The room at the bottom of the stairwell was brightly lit, with a polished counter and shelves of leather-bound books. But the air was hot and oppressive, and the smell lingered in the room like stale pipe tobacco. Lin shuddered. She could only imagine how uncomfortable Isvan must have felt down here.

"Good evening," Rufus said, and stepped up to the grey mouse who sat bent over a ledger. His tall, vaulted forehead gave him a look of continuous surprise that widened into worry when he saw the hooded figure of Lin.

"Good evening," said the mouse in a voice so soft it was almost a whisper. The sign on the counter said CALCULATION CLERK and beneath, someone had neatly taped a strip of paper that said NIT.

"My name is Rufus, and I work at the House. I wonder if I could take a peek at your records for September and October. You do keep records around here?"

"Yes," Nit said, glancing at a metal door that led from the office. "I keep lists of all requests and deliveries. But I'm not sure Mrs. Zarka would approve if I showed them to you."

"Oh, she won't mind when it's House business," Rufus said. "There's nothing suspicious in your books, is there?"

"No, of course not," Nit said. He cleared his throat and started leafing through the ledger. "Pomeroy asked for strawberries and vanilla pods. Puskas asked for gold leaf. Ingebrikt asked for an ebony chess piece . . ."

He listed all the requests that had come in, but none of them had been made by Isvan. Rufus drummed his fingers on the counter. "You're sure that's all there is?"

Nit nodded quickly.

Lin pinched Rufus on the upper arm, three times in a row. The triple pinch was a signal she and Niklas used when they needed to stay silent: go further, search harder, there's something there. Right now, she was sure the little calculation clerk was lying.

Rufus hadn't forgotten the signal. He stiffened for a moment, then pried the ledger gently out of Nit's paws.

"May I?"

Nit pursed his lips, but he didn't object.

They skimmed column after column of Nit's even handwriting. There! Between the twenty-eighth and the thirtieth of September, a page had been very carefully cut out.

"What happened to the twenty-ninth?" Rufus asked.

"Nothing." Nit took the ledger back and closed it. He looked frightened.

"You're not in any trouble," Rufus said. "We're just trying to find someone. Maybe you know him? It's the young Winterfyrst, Isvan."

Suddenly the metal door slammed open and a stench belched out from the room beyond. On the threshold stood a speckled owl with green eyes the size of saucers. She wore a black cogwheel on a chain around her neck, and when she lifted it to her eye, Lin realised that it was a monocle.

"Isvan!" the owl wheezed. "How good of you to finally drop by." She advanced toward Lin, feathers rising. "We should start taking your measures immediately." Her beak was stained by something black and sticky, and her breath stank of putrid candy as she nipped and pulled at Lin's chaperon.

"Stop that!" Rufus cried, wedging in between them. "This isn't Isvan!"

Mrs. Zarka paused. "Excuse me?"

"She's a fresher," Rufus said. "Just arrived tonight. I'm showing her around."

"I see." The owl closed first one eye, and then the other. "My mistake. Well, since you're on a tour, let me make amends by offering you a demonstration. The Zarka-Heidelsneck Reconstruction Mechanism is the most magnificent sight in this outpost town."

Lin yearned to get away from the unctuous air, but Mrs. Zarka was clearly involved with Isvan in some way. She pinched Rufus again: go further, search harder. He nodded. "Thank you. We would be honoured to see the Machine."

"Excellent. Nit! Fetch me a shoe from storage!" The owl huffed back into the Machine Vault, leaving the door open for them. On the threshold, Lin almost staggered. The air inside felt like a rotting barrier. But even worse

was the thin keening noise that rang through the cavern-
ous room.

"Enter!" Mrs. Zarka intoned. A fireplace roared at
one end of the chamber, and next to it there was a desk
and a painting named *Wichtiburg* that showed a city of
towers and chimneys. But these tokens of civilisation were
dwarfed by the hulking monster that filled the entire
opposite end of the vault.

The Machine was riddled with wires and tubes through
which a sluggish dark liquid flowed. Tiny, red lightbulbs
turned on and off, chasing each other across the metal
surface. At either end there was a large compartment
behind a dirty glass door, and between the compartments
ran a glass tube.

Mrs. Zarka was standing by a control panel in the
middle. Rufus plodded over to her, whiskers wide.

"It's enormous!" he said, reaching for one of the switches.
"How does it work?"

Mrs. Zarka swatted his hand away.

"Do not touch anything! The control panel is not for
Rodents or other incompetents!"

"Excuse me," said Rufus. "I may be a Rodent, but I'm
not incompetent."

Mrs. Zarka stared down her beak at him. "Really? Then
you are not as uneducated as everyone else in this un-
healthy cold? Perhaps you have studied Technocraft at the

university in Wichtiburg?" She opened her beak wide. "Do you even know the first thing about shred science?"

Rufus was forced to take a step back.

"I thought not," Mrs. Zarka said. "So stop pawing and observe. Today we will make this." She held up a photo of a Feline shoe under Rufus's nose. "But my Machine can make anything you wish for—spices, gems, fine clothes. Even living creatures, I believe, though Teodor will not allow it, that old-fashioned fool."

Mrs. Zarka lifted her monocle and glared across the room at Lin.

"Well, fresher? Are you going to loiter by the entrance all day? Come closer!"

Lin reluctantly left the door and its promise of fresher air and walked to the middle of the room. There she stopped, swaying. Rufus finally noticed that something was wrong and joined her.

"You're all pale!" he whispered.

"How can you stand it?" Lin groaned.

"What, the smell? It's not exactly pleasant, I'll give you that, but . . ."

"No, the noise!"

Rufus started to say something, but Nit poked his head through the metal door. "Forgive me, Mrs. Zarka," he said unhappily. "We don't have any shoes that are calculated and ready for shredding. But perhaps this might do?"

He produced a limp piece of brown leather and held it up for Mrs. Zarka's approval. "I dare say it's a peculiar one, too narrow to be a Rodent model."

"Excellent," Mrs. Zarka hooted, launching herself at the door so she could snatch the piece of leather out of Nit's grasp. Lin got a glimpse of it as the owl rushed past, and she was glad her hood hid the shock on her face.

It was her slipper, the one she had lost when they fled from the Winnower's cottage. "If you'll just let me do the basic calculation . . ." Nit called after her, but Mrs. Zarka waved him to silence.

"We shall make an exception. It is common sense that a slipper and a shoe must be close together in numbers."

She shut the slipper in one of the Machine's compartments and strapped a headgear made of metal bands and suction cups to her head. "This brain goggle will pluck the image of the shoe from my mind." Next, she picked a bottle of dark liquid from a rack, emptying the contents into a spout in the Machine. "Now that I have injected the Machine with Thorndrip, I can . . ."

She pushed a large lever to the floor, and the rest of her sentence drowned in a piercing wail that seemed to come from the depths of the Machine. Lin tried to protect her ears with her mittens, but the wail was in her head, stabbing her. Through leaking eyes, she watched her slipper begin to slowly dissolve from one end. The long glass tube filled with a pearlescent light. In the second compartment, a perfect shoe appeared out of nothing.

But still the slipper was almost whole.

The shoe rattled. Small blisters boiled across its surface, gathering in larger cankers. Then it exploded into black specks that melted off the glass door.

Mrs. Zarka's headgear buzzed and sparked, and the owl flopped backward to the floor.

Even through the terrible scream, Lin heard an alarm howling. The entire Machine vibrated now. Vials of Thorndrip fell down from the rack and broke, and the red lights started to burst, one by one. In the long glass tube, a web of fine cracks had appeared, spreading out like veins in pale skin.

Rufus ran over and pulled hard at the lever. It wouldn't budge.

Lin swallowed, trying to focus. There was a strange, metallic taste in her mouth. The door to the office was open, and a slack-jawed Nit stood in the doorway. "Help!" she yelled at him, and he came tottering over the heaving floor. But instead of shutting the Machine down, the mouse began pulling the unconscious Mrs. Zarka toward the exit. Behind the painting of Wichtiburg deep fissures ate across the wall. Lin had a sickening feeling that getting out of the vault might not be enough to escape.

"He's right!" she screamed at Rufus. "We have to leave!"

But Rufus was busy hauling a fire poker and the heavy desk chair across the floor. With all his strength he launched the chair at the glass compartment.

Lin crouched down and covered her face. Glass rained around her. She peeked out between her arms as Rufus lifted the poker like a baseball bat. He didn't even flinch when a large shard flew by, grazing his whiskers, but swung the metal rod and hit the slipper out of the compartment with a precise strike.

The pearlescent light flashed one final time and disappeared. The noise died down, leaving a ringing in Lin's head, and the alarm was cut short in time for the slipper to give a wet slap as it hit the wall. A thick silence filled the vault, until Rufus began gasping for air.

"Rats!" he panted. "That was close! Are you OK?"

He turned to Lin, lifting her hood so he could see her face. His jaw dropped first, then the poker. "What happened to your nose? Were you hit by the glass?"

Lin touched her nose. Her fingers came away bloody. "I don't know."

Rufus sniffed at her. "Oh no, your ears are bleeding, too! Are you in pain?"

Lin rubbed her temples. Her ears ached dully, but she felt a tremendous relief that the keening sound was gone.

"I think it was the noise."

"You mean the alarm?"

"No, the other noise. The screaming one," Lin said.

"That's what I was trying to tell you before Mrs. Zarka started the Machine! There is no other noise!"

"But there was!" Lin said, confused. "It's gone now, but it was terribly loud!"

Rufus sniffed at her again.

"I think we'd better have Doctor Kott examine you, just in case. Let's get you out of here."

He pulled Lin's hood back into place and put a sheltering arm around her. But before they reached the door, Mrs. Zarka burst back into the vault, feathers smoking. She searched the scene, registering the shards on the floor, the spilled liquid, the shattered compartment, and the cracked glass tube. Finally she spied the slipper, which lay on the floor, looking for all the world like any old scrap of leather.

"Nit!"

Nit appeared behind her, trailing a length of bandage. "Yes, Mrs. Zarka?"

"To whom did that slipper belong?"

Lin kept very still. Because of Nit's comment on the peculiar shape of the slipper, she had given no sign that she recognised it before, and she certainly dare not claim it now.

"I . . . I don't know," Nit said. "One of the gatherers found it in the woods earlier today."

Mrs. Zarka's voice dripped with acid. "I do wish you had thought to inform me of this before you made me feed an unknown object into my delicate, invaluable Machine." She poked her talons in his direction. "You screw-cogged idiot! You deserve to be raked!"

Nit bowed his head, shivering, and Lin realised with a pang that he was expecting some sort of punishment. She couldn't bear it anymore. "Actually, Mrs. Zarka, I think you have it wrong. You would be badly injured if Nit hadn't risked his life to save you. He's a hero."

Nit looked up, forehead all lined with astonishment. Rufus chewed his tassels as he watched Mrs. Zarka, but Lin pressed her lips together. She would rather be exposed than discover what it meant for someone to be raked.

Mrs. Zarka lifted her monocle. Lin could feel the one-eyed gaze trying to burn through her hood. "Is that so?"

Lin stood her ground. "Yes."

"Then I suppose we shall make an exception." Mrs. Zarka turned her back on all of them to fetch a pair of tongs from the fireplace. Gently, gently, she used them to pick the slipper off the floor. "What are you?" she muttered. "Not what you appear, that much is certain. No rune marks, or any Technocraft enhancements. Yet magical you are, magical enough to almost ruin my beloved Machine."

She turned to Nit.

"Send for a glassblower immediately! That pretty Feline if you can find her. She is the best."

Nit vanished, and without sparing Lin and Rufus a thought, Mrs. Zarka brought the slipper over to her desk and sat down to work.

Rufus swished his tail. "Lin is bleeding. I'm taking her to Doctor Kott."

"Yes, yes," the owl said, dismissing them with a wave of her wing.

"One question before we go, though. Why were you expecting Isvan?"

That got Mrs. Zarka's attention. A greedy light kindled in her green saucer eyes. "Isvan? The Winterfyrst? You have seen him?"

Lin and Rufus shook their heads in unison. Mrs. Zarka wheezed, and Lin couldn't tell if she was suspicious or just annoyed. "I have sent for him several times, I require his skull measurements."

Rufus's fur bristled. "*Skull measurements?* What do you need those for?"

"That's confidential," Mrs. Zarka said. "Not even Nit is allowed to assist me on this project. It is not suitable for the uneducated."

That was the last drop for Rufus. "I don't know why the House let you build this ugly Machine in the middle of Sylveros, but I'm going to tell everyone how dangerous it is. And how you treat poor Nit and everyone around you!"

Mrs. Zarka closed first one eye, and then the other.

"No need for that," she wheezed. "Isvan has nothing to fear. The device is entirely for his own good. Besides it has all been approved."

"It's been . . . *approved?*"

"Oh yes," Mrs. Zarka said. "By the House."

On their way back up the stairwell, Rufus stomped so hard on the metal steps that they almost didn't hear it, a small voice rising from the bottom.

"Wait!"

Nit's forehead made a growing, grey moon in the murk as he climbed up to join them, clutching a piece of paper to his chest. "I wanted to thank you for defending me. No one has ever done that before." He swallowed nervously. "And I wanted to tell you that Isvan did come here that day."

"The day that was missing from your ledger?" Rufus asked.

Nit nodded. "September twenty-ninth. Mrs. Zarka instructed me to take his entry out since we couldn't grant his request."

"Why not?" Rufus said. "I thought the Machine can make anything you want."

"It can, but only if you feed it something equally powerful. And Isvan wanted this." Nit handed them the brittle paper.

It was an illustration of an ice axe. Swirly carvings curled up the long handle, and the head was transparent like ice, engraved with the Winterfyrst snow crystal. Beneath the drawing there was a name: FROSTFANG. ALLOWS THE BEARER TO CONTROL THE SUBSTANCE OF ICE.

"September twenty-ninth was three days before he stole Lass's axe," Lin said.

"He got so upset when I said we couldn't help him." Nit rubbed the back of his head. "I said we should ask Mrs. Zarka, but he knocked me down and ran. There were icicles all over the counter afterward."

"Control the substance of ice," Lin whispered. "Does that mean what I think it means?"

Rufus whistled softly through his teeth. "Frostfang is magical!"

CHAPTER THIRTEEN

Doctor Kott lived in a part of town particularly favoured by the Feline clan, a tall hill wound around with narrow alleys, overlooking the Great Square. The doctor's house perched above a small widening at the hairpin turn of a street, and his lights were on under the stethoscope sign. But the good doctor had failed to answer the door, and neither did he appear at the mead house next door, where he liked to have his dinner. Under the sleek, typeset sign of the RED CAT, Rufus pulled his whiskers in dismay. "Where the rats is he?"

Lin sighed. "I said it's okay. I'm not in any pain."

"And I said I don't care. You're seeing the doctor." Rufus peered through the mead house window, nostrils flaring. "The salt fish and hot pepper chowder is almost ready in there. Doctor Kott won't want to miss that."

Lin crinkled her nose. "I don't think we have time to wait for him."

"He brews all his medicines at the Remedy Chamber down at the House. I bet my tail that's where he is."

"Well, we don't have time to run around and search for him, either!" Lin's irritation was rising to the surface. Since the ear-bleeding thing, Rufus had gone into some sort of worrying frenzy, stopping to peer into her ear every twenty steps.

"You're right. But maybe we could do both." He tugged Lin into the square of light from the mead house window. "Stay here where the Red Cat patrons can see you. I have to report those cracks in the Machine Vault. They should be secured, or the whole barn could come down on someone's head. I was going to leave you here with Doctor Kott while I went down to the House, but I guess I'll have to find him while I'm there."

"Then I'll come with you!"

Rufus shook his head. "That's just the thing. I can't take you. The Canines that work in the reception hall are bloodhounds. They would smell you in a heartbeat. You understand that, don't you? Of course, you could wait in the Square, but then you might as well stay here, away from the crowds, in case the doctor comes back."

Lin started to protest, but Rufus put his knuckly fingers on her mouth. "Blood doesn't come out of people's ears for no reason. I need you to see the doctor. Please? Just wait here, and I'll be back in no time."

He set off down the hill on all fours, and soon his rusty tail whipped around the next bend and disappeared. Lin crossed her arms and leaned against the wall. The lilting voice of a willow flute trickled out from the mead house to nag at her. This whole exercise was really pointless. The pain in her ears had diminished to a cotton-ball feeling, and her foot was as good as new. Besides, if Doctor Kott were to examine her, one more Sylvering would know about the human girl.

Not far away, a bell tolled five times. Five o'clock, and still they had no idea where Isvan was. Her father always said: "If you want to make a plan, start with what you know." Inside her mitten, Lin counted off the information they had gathered. First, there was the letter they had found in Isvan's pillow, which may or may not be the reason for his falling out with Teodor. Second, there were the mysterious bite marks in his home, and the fact that someone had been there when Lin and Rufus arrived. Someone who had fled out the back stairs. Third, both Lass and Nit had thought Isvan's behaviour seemed strange, as if he were scared. And fourth, Figenskar and Mrs. Zarka both wanted the Winterfyrst for some reason.

She frowned at her mitten, but she didn't take it off. Cold was seeping through her trousers, numbing her thighs, and she had to get away from that willow flute. She began pacing the little street instead. *Start with what you know.* Well, the only thing she knew for certain was that Isvan had disappeared sometime after October third, and that he had wanted a magical ice axe. What she didn't know was why.

All the way up here, she had tried to convince Rufus that they should go and see Teodor. But Rufus had refused. "I don't trust him with this," he had said. "In fact, I don't trust him at all." Lin didn't trust Teodor either, but if anyone knew something about that axe, it would be the old fox. She grimaced as she made another turn, and there she froze.

She was not alone in the street. She hadn't seen him, withdrawn in the unlit lane between Doctor Kott's house and the Red Cat, poised at the edge of his stone base, leaning forward. A statue of a boy with slicked-back hair and a pinched nose. A fellow Twistrose, crowned with old snow.

"Why aren't you on Eversnow Square with the others?" Lin brushed the snow off his plaque.

Edvard Uriarte. 1919.

None of the Twistrose statues she had seen featured their Petlings, but this boy had a crow at his feet. A bird, not a Beak, and it lay on its back, as if it were dead.

"I suppose you solved your puzzle, since they made you into a statue. Any tips on where I can find Isvan Winterfyrst?"

The statue stared past her under hooded lids. Lin turned to see what he saw. Edvard Uriarte might be hidden in the shadows, but he had a magnificent view of Sylveros.

The snowy roofs spread out before them, slashed by the dark river. Some neighbourhoods remained hidden in the folds of the town, but the domed palace to the north of the town was easy to locate, and so was Heartworth and the House with its spires and the belfry. Already the Great Square milled with Sylverings, queuing at the popcorn carts or cocoa stands, or dancing in the pavilion. She thought she saw Pomeroy fussing over his gold-striped stand, but she couldn't find Rufus in the crowd.

All of a sudden she had a feeling that she should leave immediately. It was almost like a push between the shoulders, or a whisper in her ear.

"Edvard Uriarte," she murmured. "I think you might be right."

Lin wasn't going to wait on Doctor Kott's steps. She was the Twistrose, and she would never solve her task if she didn't spend her time more wisely. Using the belfry and Main Road as a guideline, she quickly located her destination. It wasn't far at all. She could even be back before Rufus.

Quite pleased with her decision, she pulled her cardigan tight and started down the hill.

She did not think to look behind her.

Chapter Fourteen

S oon she was standing under the quill sign in Peppersnap Nook. There was a heavy ring engraved with a
fiery pattern on the door, and Lin used it to knock.
She waited, kicked some ice off the steps, knocked again,
and waited some more.

No one came.

Had everyone in this town gone to the feast? Carefully
she tried the handle. Locked. But through the red glass
window she could just make out a flickering light, and
from the chimney by the turret there was a wisp of smoke.
She was sure Teodor would not have left the house with
candles and fires lit.

The backyard gate was ajar. She hesitated for a moment
before she stepped through it, trying very hard not to
appear like a trespasser.

"Teodor!" she called loudly. A quick peek inside Fabian's

stables revealed a rose-painted stall with lacy curtains and a gilded crib, but no Fabian. The belled harness hung on the wall; the sleigh with the carved fox masks stood dripping beneath it. Then they weren't out driving.

She found the kitchen entrance to the house, and knocked three times before she entered. "Is anybody home? It's me, Lin!"

The small kitchen was unlit, but the snow in the backyard reflected the light from the Wanderer through the doorway, outlining a plate of oatmeal cookies and Teodor's porcelain cup on the table.

Lin left the door open in case of a quick retreat and sidled into the room. She removed her mittens and stuck a finger into the cup. The tea was cold.

"Teodor," she called again. The only reply she got was a faint tick from the table clock in the library.

In the hallway, Lin discovered the source of the flickering light: a candle on a dresser. It had almost burned down, and the wax had spilled onto the tablecloth. A fire waiting to happen. She hurried over to the dresser and pursed her lips to blow it out . . . but didn't.

It was most certainly risky to snoop around the house of someone who might turn up at any moment, especially when that someone was an old Wilder with a nasty temper. But she had come here for answers, and since Teodor wasn't around, she should try to find one or two herself. She picked up the candle and walked into the library.

The armchairs cast black shadows across the carpet. The table clock on the desk showed four minutes past five. Lin lifted her light toward the bookcases that reached from floor to ceiling. There must be thousands of books in here, and many of them didn't even have a title on the spine. She pulled one out at random, leaving a trail in the thick dust on the shelf. It was printed in an old-fashioned type that she couldn't read. This was no good.

"Bring your brain to the party," she muttered to herself. Where would Teodor keep books on magical items or Winterfyrst lore? Books that he perhaps wanted to keep secret from both her and Rufus? Not in the room where he had repeatedly left her alone tonight, to get milk and warm clothes and to check something in . . .

The turret.

Melting candle wax spilled over her hand as she crept up the stairs. "Teodor? Are you up there?" But she had a feeling he wasn't, so she kept her voice to a whisper. When she passed the Twistrose girl of the painting, poised on the threshold to darkness, she nodded in silent recognition.

The turret chamber had windows facing in every direction, three round ones and one square. Under each of the round windows a three-leafed symbol had been carved into the wall, the same kind she knew from the Hall of Winter and the table clock. The east and south symbols were cracked and smudged by soot, and only the one to the north looked clean and whole.

Under the square window that faced the belfry and the lake beyond, the wide sill doubled as a desk. On it sat a single book, a fat tome with leather binding. Lin put the candle down and lifted the book gently.

The title page said *The Book of Frost and Flame*. On the next page, there was a little poem, written in beautiful longhand.

> Ever bound, ever sworn,
> To the Realms of the forlorn.
> Frost and Flame,
> One and same,
> Hidden guards of Dream and Thorn.

Beneath the poem, two symbols were drawn, one above the other. Lin had seen them both before. The lower symbol showed three leaping flames, exactly like the stained-glass window in Teodor's front door. The upper symbol showed three blue icicles, like the window in the Winterfyrst mansion. They fit perfectly together. How could she have missed that?

She skimmed through the first chapter. Frost and Flame was the name of a secret order founded nearly fifteen hundred years ago, sworn to protect the Realms. The servants of Frost were warriors called Frostriders. Their task was to protect caravans and border farms, walls and mountain passes, and if need be, to give their lives for others. The members of Flame were called Flamewatchers. They kept chronicles of everything that happened in the Realms, but they were also runemasters, which seemed to be some sort of sorcerer.

Lin lowered the book, wide-eyed.

Teodor was chief chronicler of Sylver. Could the glass painting in Teodor's door mean that he was a Flamewatcher? If so, the old Wilder knew magic. And those three leaves of the carved symbols – could they not be leaping tongues of flame? Rufus would never get over this!

Down in the library, the table clock ticked. With a pang Lin imagined Rufus arriving at Doctor Kott's house, only to find the street empty. It was silly of him to refuse coming here, but she didn't want him to worry. She let the rest of the pages run through her fingers. Halfway in, she felt a snag in the flow, and when she saw what caused it, she caught her breath. At the end of a chapter on Frostrider artifacts, she read:

"'Some number this magical axe among Frostrider heirlooms, but they are wrong. In truth, it belongs to our long-standing members, the Winterfyrsts of Sylver. The axe, which bears the name Frostfang, is not only a most powerful weapon of defence. It also unlocks the sacred Well of the Winterfyrsts.'"

The next page had been ripped out.

Lin brought out the illustration Isvan had taken to the Machine Vault. A match.

"So you were here too, Isvan," Lin muttered. He must have sneaked into the turret while Teodor was out, because Lin was pretty sure that Teodor would never have allowed anyone to damage his books.

"Sadly, old fox, you are not here for this, either." She tore the other page out and tucked both of them into her right pocket. "One point to Miss Rosenquist!"

Somewhere in the house, there was a faint creak.

Lin started, knocking over the candle. It toppled off the desk and died, leaving her only the Wanderer to see by. She padded to the top of the stairs.

"Teodor? Is that you?"

She hurried down the steps, sorely tempted to bolt into the kitchen and out through the backyard. But she had already revealed herself, so it was probably best to try and explain. She hesitated on the library threshold. Over by the armchairs, she thought she saw a movement. "I . . . I found the back entrance open, and I only wanted to speak to you . . ."

The embers in the fireplace spat and flared, but there was no answer. Lin walked slowly over to the chairs, and there she discovered what they had concealed since she entered the house.

Teodor's briefcase, which he had kept so well protected, lay on the floor. A letter stuck halfway out under the lid.

It was addressed to Teodor and had already been opened. Lin eased it out of its envelope and read it. As she did so, the blood drained from her fingers and lips.

Dear Mr. Teodor,

Thank you so much for your letter, and for overcoming your doubts about my craft. We have wasted too much time quarrelling when we should be combining our powers for the good of Sylver and all the Realms. Allow me to propose a Technocraft solution to the Winterfyrst plight.

For another client, I have been working on a design inspired by Heidelsneck's classic Thorndripper. But I have improved the device so it fits the child instead of a sparrow's chest. The Brain Tapper spikes will be inserted into Isvan's skull until they touch his brain. When the spikes are charged, the Technocraft tension should bring forth the Winterfyrst knowledge locked inside his mind.

To save time, it might be best if you send the boy to me immediately so his skull can be properly measured. I enclose my drawings.

Your servant always,
Rosana Zarka

Lin sank into the nearest armchair. She could hardly breathe.

The first drawing was titled "Thorndripper" and showed a little sparrow caught in a gruesome contraption, a metal ring with three slim thorns that pierced its chest. Blood leaked down the thorns and into a linked set of pots and tubes until it ended in a bulbous glass vial as a black, thick liquid.

The second drawing was titled "Brain Tapper" and showed a helmet of thin bands, much like the one Mrs. Zarka had worn when she operated the Machine. But instead of suction cups, this one had three long, sharp spikes that pointed toward the middle.

The third drawing showed how to use the helmet. It was strapped to the head of a boy, and the spikes were driven into his head. The boy was biting down on a piece of rubber. His eyeballs were white, yet he was sitting upright, writing on a piece of paper.

Horror sluiced through Lin's veins. This was Mrs. Zarka's secret experiment? And Teodor had ordered it? Rufus was certainly right not to trust him. Could Isvan have seen this letter? No wonder he had been scared of his so-called guardian!

She had just regained her breath when a voice sounded behind the armchair. It was silky on the surface, but so cold underneath that Lin's spine was filled with ice.

"Little Lin. Little *Rosenquist*, hmmm? Oh yes, I heard your little cry of triumph up there, and now I know your full name. But don't be so terrified! Come to Figen-skar!"

And darkness fell from the ceiling and caught Lin like a mouse in a trap.

CHAPTER FIFTEEN

There was no way out.

Lin flailed around, but all she felt was coarse, chafing fabric. It was a sack, she realised. A burlap sack big enough to fit her inside!

Something hit her shoulder and knocked her over. Down by her feet she spotted a glimmer of light that must be the opening. But even as Lin twisted around to reach it, it closed up with a hard tug.

Dust and fibres stuck in her throat, and her screams for help came out as stupid croaks. She could hardly hear them at all, her pulse pounded so loudly in her head. The sack opened up again, and Figenskar's dusk-blue needle teeth appeared. "Easy now, little girl!"

He held her down and tied her hands tightly at the wrists. Then he brought out a wrinkled rag, spattered with some kind of dried-up, black ichor, and pushed it at Lin's lips. It smelled sweet and cloying with a sting of liquor. Figenskar pinched her nose between two claws, and when she had to gasp for air, he jammed the rag into her mouth.

Cocking his head, he inspected his work. "What were you doing sneaking around in the chief chronicler's home? Looking for signs of Isvan, hmmm? Did you find any?"

Lin glared at him.

"Cat caught your tongue? Don't worry. You will have your chance to tell." Figenskar's grin grew wide and hard. "Oh yes, little Twistrose," he murmured, pushing back Lin's chaperon so he could study her face. "You may not think so now, but you will tell. Everyone sings before the Margrave!"

The Margrave! Lin made a mewling sound into the rag. Figenskar knew something about the soothsinger prophecy? His pleased expression was the last thing she saw before he closed the sack over her head.

The three steps of Teodor's backyard stairs slammed mercilessly into Lin's back. She was lifted onto something hard. Icy air seeped in through the weave of the burlap.

"We're going for a little evening stroll," Figenskar snarled next to her head. "But first I want you to know what will happen if you do any more squealing or squeaking or try to draw attention to yourself in any way. One night, when you are gone, I will pay a visit to Rufus's grubby little den in Stitch Lane. He's quick, I'll give him that. But I am a Feline and a hunter. I can be quieter than the first light of dawn. I will bend over his pathetic sleeping pocket and take my time finding the weakest spot on his little Rodent neck. And with a simple snap . . . Pest control. Do you understand?"

Lin lay very still. She understood, but she couldn't believe it. Hadn't Teodor said that only creatures once loved by a child lived in Sylver? Who on Earth could have loved this dreadful cat?

The darkness deepened as a heavy cover was pulled over her body. Soon she heard the sound of snow beneath runners. A sled, then. Dread gathered into a lump in Lin's throat. How would Rufus ever be able to track her down if there were no footprints in the snow? Come to think of it, how would he even know where to begin his search?

They moved fast, always uphill. Lin listened to the creaking of Figenskar's boots in the snow, trying to guess where he was taking her. Several times she heard voices, but none close enough to be of any good to her. But at last someone called out, not far from the sled. "Figenskar!"

Lin knew that curt voice! It was Lass the gatherer. The sled and the footsteps stopped.

"Evening stroll, Figenskar?" the Canine said. She was very close now. Lin could hear her loll-tongued breaths right above her head.

"Stroll, yes," Figenskar said smoothly. "What can I do for you, Gatherer?"

"I have gatherloot for Ursa Minor, but he has managed

to fall off the map on his way to the Machine Vault. Have you seen him?"

"I'm afraid not."

"I went to the vault. They were cleaning up after some sort of accident. I thought for sure it was Minor's doing, but Nit said he never showed up."

"You don't say," Figenskar said.

"And that's not the only strange thing that has happened, either. I had a chat with Ronia at the Bowl and Biscuit. She told me that two different customers had seen a blue flash coming from old Teodor's turret a little while ago. And afterward he came running out of the house, staring toward the mountains like he had seen a Nightmare. And he got on his horse and galloped off toward the woods!"

Figenskar didn't answer. His tail lashed against the sled.

Inside the sack, Lin's heart pounded. What would happen if she called for help? Lass would hear, even through the rag. But Figenskar knew where Rufus lived. Had been there, even, since he knew about the sleeping pocket. And he had promised to kill Rufus if she didn't keep quiet. No, she couldn't risk it.

Lass yawned. "Well. I'd best keep looking. See you in the Square." The snow groaned under her feet as she turned to leave. But abruptly she stopped and snorted. "What's this you've got on your sled, anyway? I could help you get it up the hill if you want. It's a mighty climb to the Observatory."

Something brushed against Lin's foot, and the heavy cover lifted ever so slightly. A pale sliver of light shone through the burlap somewhere by her left knee, and for a moment Lin thought she would be saved. But Figenskar briskly tugged the cover tight.

"A surprise," he purred. "For Wanderer's Eve. I'd best take care of it myself, hmmm?"

Lass hesitated another moment, but she said good-bye and hurried off.

Figenskar hissed softly. "Well done, little Rosenquist, for not squealing. You must like your Rodent more than he deserves." He walked in silence for a little while before he added: "You can't imagine my delight in finding you here this evening. You just might save both my deal and my tail. I'm sure the Margrave will find you to his liking. After all, you and he have much in common. You are kin, hmmm?"

Lin flinched. It had just dawned on her that the Margrave Figenskar spoke of was not at all the Wanderer called by a different name, but a person. And by the strain in Figenskar's voice, the Feline was scared of him.

"Oh, you don't think so?" Figenskar's laugh had a brittle ring. "Well, you shall see for yourself before long."

Lin didn't respond, but in the darkness of the burlap sack, she wondered. See what? How could anyone in Sylver be her kin?

The air changed. It was crisper, no longer laced with woodsmoke. Lin chewed over Figenskar's hints about the Margrave, but without more information, she couldn't make them fit. Instead she turned her thoughts to a detail she could make use of. Light had shone through the burlap when Lass lifted the cover. Lin may not be able to run without risking Rufus's life, but there was a tear in the sack, and that changed everything.

She felt around with her bound hands until she discovered the hole. It was small, but it would do. Inch by inch, she pulled the chewed, old drawstring out of her cardigan collar and tied a double knot. The troll-hunter signal for "I am here." Holding her breath, she pushed the green string through the tear. There were creaky steps and sliding runners and her pulse whooshing in her ears, but no sign that Figenskar had noticed. Now all she could do was hope that Rufus would find her message.

They stopped. Lin thought they must be close to something massive, because she felt it brooding over her, at once sound-stealing and full of faint echoes. A door creaked open. Figenskar dragged her off the sled and across two thresholds before he dropped the sack to the floor with a snicker. "Success."

Lin could tell from the silkiness of that one word that there was someone in the room with them.

"Success? The boss has found the Winterfyrst?" The stranger had a brassy, blaring voice.

"No. But I have caught the Twistrose instead, and I think she will do quite nicely. Cold child, warm child, the difference is not great. Did you perform your little task?"

"Little task," the blaring voice said. "Yes. It's cracked now. Dead and destroyed."

"Excellent," Figenskar said. "I shall finish the last one myself later tonight. Teriko, my good lieutenant. You may ready the casks and burn the evidence. Operation Corvelie is back on track."

"Back on track!" said the one named Teriko. "You're a genius, boss!"

"The Sylverings will never know what hit them," Figenskar said smugly. "And as for this little bareskin . . ." He nudged Lin with the toe of his boot. ". . . she can ripen while we finish our preparations. Put her in the cage."

"The cage? Right you are, boss. She'll sit pretty there," the stranger cackled.

"Remember, little Rosenquist," the cat purred in Lin's ear, "you're caught, like a worm on a fishhook, and you can spare yourself any wiggling, hmmm? This is the Observatory. You're in my house now."

Lin was hauled off again, this time in violent jerks, down a long flight of stairs, and along a pebbly tunnel. By the time they stopped again, she hurt all over. She heard a jangle of keys, followed by a rasping click that echoed off the walls.

The sack opened, and as Lin struggled free of the burlap, metal banged against metal. She sat up, blinking.

She was trapped inside a cage inside a cave. Smoking torches lit the bottom, which was soiled like a neglected barn floor and reeked even worse. Tree-trunk perches covered in dirt and old feathers crisscrossed the cage, and in the middle hung a fat, rusty chain that ended about twenty feet above the ground. Fastened to the chain with a thick rope was the only clean object in the entire cave: a large, gleaming mirror.

Right in front of Lin there was a door of metal bars, and from outside it, a perfectly round eye stared at her. It sat next to a flat, strong beak that curved viciously at the end, surrounded by shiny feathers in deep blue, green, and yellow. Figenskar's lieutenant was a parrot.

"What a lucky little girl!" the parrot cawed. "Not everyone gets to borrow Teriko's home sweet home." He poked a claw through the bars. Lin scrambled away.

"Now, now, bareskin. Teriko will unstuff her mouth. Or does she like the taste of rag?"

Scalp prickling, Lin allowed the bird to pick the rag out of her mouth. She lifted her bound hands to her jaw, coughing and spitting. The parrot turned his back and hopped toward the craggy archway that led out of the cave.

"Wait!" Lin said hoarsely. "Don't leave me here! I have to finish my task!"

Teriko turned one unblinking eye toward her and gaped wide and high. "Task! Stupid little task!"

"But it's important! I'm a Twistrose! Rufus knows, ask him! Or ask Teodor!"

"Teodor," the bird spat. And with that he left, hop, scrape, hop, scrape, sweeping gravel with his tail feathers.

Lin kicked on the cage bars and yelled after him, "Sylver is in danger. You have to let me out!" But the only answer she got was the slamming of a heavy door in the distance.

Her legs buckled. She couldn't bear lying down on the muck-encrusted floor. Instead she sank down on her haunches and hid her face in her throbbing hands.

Rufus would never find her, not in this wretched dungeon. Nobody knew where she was, except for a malicious Feline and a gloating parrot. Nobody knew where Isvan was, either. There would be no statue in her name. She would never see Summerhill or her parents again. Instead she would see the Margrave, who had taken his name from a star, and who scared even Figenskar.

"I'm sorry," Lin whispered, and she was. She was sorry she had left without telling Rufus. She was sorry she had been so cross about moving to Oldtown. But most of all, she was so very sorry that she hadn't stayed to taste her mother's rice pudding.

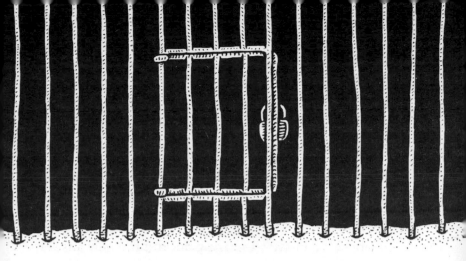

CHAPTER SIXTEEN

Two troubled voices found their way down the slanting corridor toward the parrot cave, accompanied by rapid footsteps.

"Really, Mirja, I hope you realise how improbable this sounds!"

"But it's true! I was waiting in line on the Memory balcony, and Memory is next to Comfort, right?"

"Yes, but . . ."

"That's where I saw her, the Comfort mirror. A human girl with messy hair and a shabby cardigan."

"Messy hair and cardigans are not uncommon on human children."

"But, Marvin, she was sitting at the bottom of a giant, filthy cage exactly like Teriko's, right here beneath the Observatory."

"The Observatory cage doesn't belong to Teriko,"

Marvin huffed. "A true Starfalcon was found trapped inside it once. He was long dead, nothing but feathers and bones, but his cage is still a site of magic. Only the chief observer is allowed down here."

"That may be," Mirja said. "But it's Teriko's now, full of Teriko's muck and Teriko's trinkets. I delivered the glass for his mirror, so I've seen it."

"Oh," Marvin said, sounding uncertain.

"Naturally, the sight of a girl in that cage appalled me. I got up to get a better view. And when I leaned out over the balcony railing, I saw her in not one, not two, but four of the magical mirrors! She was crouched on the ground, the wretched thing. Suddenly her eyes bulged in surprise, or in pain. And that's when the mirrors all went blank."

Marvin cleared his throat. "That was unusual, I agree, but the mirrors rekindled instantly. It was probably a natural fluctuation of magic. We were told to expect them on Wanderer's Eve."

"Rubbish. Even I know what it means when a human child appears in several mirrors at once."

"It means she is in dire need," Marvin said breathlessly.

"Exactly."

They walked in silence for a moment before Marvin said, "Even so, it must have been a different cage. There are no human girls in Sylver."

"There is one tonight! I saw a hooded stranger at the

Waffleheart a little while ago, wearing a cardigan. She didn't smell like a Petling. She smelled like a child. I'm telling you, a Twistrose has come."

"But what would she be doing down here?"

"I know what I saw."

Someone stumbled on a loose rock, and Marvin complained, "I do wish you had made a note of the girl's name."

"I think it began with an L. Laura? Liesl? But I didn't catch her last name."

"Oh dear. I just hope Mr. Figenskar doesn't find out we took his keys to get down here. He gets so frightfully angry. . . ."

Two persons appeared in the cave opening. One was a guinea pig with horn-rimmed spectacles, a red woollen vest, and generous bangs slicked down with pomade. The other was the pretty Feline from the Waffleheart. Both stopped in their tracks when they spied the cage.

"She is gone!" Mirja said. "She was sitting right there. . . ."

"This is not good," Marvin squeaked, searching through a crowded key ring. "Not good at all."

The rasping click sounded, and Marvin took a few steps into the cage. With trembling hands he picked something up from the ground, lifted it up against the torch light, and straightened his glasses. "But this is . . . Oh, dear me!"

He dropped the object and rushed out of the cave. His little feet pounded up the long corridor like drumsticks. Mirja whirled about and ran after him.

Broken glass littered the cage floor. The largest shard, the one Marvin had picked up, dripped with fresh, red blood.

CHAPTER SEVENTEEN

The door at the top of the stairs slammed. Lin let out a long, shivering breath. She had intended to reveal herself to the two Petlings and beg them to save her from Figenskar. But when they walked into the cave, she just couldn't. In her head she kept hearing Figenskar's gloating hiss: "You're in my house now." Marvin worked for him. What if he delivered her straight back into his claws?

So she had kept her silence as she dangled high above them, clinging to the chain that carried Teriko's mirror. Or what was left of Teriko's mirror, a clunky metal frame and a few bits of glass around the edges.

While she was crouched on the floor, Lin had heard a clear ringing noise, like a gong struck in the distance. She had raised her head and noticed something in the slime on the cage bottom: a rock covered in parrot turd. Almost without considering, she had picked it up, weighed it for measure, and hurled it at the mirror.

On her first attempt, the mirror cracked. On her third attempt, the glass had shattered into hundreds of pieces that rained down on the floor. She had cut the rope on her hands with the biggest shard. But when Mirja's and Marvin's voices sounded in the tunnel, she had started so badly she cut her wrist, too. She still had no idea how she had managed to climb from perch to perch and onto the mirror with hands that were slippery with blood.

Lin eyed the nearest tree-trunk perch, which was slick with excrement. She wasn't at all convinced she could jump that far again, and it was a twenty-foot drop to the floor. But if she wanted to get out of the cage, she had no choice but to risk it.

The very instant she made her decision, there was another boom from the door.

"But Mr. Figenskar! I assure you, she was gone when we got there!"

There was no way she could get down in time to get out through the cage door. There was no way she could escape at all. Unless . . . Lin looked above her. The red glow from the torches didn't reach the top of the cage. The dark might be deep enough to hide her up there.

Using her legs to push and her one good arm to hold

on, she began to climb. The voices approached quickly, Marvin's simpering and worried, Figenskar's deep and furious, and just when she thought she had better stop climbing, Lin bumped her head into something hard. She had reached the end of the chain.

Far below, Figenskar stepped into the circle of light with a flashlight in his paw, and Marvin trailing behind. Shoulders hunched, the chief observer walked around the mirror shards, setting them alight with the white beam. His boots made sucking noises in the muck.

"Who broke the mirror?" he said, so softly that Lin almost didn't catch his words. "Was it you, *Rodent*?"

"What? No! It was already smashed when we arrived!"

Figenskar whirled about and sent the flashlight beam straight into Marvin's face.

"You expect me to believe that? After you left your post, after you came down here even when I expressly forbade you to?"

"It's true!" Marvin squeaked, cowering against the bars. "I swear it!"

Figenskar glared at him for a long, cruel moment before he turned his attention back to the glass. He picked up the bloody shard and ran a claw along the edge. "She can't be far away. How fortunate that you encountered Teriko in the corridor, hmmm? She won't have got past him."

Figenskar sniffed the cave floor outside the open door.

"I don't see her marks anywhere. Rodent! Search the tunnel for footprints!"

"It's too dark, Mr. Figenskar. My night vision isn't what it used to be."

"Then take one of the torches, for winter's sake!"

Lin dropped her jaw. The torches! There were at least twenty of them along the wall, and they all gave off black smoke. The air in the cave ought to be thick with it, but it wasn't. That could only mean that the smoke was escaping somewhere. Maybe there was another way out after all.

She squinted at the craggy rocks in the ceiling. The end of the chain was fastened to a hook. To its left, there was a ridge, big enough to hide a crack. She leaned out.

One point to Miss Rosenquist!

It wasn't a crack; it was a tunnel opening. Even better: Inside the tunnel, she could just make out what appeared to be the bottom rung of a ladder.

Lin reached out as far as she possibly could. Her fingers locked around the metal bar. She could do it. She had climbed the highest branches of the morello tree outside her window on Summerhill a hundred times, she could do this. Before she had time to reconsider, she let go of the chain and flung herself at the ladder.

It was a terrible mistake.

Her injured hand couldn't carry her weight. It slipped, and just like that, she was dangling lopsided from the ceiling, ten yards above the ground. Her sudden jump set the chain to quivering, and the mirror frame danced back and forth above Figenskar's head with tiny movements.

The chief observer was bent over picking shards up from the floor. His ears turned backward as if to pin down some irksome noise. His tail flicked. Lin winced and waited for the "hmmm".

But it didn't come. Instead he called Marvin back into the cave. "Alert the clerks! Tell them her name is Rosenquist. Lin Rosenquist. You know what to do."

"Yes, Mr. Figenskar." Marvin pushed his glasses back, looking very relieved to be dismissed.

"Wait! First hand me my keys. I don't want any more meddling."

"Yes, Mr. Figenskar."

Marvin approached his boss warily, holding out the keys. But before Figenskar could seize them, the guinea pig pulled back his hand and touched his neck, as if something itched there. Slowly, he turned his broad face upward, staring straight toward Lin. She expected him to cry out in alarm, but instead he jumped as something dark spattered onto his glasses.

Blood from the cut on her wrist.

Figenskar hissed, veering about with his flashlight. The beam rose along the cave wall like a hungry spotlight.

Suddenly Lin found the strength she needed after all.

Ignoring the pain, she hoisted her weight up so she could reach the next rung on the ladder. And the next, and the next.

Just as the flashlight beam swept by, she pulled her legs up into the tunnel. Clinging to the ladder, she hugged her injured arm to her chest.

She had no way of knowing if Figenskar had seen her or not. But deep below there was a terrible snarl.

CHAPTER EIGHTEEN

A t first it hadn't occurred to Lin to count the rungs.
But the tunnel was so dark it felt like climbing
into nothing. Counting made it seem like she
was going somewhere. She reached for the next metal bar
and pushed with her legs.

Thirty.

The injured arm blazed with pain. Cold, smoky air blew
up the narrow shaft, chilling Lin's stiff and trembling legs.
She rested her head against the rock. Beneath, a red circle
marked the opening to the parrot cave. It had grown quiet
down there. Maybe Figenskar hadn't figured out where
she had gone. Or maybe he knew where the tunnel ended
and sat there waiting, like the Summerhill cat by his favourite mouse hole. Well, if he did, he did. There was nothing
Lin could do but keep climbing.

At forty-three, the ladder ended and the tunnel split in

two. One fork continued upward with the draft. The other slanted to the side, ending in a pink glow. Lin crept into the side tunnel and lay down for a moment, to stretch her sore limbs and examine the cut on her wrist.

There was a piece of glass wedged in the wound. No wonder it was painful! Lin picked the shard out and tossed it on the tunnel floor. The cut began to bleed again, but it hurt less. Encouraged, she crawled toward the end of the tunnel.

The opening was covered by a heavy fabric. It yielded slightly to Lin's touch, letting in a glimpse of light and the crackle of a lit fireplace. She waited, listened. Nothing but the sputter and hiss of the fire.

Lin pulled her hood back up, lowered herself to the floor, and inched along the wall to peer around the edge of the curtain.

No pouncing Feline in sight. Just a large office of white-washed plaster with a fireplace, a small chest, a desk with an ancient gramophone, and two doors. Golden lamplight fell on a sign next to the gramophone: CHIEF OBSERVER FIGENSKAR. The curtain turned out to be a tapestry of a white bird soaring in a sky of faded ruby, rose, and scarlet. If she didn't know, Lin would never have guessed it concealed a tunnel opening.

She crossed the room and put her ear to the first door. Muffled, urgent voices in the distance. Behind the second door, there was only silence, and the wood felt cold against her skin. In a puddle of water by the threshold lay a frayed burlap thread. This must be where she had been brought in, which meant it was the way out.

With her hand on the doorknob, Lin paused. Figenskar had been searching for Isvan. He needed him for some sort of secret operation, something to do with the Margrave, something he said would *hit* the Sylverings. And here she was, alone in Figenskar's office. What kind of Twistrose would waste an opportunity like this? Legs jittering, she turned around, away from the exit.

She found the drawers of the desk empty. Not so much as a scrap of paper in them. But the pile of ashes in the fireplace seemed conspicuously big. *Burn the evidence,* Figenskar had told Teriko. Whatever they were planning, it would happen soon.

Lin found a poker and raked through the embers.

Teriko may have been obedient, but he had also been sloppy. At the bottom of the ashes an object had survived the flames: a small, slim leather cylinder engraved with a bird of prey. The metal top was too hot to touch, so Lin set the cylinder on the edge of the hearth to cool off.

Next to the fireplace stood a carved, wooden chest. Or by another name: casket. Figenskar had also told Teriko to *ready the casket.* What was in this thing? Lin pushed at the lid, but she couldn't shift it. She peered into the empty keyhole, but she had no idea how to pick a lock. No points to be earned there.

The final object to be examined was the strange gramophone. It had a black horn and on the turntable lay a peculiar record, fat with wobbly grooves and lined with small glass pebbles.

Lin turned the crank. Nothing happened. She had a feeling there was something missing, something that ought to fit into a small, scorched hole in the side of the player. But then her hand grazed the needle, and with a nip of electricity, it lit up with red lights and swung over the spinning turntable.

The whining noise the needle made as it carved into the disc made Lin's flesh crawl. Or perhaps that was the voice that streamed out of the horn. Deep and wheezy, it sounded toneless and somehow dead in the thick static that kept tearing pieces out of the sentences.

"Figenskar," the voice grated. "The prophecy says my elixir . . . made from the Child of Ice. The Soothsinger . . . warning to the Vulpes of Lucke . . . He must not see the song. Intercept the falcon messenger . . . Bring the child to me. On Wanderer's Eve, I shall have the Nightmares ready . . . From the ashes of Operation Corvelie, a new lord will rise."

A deep, whistling breath, another burst of static, then the voice was gone, leaving only a burned smell. Lin hurried over to the hearth and picked up the cylinder. It could very well be a message tube, and the engraved bird of prey could be a falcon. Figenskar had succeeded. Lin stuck the message tube into her boot. Time to escape.

She had just placed her hand on the cold doorknob again when she heard someone speaking on the other side.

"You are sure she has not come this way?" It was Figenskar, approaching fast, and there was murder in his voice. "I want her found!" he said. "Now!"

Lin leaped back. She had to hide, immediately. No time to crawl back behind the tapestry. The only way was forward, through the other door, deeper into the bowels of the Observatory.

Quickly, she slipped through into an empty corridor lined with doors. At the far end there were double doors marked as the Observatory hall. Through the foggy glass windows Lin could only see a silvery light with shadows flitting by. But she heard plenty: clipped shouting, airy swooshes, and a deep, rolling sigh, like ocean waves in a seashell. Her ears itched as she ran down the corridor.

Hop, scrape, hop, scrape.

Lin recognised the footsteps. Teriko. She leaped through the closest side door just in time before the double doors burst open.

"Find her! Find the little treat!"

Holding her breath, Lin cast about. She was in a stairwell now, also brightly lit, with winding stairs of latticed metal. Still nowhere to hide. The stairs were her only chance. She climbed them silently, and found another long hallway, a cramped passage that curved off to either side, with red lacquered doors on the inner wall. It didn't take her long to realise it was a closed circle.

Down in the corridor, Teriko cawed, "Blood on the floor! Boss! Boss! This way!"

Lin's heart pounded. Stupid blood! Taking care to keep her bleeding wrist away, she opened one of the red doors. It had a sign that said LUCK, and behind it she found a covered balcony cast in shadow. A music stand and a telescope were mounted on the railing, and beyond it . . .

Lin stepped through the crack to gaze out into the bright room.

The Observatory hall.

Above her, a dome of milky glass shone brilliantly, as if lit from the outside by a high summer sun. Thousands of black specks were etched in the glass, some connected by straight lines; constellations plotted on a reverse colour map of stars, and Lin found both Orion and the Big Dipper. It was the Earth night sky.

Under the dome, the room formed a courtyard in the shape of a hexagon. High up on each of the six walls hung a covered balcony like Lin's, with carved railings and plaques marking them as Hope, Courage, Comfort, Strength, Luck, and Memory. Farthest down on the wall of Hope, Lin spied something that made her belly lurch. Another way out.

But how was she going to get there without raising the alarm? The stone floor of the hall teemed with workers. Petlings of all clans sat behind tall counters with telescopes, watching the walls, scribbling in ledgers. Others sorted papers or rummaged through rows and rows of archive cabinets. The air was crowded, too: whole flocks of finches and canaries milled about below the dome.

Wings flapped, archive drawers banged, voices buzzed, and beneath it all was a hum, as if high voltage wires riddled the bones of the building.

Yet the loudest noise, the one that made Lin's eardrums itch and her pulse flutter, was the rolling sigh she had heard through the double doors. When she realised where the sound was coming from, she forgot all about escaping for a moment. Mesmerised, she walked to the railing to use the telescope.

On the walls hung huge, framed mirrors. Rather, they resembled mirrors, but instead of the bright hall, they showed a blue mist just shy of black. Ghostly, grey creatures moved in the glass, and they weren't finches or canaries. None of them belonged here, not in the Observatory, and not in Sylver.

For the ghostly creatures were children. Hundreds of human children, speaking or singing, crying or sleeping, with no other sound than the soft, rolling murmur from the glass. Below each child there was a light blue square with a name and a number. After a while, the children retreated back into the darkness, and new faces appeared, like captured water lilies released from the bottom of a pond.

Lin pointed the telescope toward a girl who was rising to the surface on the nearest wall. The girl lay in bed, writhing. Pearls of perspiration formed on her brow, and a menacing blotch grew on the chest of her nightgown.

One of the flying Sylverings, a nimble finch with a gold ring in her beak, wheeled past the girl a few times before diving down toward the closest counter. "Katerina Millner," she sang to the clerks. "Eight years. Foreground on Courage. Sick, by the look of it!" Beating her wings, the finch rose toward the shining dome again. One of the clerks wrote something in his ledger. Above them, Katerina Millner was already sinking back into the darkness.

Lin let go of the telescope, but she held on to the railing, feeling woozy. The Observatory was a place where the Sylverings could watch their human children! She remembered what Mirja had said on the way down to the parrot cage: *I saw her in not one, not two, but four of the mirrors!* Could it be true that they had shown her, Lin Rosenquist?

"Lin Rosenquist!"

Figenskar's voice cut through the din like a whip. Horrified, Lin scanned the hall until she located Figenskar's liquid shape, expecting to find his needle-toothed grin glinting up at her. But Figenskar had his back turned and was towering over an archive clerk, tail lashing. "Then try all variations!"

Lin backed into the deepest shadow of the balcony.

But she was not safe there. "See you in the Square," said a husky voice as the red door swung open, and in came a piebald rat. He took up position at the telescope, placing a binder on the music stand. By a stroke of luck, Lin had wound up behind the door when it opened. But now it was swinging back. The rat whistled to himself as he adjusted the telescope. He didn't turn as Lin sneaked around the closing door and out into the hallway.

Someone was climbing the stairs. Lin turned and ran, but stopped short when she heard another pair of feet coming toward her just around the bend. She had no choice but to try the next door, where the sign said MEMORY.

This balcony was larger and flanked by velvet curtains tucked on the inside of the railing. The floor sloped down with rows of linked plush chairs, like in an old movie theatre. The seats were occupied by Petlings, none of whom noticed when Lin entered. They stared intently at a slide projector and the guinea pig next to it.

Marvin's bangs had rebelled against the pomade and poked out in all directions. He was fingering a bunch of small, grey cards, looking quite upset. Lin crept behind the velvet curtain so she could watch without being seen.

"So sorry for the wait. Let's move on, shall we?" Marvin peered over the rim of his glasses at his audience. "Who's got Jimmy? Ah, Bonso, of course."

The Saint Bernard from the Waffleheart got to his feet. "Here!"

"The lad is seven already? Goodness, time flies." Marvin winked at Bonso and fed the card into the projector, which ate it with a whirr and a click. A dusty beam of light streamed across the hall to the mirror on the opposite side. Out of the blue darkness, a freckled-face boy came floating to the surface, marked by the text box as JIMMY HALDER, AGE SEVEN. He was sitting at a desk, wrapping a present. The tag said "Happy birthday!"

"Will you look at that! Spelled right and everything!" Bonso wagged his tail. "I keep forgetting about those sweet freckles."

The guinea pig pressed a button on the projector. It ejected the card, and Jimmy melted away. Lin slipped her hand in her left pocket, swallowing hard. Now she understood how Rufus knew about the long, lonely afternoons by Mrs. Ichalar's rosebush. He had come to this balcony to watch over her.

"This is yours, Sofie, we all know that." Marvin picked a new card out of the bunch. "You do keep a close watch."

A pair of long rabbit ears pricked up from the second row, and Rufus's seamstress landlady rose slowly. "I'm worried, that's all," she said.

Marvin inserted the card, but the projector spat it back out. The Petlings on the balcony gasped. Stroking his bangs, Marvin tried it one more time, with the same result. "I'm sorry," he said. "It's a cruel night for it, but the card is rejected."

"No," Sofie whispered. Her whiskers trembled. "Try it again."

"It will do no good, my dear. . . ." Marvin's eyes brimmed in sympathy. "The projector doesn't lie, you know that."

"Just try it! Please!"

But Lin could tell from the hung heads in the seat rows that everyone agreed with Marvin. It would do no good.

The door to the gallery slammed open. Lin's limbs filled with lead, but somehow, she managed to pull the curtain closed. Hollow footsteps clacked on the balcony, accompanied by the unmistakable hop, scrape, hop, scrape.

"Marvin," Figenskar said, "be so good as to show me this girl. She seems to have escaped . . . my list."

Marvin cleared his throat and said: "As you wish, Mr. Figenskar."

Mercilessly, the projector whirred and clicked. Lin's ears started to itch, then sting, then throb with pain.

"Is that . . ." Sofie sounded half-strangled. "Is that *us*?"

An astonished clamour broke out among the Petlings on the balcony as they recognised themselves in the Memory mirror. Excited parrot squawks pierced through the noise. "The curtain! She's behind the curtain!"

The velvet was ripped aside, and Lin looked up into a pair of inky eyes below a three-cornered hat.

"*Lindelin* Rosenquist! What a pleasant surprise!"

"Surprise!" Teriko screamed.

Figenskar tore her hood off and another wave of shock rolled through the hall. "Where is it," he hissed, blasting Lin with fishy breath. She clutched desperately at the railing, but Figenskar was much stronger. He sank the claws of one hand into her cardigan, lifting her until her boots dangled, patting and clawing at her pockets with the other hand. "Where have you hidden it?"

Lin kicked and struggled, choking on the lump in her throat. Her gathered clues and papers fell to the floor. "Help me!" she cried. "He's planning something terrible! Don't let him take me to the Margrave!"

The door thundered open again. And when Lin saw who was standing on the threshold, dark of eye and bristling with fury, she couldn't help herself. Tears leaked down her cheeks.

"Let go of my girl, you mangy excuse for a cat! Or I'll mouldy well make you!"

Chapter Nineteen

Figenskar stared at Rufus, and Rufus stared at Figenskar. The air on the balcony simmered with rage.

"Let her go! Now!"

On the opposite side of the Observatory, the Memory mirror was still showing Lindelin Rosenquist, age eleven, pale and bloody before a menacing figure with a three-cornered hat. After the first cries of shock, a breathless silence had unfolded down among the counters, broken only by the rising and falling sighs from the mirrors.

Figenskar's ears turned toward the hall, to Marvin, to the other Sylverings on the balcony. Then he retracted his claws and Lin fell to the floor. Knees weak with relief, she scrambled to Rufus's side. "You found me!"

"You're soaked in blood." Rufus was trembling, but when he addressed Figenskar, his voice was as chill as spring frost. "Mr. Chief Observer. That's the second time I've found you pestering Lin tonight. It seems you're not clever enough to be afraid of Rodents, but Lin is a House guest. If you so much as poke another whisker in her direction, there will be consequences."

"I see." Figenskar arranged his lips into a smile. He held out a paw in the direction of the projector. "The index card." Marvin looked like he was about to faint, but he hammered on the button until it ejected Lin's index card. Figenskar caught it smoothly.

As Lin's image faded from the Memory mirror, a rush of whispers filled the hall.

"There appears to have been another misunderstanding, hmmm?" Figenskar put his hands behind his back.

"Misunderstanding?" Lin croaked. "You kidnap me and stuff me in a sack and lock me in a filthy cage and try to hand me over to some mysterious Margrave, and you call it a *misunderstanding*?" Her voice caught with fury.

Figenskar's smile gave way to a humble, chagrined expression. "You must forgive me, Miss Rosenquist! I only wanted to protect the good people of Sylver from your thieving, spying ways. After all, you had broken into Teodor's house. Perhaps I am mistaken, hmmm?"

"Yes! Or I did go into his house, but Teodor was out, and . . ."

Figenskar snorted, smiling squint-eyed at his audience, the way grown-ups do when they think children are adorable. Stupid, but adorable. "Oh, he was *out*? How *could* I confuse you with a thief!"

"Thief!" cried Teriko.

"Hush," Figenskar told the parrot gravely. "You mustn't upset the girl, hmmm? Wait, what have we here!" He bent down to pick up Lin's gathered evidence. "More personal papers that do not belong to you tumbled from your pockets!" He riffled through them greedily.

Lin gaped. She was so mad her thoughts sizzled like butter in a frying pan. Rufus stalked over and snatched the papers out of Figenskar's hands.

"We don't have time for your false accusations," he said. "But do not for a moment think that we are done with this."

"Oh, I wouldn't dream of it," Figenskar said, all silk and frost.

"Good." Rufus led Lin toward the hallway. On the threshold, he halted. "By the way, we'll take that index card."

Figenskar's tail twitched. "The index card belongs to the Observatory."

"The index card belongs to Lin," Rufus retorted, "and she needs it. Now."

Figenskar glanced around and found nothing but frowning faces. He flung the card to the balcony floor. Rufus picked it up and hid it in his scarf. "Let's get out of this cat nest."

All the workers on the floor gawked at them. "It's her! It's the child!" they murmured among themselves, and as Lin and Rufus passed under the archway and into the foyer beyond Hope, there were whispers of "Twistrose".

Night had fallen.

While Lin had crept through the bowels of the Observatory, the sky had grown black as tar. How much time had they lost because she had got herself caught? She stole a look over her shoulder. Up close, the Observatory no longer reminded her of a palace, but of a mausoleum, with marble columns and no windows. She ought to be grateful she had escaped at all. "I can't believe you found me."

By her side, Rufus was limping heavily. "I wouldn't have if Lass hadn't told me about Figenskar and his heavy sled. And then I stumbled over this on the hill." He held up a sodden, tasselled string, chewed at the ends and tied in a double knot.

Lin grinned. "The twice-bound knot! You found my signal!"

Rufus didn't share the smile. "Did Figenskar tell the truth about finding you in Teodor's house?"

"Yes. But I discovered a thing or two before he showed up." Lin began a hectic account of everything that had happened and everything she had found out since they parted: the turret and the secret brotherhood and Mrs. Zarka's Brain Tapper plans and the Margrave and the cage. Rufus listened without question or comment as they wove their way down Observatory Hill and into the alleys and back streets of the town. When she had finished, he nodded once. "Do you want your drawstring back?"

"What?" Lin stared at him. All that excellent investigation, and no points for Miss Rosenquist.

"Suit yourself." Rufus shrugged and put the string into a scarf pocket. "Doctor Kott is waiting for us in Winderside by the Lake."

"Rufus, what's wrong?"

"Do you have any idea how scared I was when I didn't find you?" His voice was rough and clipped.

She felt her cheeks heat up. "You're the one who left first. In fact, you left me for the second time. And both times I ended up in Figenskar's claws."

"That's not fair!" Rufus tugged at his scarf. "I told you to stay outside the Red Cat, where you could be safe and seen! And I left to get you help, not because I didn't trust you or thought you wouldn't listen."

"You *wouldn't* listen!" Lin said, picking up her pace so Rufus fell behind. "I told you we needed to confront Teodor, but you kept refusing."

"You don't understand."

"You're right. I don't!" Lin whirled about to face him. Rufus's eyes were liquid and pained, and his hands were trembling. After a moment, she added, softer, "So explain it to me. Please."

"Remember when you found me in the mountains above Summerhill? That burrow was a fox's den. He had me pinned and I knew I was dead. But then you came along, all noisy and stomping in your human way, and you scared him off."

"Oh." The silver scar on Rufus's bad leg reached all the way from haunch to heel. "A fox did that?"

"I know I'm supposed to let all that go here in Sylver. But I'm not like the other Petlings. I can't settle for waffles and tea and visits to the Observatory. What's worse, I keep acting on my instincts, like some first-day fresher." Rufus sighed. "Teodor has had my guts in a knot from the moment we met. But I shouldn't have let that get in the way of our investigation. I'm sorry. And I'm sorry for leaving you. It's just . . . Up until tonight, you were always so *big*. Sometimes I forget that you're not anymore."

"I thought your old memories were fading," Lin said. "That you are forgetting everything from *before*."

Rufus looked crestfallen. "No! Not you. I remember everything about you. I've spent almost as much time up on that balcony as you have by the rosebush."

Lin shook her head. Why were they quarrelling when she really wanted to give Rufus a hug? She reached up and buried her fingers in the soft fur by his ear. "Then I think we should stop leaving each other," she said.

Rufus's whiskers perked up. "You've thought about my idea?"

"I'm still thinking." Lin's smile was quick. "But your logic makes sense. Disasters don't occur every ninety-four years on the dot in time to fit with a Wandergate. There has to be another way."

"Let me see that," Rufus mumbled, taking Lin's injured hand in his. The cut from the shard had stopped oozing blood, but it looked awful and hurt worse. "You climbed a chain with this? You're no softie, Miss Rosenquist." He winked at her. That was medicine as good as any.

"No," she laughed. "I'm a lot harder than you'd think."

"But not as hard as dung-covered rock!"

CHAPTER TWENTY

The lake was dark and free of snow, and Sylverings skated around the Wanderer's reflection like silver moths circling. A cold breeze came sweeping over the ice to tug at the low houses along the Winderside shore. Lin and Rufus huddled by the outmost building of them all, the mead house called the Burning Bird, Rufus's favourite.

"I told Doctor Kott to meet us here." Rufus peered in through a window. "But I had no idea your cover would be blown so spectacularly. Everyone at the Observatory saw you. Someone might very well have made it here with news already."

He was right, their careful route through Sylveros had cost them some time. Lin frowned at a Rodent with flaring pink ears who gesticulated eagerly to a group of Hoofs at the bar counter. Was he talking about her? Warning them that a Twistrose had been called?

"Then maybe we shouldn't risk it," she said wistfully. "Didn't you say Figenskar is a regular here? I don't want word to reach him that we came this way." She would have loved to go inside. Laughter and fiddle tunes drifted out from the rose-painted booths, along with a lovely smell of savoury pastries.

"Well, it's true what they say," Rufus muttered. "Rumours spread faster than fleas, especially here at the Bird."

"What a gruesome name, the Burning Bird."

"True, but it's the best place for storytelling in all of Sylver. The name is taken from a legend about a scream-ing red bird, who flies through the heavens with wings on fire. If you betray someone, and the betrayal is horrible enough, the burning bird will come plunging out of the sky to die at your feet."

"That *is* gruesome." Lin cradled her injured arm. The cut throbbed viciously now.

Rufus saw. "Come on. I have an idea."

He took her to the back of the building and into a stor-age room that smelled of old skates and sawdust. Yellow light spilled under a door on the opposite wall, highlight-ing a chopping block on the floor. Rufus barred the exit and blew life into a lantern on the rough block.

"Now, I really wish you didn't have to wait here," he

whispered, listening at the entrance to the common room. "I wanted you to hear the seven Twistrose legends."

"Eight," Lin said. "Eight with the boy by the Red Cat. There's another statue hidden in the lane outside."

"There is?" Rufus wrinkled his brow. "I'll have to take a look at that. I don't think I've heard of an eighth Twistrose." He laid a finger over his mouth and cracked the door open for a very quick moment, letting in a burst of loud voices and delicious smells. "All clear. I'll just go right inside, fetch the doctor and the key to this door. But I won't turn my back for a heartbeat. I promise."

He sneaked through. Just as the crack closed, a guitar chord strummed and a voice began to sing. It was a melancholy tune that rose from dark to light and ended in a deep sigh. Lin knew it immediately. "The Margrave's Song."

The Margrave wandered in woods winter-wild.
Stole through a gate for the heart of a child.
The boy gave to them his heart to devour.
A Winter Prince lost in the Wanderer's hour.
Roses will wilt as the eve grows old.
Silenced and caught in the secret cold.

She drifted closer, shivering at the words. Did the singer know what she did? That the Margrave was not just a figure in an old song, but someone who this very night waited for Figenskar to bring him a child?

Lin took a quick step back. What had the wheezy voice said? *The Soothsinger has sent a warning to the Vulpes of Lucke. He must not see the song.* She stuck her hand into her boot, and there found a slim leather tube. The falcon message that Figenskar had intercepted.

With icy fingers she eased the letter out and unrolled it in the muted glow of the lantern. She had guessed right, this was "The Margrave's Song". But it was not the same verse Teodor had sung in the woods.

> *The Margrave hunted in riddles and lies,*
> *Seeking his draught in the Child of Ice.*
> *Thorns of gold through flesh and marrow,*
> *Who then will suffer the death of a sparrow?*
> *Stronger than Falcons and made of a child,*
> *A Blood Lord wakes in the Winter Wild.*

Below the song, the author had added a postscript in spindly letters.

> **My dear old Vulpes of Lucke. I know you have been searching for answers. This came to me in fitful dreams. It is a variation of "The Margrave's Song", the one sung by my grandmother many years ago. I believe the verses complement each other.**
>
> **As always, the words of the prophecy are**

not mine to understand. But it seems to me
that a new lord will be made on Wanderer's
Eve, one whose magic will be more powerful
than we have seen since the last Starfalcon
left. If I were you, I would keep a close watch
on the Child of Ice.

Raymonda, Queen of Soothsingers

Lin stared at the letter. What was it the gramophone
message had said? *From the ashes of Operation Corvelie, a
new lord will rise.* The Margrave wanted to become this
Blood Lord? And he wanted Isvan to make a draught of
some sort? And who was this Vulpes? Had he taken Isvan?

The door opened briefly, and Rufus returned with the
key. Sadly, he had brought no pastries, but he clutched a
steaming mug. When he saw Lin by the chopping block,
he cocked his head. "That's promising. You've got your
quizzy face on."

Lin lowered the falcon message. "My what?"

"Your quizzy face. With the lifted chin. That you wear
when you're about to figure something out."

"My father has a quizzy face. I don't."

Rufus laughed and gave her the mug. "Here. Something to keep the cold at bay."

The drink sparkled silver in the cup, and it tasted of
cardamom and fireworks. After two sips Lin already felt

much warmer. "This is wonderful!" she mumbled into the mug. "What is it?"

"Starmead. No one but the owner of the Burning Bird knows what makes it shine. The caravans buy it by the barrel. What have you got there?"

Lin handed him the parchment roll. "The message I found in Figenskar's office. The one Teriko had tried to burn."

Rufus twirled his whiskers as he read the song. "I don't like all this talk of thorns and flesh and marrow. Lin, do you think there's any chance this Child of Ice is *not* Isvan?"

They both jumped at the knock on the door, two quick raps first, then a third. Rufus rolled up the message swiftly. "That'll be Doctor Kott."

He opened up for a tall Feline with a large, black bag. "Now then, Rufus," the doctor said as he stepped through, "what is the meaning of this?"

Rufus closed the door and turned the key quickly. "Sorry about the secrecy," he said. "But at the moment it's not . . . convenient for us to visit the Bird. Lin, take your hood off."

"Quite," the cat said at the sight of Lin's face. "May I?" He pressed along the edges of her wrist wound, causing eels of pain to slither up her arm. "This requires stitches. How did it happen?"

Lin glanced at Rufus. She had no idea how much the doctor knew.

"Figenskar," Rufus said darkly.

"Quite," Doctor Kott said again as he washed the blood from Lin's face and arm. "That man has a violent streak. I've heard him at the Red Cat. He has grand ideas about Feline excellence, and not so grand opinions of the Sylver Pact."

"Figenskar is against peace among the clans?" Even after all that had happened at the Observatory, Rufus sounded shocked. The Sylver Pact was the foundation for Sylver's way of life, the very first thing they taught freshers when they arrived.

"He claims it's unnatural," Doctor Kott said. "But I never thought he would go so far as to openly attack someone."

"He didn't," Lin said. "Not openly."

Doctor Kott poured a clear liquid into the cut. It stung, but the pain quickly dulled to a strange pressure. Then he threaded the needle.

It wasn't the first time Lin needed stitches. She had three in her brow after she and Niklas tried to dive for emeralds in the Summerhill stream. That time there were local anaesthetics and her mother to accompany her. And Niklas. "Not bad, Rosenquist," he had said. "Are you sure you're not that girl from your mother's ballads after all?" Of course, after that, there was no way she could complain.

She didn't complain now either. But she had to fight the urge to wrench her arm back and run as Doctor Kott poked the curved needle through her skin. The thread resembled spider legs creeping along the wound. "Tell me," Doctor Kott said as he pulled a stitch tight. "Is Figenskar to blame for the blood on your face, too?" Lin grunted, concentrating on breathing.

Rufus stirred from his watch over by the door. "No, that happened earlier, in the Machine Vault. She just started bleeding during a demonstration. Do you have any idea what might have caused it?"

The doctor put a strip of blue lichen over the wound and wrapped it in a bandage. "There were no other symptoms?"

Lin winced. "I heard this loud sound that no one else seemed to hear. Right before. And my head hurt."

"I'm afraid the anatomy of humans is not my strong suit," Doctor Kott said, examining her nose and ears. "But I believe this is a case of magical otopathy."

Rufus clicked his tongue. "Magical otopa-what?"

"Extreme sensitivity to magic, also known as magic ears, because of the symptoms. It is a rare and very coveted talent, especially in Wichtiburg. But if the magic is very powerful, or in some other way puts too much strain on you, it can cause bleeding and severe headaches." He sighed as he packed up his tools. "The willow drops and withermoss should ease the pain in your wrist, but be careful. Stay clear of Figenskar while you are here. And more importantly: Stay away from whatever magic it is that makes you bleed."

Rufus stepped aside, whiskers tight with worry. "Thank you, Doctor. We will try."

Before he slipped out, the Feline paused at the door.

"You were right not to bring her inside. Apparently, the rimedeer are spooked, the Machine Vault nearly blew up, and Teodor just galloped up the Caravan Road as if a pack of Nightmares were on his heels. On top of which a human girl is rumoured to be in town, which has everyone wondering if a Twistrose has been called. They're rather worked up in there. Like I said: Be careful."

A wave of excitement rose in the common room. At first, Lin thought someone must have seen the doctor come out through the door. But then she heard the footsteps, hop, scrape, hop, scrape across the floor, and a blaring voice, screeching through the din. "Blue and white! She is wearing blue and white, and hides her face in a hood. Has anyone seen her? Has anyone seen the thief?"

CHAPTER TWENTY-ONE

L in and Rufus held their breath, watching each other, their faces pooled with shadows. But in the common room, no one spoke up to answer Teriko. It seemed Doctor Kott had no intention of betraying them. Rufus ghosted over to the door and turned the key in the lock. Lin thought the click sounded painfully loud.

"Now what?" she whispered.

"Well, my first choice would be to get you away from here as soon as possible."

"I can't just run!" Lin rubbed her forehead. Teriko's cackles almost made her feel as if she were back in the cage. "I have a task to complete."

Rufus nodded. "I know you do. So before we leave, we're going to make a new plan. A better one." He gave her the cup of starmead. "First, you can finish this. Then you tell me everything you found out one more time. It's time for you to put on your quizzy face."

Lin smiled at him over the rim of her mug. "Which I don't have," she whispered.

"Then bring your brain to the party, or do whatever it is your father always tells you."

Quietly, so quietly, they placed all the scraps of papers, letters, and evidence on the chopping block. Rufus added wood chips for everyone they knew had been trying to find Isvan: Mrs. Zarka, who wanted him for her experiment; Teodor, who wanted him for the Wandersnow; Figenskar and the Margrave, who wanted him for their mysterious Operation Corvelie.

Rufus poked at the chip that represented the Margrave. "I wish we knew more about him, other than that he has a wheezy voice."

He is my kin, Lin thought, at least according to Figenskar. But she said softly, "We know that he wants to become a Blood Lord, whatever that is. And that he wants to make an elixir."

"Seeking his draught in the Child of Ice," Rufus quoted from "The Margrave's Song".

Their eyes met over the chopping block. Out in the common room, Teriko screeched.

"At least they are all still searching for him," Rufus whispered. "Let's hope it means that none of them have him."

Lin bent over the papers. "Let's start with what we know." She frowned at the illustration of Frostfang that Isvan had brought to the Machine Vault. "Isvan wanted this axe. Not just any axe, but this one, the one Lass had found on the Cracklemoor."

Rufus twirled his whiskers. "Go on."

"He went to great lengths to get it. First he tried at the Machine Vault, even though he must have been suffering in the heat down there, and even though Mrs. Zarka scared him so much that he panicked and knocked down Nit."

"And don't forget that he sneaked into Teodor's turret and vandalised a secret book to get this illustration." Rufus shuddered. "That takes some serious motivation."

Lin winked at him. "If you say so. Then, when Nit turned him down, Isvan trespassed into the backyard of Lass the gatherer to steal the real axe. Twice he did that, even though Lass terrified him, too, and even though she would know he was the culprit."

"Yes," Rufus whispered. "So he wanted Frostfang. But why?"

"Well, Lass did say it's an excellent weapon. And even better, it's magical and can control ice."

The door handle moved. Once, twice, harder, until the whole frame rattled. Lin's breath caught.

"There's nothing in there," came Doctor Kott's calm voice from outside. "Just skates and wood."

"Skates and wood," Teriko cawed. "And a little thief, maybe! Bring me the key to this door!"

"Quite. Give me a moment to unearth it," Doctor Kott said. The rattling stopped.

Rufus put a finger under Lin's chin and turned her face away from the door. "Forget about the parrot," he said very softly. "Think about Isvan."

Lin let the air in her lungs out. She nodded. Isvan. Isvan sitting in his windowsill. Isvan sneaking into Lass's backyard. Isvan at his lonely table outside the Waffleheart.

She picked up the Waffleheart receipt where Pomeroy had scribbled down the date of Isvan's last visit: October third. "The waffles," she said. "Isvan ordered fifteen rounds of waffles!"

Rufus scratched his ear. "Now you've lost me."

"I don't think anyone has taken Isvan." Lin swept the wood chips aside. "I think he left. The waffles were provisions for the road."

"To go where?"

Lin tapped the page she had ripped out of *The Book of Frost and Flame*. "Listen to this: 'The axe, which bears the name Frostfang, is not only a most powerful weapon of defence. It also unlocks the sacred Winterfyrst Well'." She lifted her chin. "That's why Isvan needed Frostfang. Not as a weapon, but as a key. Isvan went to hide in the Winterfyrst Well."

Rufus snickered softly. "You want one of those points now, don't you, Miss Rosenquist?"

Lin put her hands up. "Not so fast. We still have no idea where to find this Well."

"Oh, I don't know about that." Rufus's eyes shone in the lantern light. "You see, there aren't many wells in Sylver. In fact, I can think of only one."

CHAPTER TWENTY-TWO

The wind rippled in Rufus's fur as he glided up along the river. White streaks trailed behind his skates, but before Lin could catch up, the scars absorbed back into the frozen water.

"Neat, no?" Rufus called over his shoulder. "The ice is like the snow on Eversnow Square. It's always flawless."

Like a mirror, Lin thought, but she didn't look. None of the skates in the Burning Bird shed had fit her feet, so she had to make do with strap-on blades. She felt about as steady as a calf in spring. But they were still moving swiftly up the valley, much faster than they would have on foot, and with every stroke, they put more distance between themselves and Teriko, not to mention a certain chief observer. And they left no trail for them to follow.

Lin risked her balance to glance up as they sped under a bridge where the road crossed the river. She must have been unconscious when they last passed it. The Wanderer shone dazzlingly bright against the night. Lin guessed that it had travelled a little more than halfway to the Sylver Fang in the west. It would be difficult to keep track of time out here. The chiming from the belfry had reached Rufus's hilltop camp, but Lin had little hope the sound would carry into the depths of the woods.

"This is it." Rufus stopped in a spray of shaved ice, rustling his map. "The ridge where we crossed over from the Tinklegrove trail. It was just before the Glass Bridge, and I remember there were a lot of silver birches." He bent down to unlace his skates. "Better get rid of these."

Lin bent down, too, fiddling with the hard straps, when she suddenly flinched back with a yelp that flew in between the trees like a startled bird. Down in the ice she had caught a glimpse of something white: a scared face, frozen into the deep.

"What are you doing?" Rufus said. "Trying to injure yourself some more?"

"No, I . . ." Lin blinked, and the face blinked back. It was just her reflection. "I thought I saw something. It was nothing."

"Well, remember what the doctor said. Be careful with those stitches."

They climbed up on the bank and crossed the Caravan Road warily. From there, they chased their own footprints backward over the ridge. Though the evidence of their previous path ran before them like a dotted line in the snow, Lin had a persistent feeling that they were going the wrong way; that they ought to turn left, or double back, or strike across the next crest. The feeling swelled in waves, always accompanied by whispered commands, like a distant chanting.

"The trees *want* us to get lost," Lin said. Somewhere in the far distance, a crow cawed. Rufus tightened his scarf. "I didn't want to spook you, but yes. It's as if the path is . . . well . . ."

". . . twisting under our feet," Lin finished. Just like in the Winnower legend.

After that, they kept their attention doggedly to the tracks until the prints grew very far apart. They had been running hard at this point. Lin glimpsed bright starlight between the branches up ahead. The Winnower's clearing.

They crept up to the ring of tall trees and huddled by a big elm root to watch for a while. The well jutted up like a sliced tower. The pieces of the lid had not been disturbed. But at the end of the parallel tracks that shot out of the wood on the north end, something was missing.

"Huh," Rufus muttered. "The sled is gone. Someone must have taken it."

"Yes," Lin breathed. "Someone has sniffed at our footprints, too."

Only feet away, the impression from Lin's body sprawled before them like a snow angel where she had fallen. A third set of footprints led from the cottage to the impression and back again.

"Whoever it is, he must still be in there," Lin whispered.

Rufus rose slowly. "Then we'd better check the cottage first. Nightmare or no, we can't have anyone creeping up on us while we're halfway down a well."

The snow creaked as they stole across the open field. Between the crooked shutters, there was no movement, and the chimney held its breath. Once more, Lin had the unpleasant notion that they were being watched. Even when they reached the cover of the timber walls, she couldn't shake it.

Up close the cottage seemed even more miserable. The stone foundation had tumbled in places, wrestled asunder by the frost. The gaps between the warped logs were wide enough to peer through. Inside, they saw bare walls and hard-packed dirt strewn with dank rushes. But no figure, hooded or otherwise.

"I don't smell anything but rime and old wood," Rufus said, relaxing his stance.

"But the tracks say someone's here," Lin said.

Rufus shrugged. "My nose says otherwise. Maybe he left on the sled? Come on. Let's search the well."

Lin did not feel reassured. The chanting seemed more coherent in the clearing, weaving in and out of range, and in the corner of her eye, something kept shifting, like a thin fabric whisked away whenever she turned around.

Rufus placed his fingers on the rim of the well. "Doesn't seem to bite."

Lin circled it carefully, as if she feared just that. Slick stones, timber crossbeam, frayed rope. But there was more to it than met the eye. The breathy mutters that escaped from the shaft proved that. She crouched down. "Here!"

Near the ground, a sign had been carved. Three leaping tongues of flame.

"That's the one from the Hall of Winter," Rufus said. "We're on the right track!"

"Maybe," Lin said. "But Teodor's table clock had the same mark, and so did the walls in Teodor's turret. He's no Winterfyrst. Quite the opposite, I would say." She peered over the edge. The starlight reached only a few yards into the shaft before it was smothered.

Rufus produced a book of matches from his scarf, lit one, and tossed it in. It spun through the air for a long moment before it fizzed out in a layer of snow on the bottom. "Rats, this thing is deep."

Deep, but apparently empty. The light from the match had revealed nothing but more stones glazed with ice. "The entrance *is* supposed to be secret," Rufus said, chewing the tassels on his scarf.

"Well, we won't know anything until we go down there and investigate," Lin said.

"Down *there*?" Rufus spat out the tassels, coughing. "I mean to say, that's a fair drop."

Lin felt her mouth open. Rufus was scared. He, who had knocked the slipper out of the Machine, who had confronted Figenskar as if he were a difficult kitten. He was scared of heights. Before, he had loved climbing, and he liked to scratch his way to the top of her head to balance sometimes. But not after he had fallen from her shoulder. She turned away, pretending to check something in her pocket. "No way around it, I think. But one of us has to stay up here, and it has to be you."

"Does it, now?" Rufus planted his fists on his flanks, trying to sound vexed, but his scruff betrayed him. It smoothed down with relief, and maybe a hint of shame.

Lin nodded at the rope. "It's our only chance at getting to the bottom. You're both stronger and heavier than me. I don't think I could manage hauling you back up, not even with two good hands."

Rufus frowned from the rope to the rusty crank to Lin. His mouth turned into a knot. "I see your point. But I don't like it one mouldy bit."

He pulled the rope all the way out, tugging and straining, until he felt sure the fibres would hold. "Keep the rope under your arms," he said, tying a big loop. "It will hurt a little, but it's the safest way, especially with that wrist of yours."

Lin slipped the loop over her head and threaded her arms through. She climbed up on the rim of the well, but Rufus held her back by the shoulder and shoved the matches into her pocket.

"You might need these to see. Oh, and we should have a signal in case you need me to pull you up fast."

"How about I call out?"

"I guess that will do," Rufus muttered. "It really should be me."

"Don't be silly. This is the only logical way." Lin dangled her feet over the edge and pretended not to cringe at the sight of the gaping hole. "Ready?"

Rufus gripped the crank with a grim nod.

She pushed herself off the rim. The loop tightened sharply and she swung to and fro as Rufus lowered her, yank by creaking yank, into the shaft.

Darkness swallowed her. She lit two matches on the way down, but all she could see was more stones and the grainy blotches of her boots. After a while, her eyes adjusted enough to make out a slowly growing disc of grey below. The bottom.

When the crank stopped with a final tug, her feet were still about a yard above it. "A little further," she called. Rufus's snout stuck out over the edge above, and there was a faint and garbled reply. Lin tried again. "I need more rope!"

The echoes faded. No more rope was given out.

If there were any answers down here, they must be hidden beneath the snow. Kicking in the air, Lin seized the rope above her head and hauled herself up enough to slip through the loop. She hit the bottom with a dull thump, got to her knees, and began brushing away the veil of snow. Nothing but black ice.

She lit another match and turned in a slow circle. No sign of Isvan, or any secret entrance, or of the magical ice axe that was supposed to unlock it. But carved into the wall near the surface of the ice was another of the leaping flame signs. Time and frost had worn it down so the cuts were hardly visible. She traced the shallow grooves with her fingertip, but pulled it back when she felt a sting, like from the electric fences around the Summerhill meadows.

The match sputtered out, and Lin paused, uncertain. In the Burning Bird, the puzzle pieces had fit so neatly. But now she couldn't stop thinking about the elegant ice and soft blue light of the Winterfyrst mansion. This well just seemed too drab and dark to be their sacred place. True, she didn't have Frostfang, which was supposed to unlock the well, whatever that might mean. But at the very least she would have expected to find the Winterfyrst snow crystal carved into it, like on the head of Frostfang, and not the Flamewatcher mark that Teodor used.

Suddenly a scratch and a hiss rent the silence, a sound exactly like the one she had heard from Teodor's turret on her first visit. The flame mark flared up, filling the well with the stink of burning. From the well stones came a long, deep groan. Lin hunched down and covered her head. The well didn't plan on tumbling down on her, did it? Another groan, and a loud crack. This time it came from below.

In the brief moment before the flame mark died, she saw that the ice was riddled with cracks.

She jumped to her feet.

"Rufus! Get me up!" She pulled at the rope, trying to get back into the loop, but she couldn't do it. Fragments of Rufus's voice swirled down the shaft, drowning in creaks and moans.

Currents roiled beneath her, and water pumped up through the cracks. Lin had never heard of ice melting this fast. A few moments more and she would fall through, and all chance of reaching the rope – and getting out of the well – would be gone.

She wound the rope around her wrists and yelled again.

"Bring me up!"

Instead the ice crunched and gave. Lin gasped as her feet and ankles plunged into the freezing water. Instantly her legs stung with pain. Her boots soaked through and became so heavy she could barely lift them out of the water.

"Rufus!" Lin screamed. "Please, hear me!"

Finally the crank creaked up there, and the rope quivered. Another creak and she rushed a foot upward. The rope bit deep into her skin. Doctor Kott's stitches were tearing. *Creak, creak, creak.* A small voice wailed above the panic, insisting that now, if the rope snapped or she let go, she would fall to her death. Lin closed her lids and told the voice to shut up, listening instead to the yammering of the crank that was bringing her back to safety.

At last, it stopped. Rufus caught her by the waist and hauled her over the edge with a hard hug. "What happened?"

"The ice at the bottom melted." Lin didn't know which hurt the most, her wrist or her shoulders. "I tried calling."

"You did? The only sound I heard was a funny echo, until that sign sparked and the whole well started grumbling. I pulled you up as fast as I could." He hugged her tight again. "Mouldy heavy, you were."

Lin snorted. "I was wet."

"And bloody," Rufus said, staring at her bandage in dismay. "Your wrist again."

Lin winced at the red stripe in the gauze. "I touched another one of those Flamewatcher signs. I think it's what caused the melting. It's as if I set it off in some way."

"But I'm guessing you didn't find any Winterfyrsts or secret entrances to secret wells?"

"None and neither."

"All right. So our theory was wrong." Rufus tried to sound optimistic, but Lin could see the weight of disappointment in his tail. "Or maybe the entrance is invisible

if we don't have Frostfang. We'll have to go back to Sylveros, get your wrist fixed again, and then we can sneak into
the Cartography Chamber, or even ask the elders. There
must be someone . . ." He straightened up, nostrils wide.
" . . . someone who knows about the . . . the . . ."

His hackles rose and he whipped around.

The door to the cottage grated. Footsteps sounded on
the porch, and then something turned the corner, lifting
its arm toward them, crowing in its high-pitched, eerie
voice.

The Winnower had come.

CHAPTER TWENTY-THREE

T he hooded figure came shuffling toward them, creaking slowly down from the porch. Rufus stepped in front of Lin, fists under chin and back straight, ready to fight. "What are you doing within the Palisade, Nightmare?"

But the Winnower reached up and pushed his hood back, and his eyes were cold mirrors.

"You," Lin whispered.

"Yes, girl," said Teodor. "What the Flame are you two doing here?"

"Funny," Rufus said. He didn't lower his fists. "We could ask you the same thing."

"We could," Lin said. "And why are you posing as the Winnower? Or . . ." She raised her chin, trying to appear unfazed. "Maybe you *are* the Winnower?"

Teodor barked, a startling, hoarse scream of impatience.

"There is no Winnower! I planted that story to scare away unwelcome visitors like you! This clearing is forbidden for those who are not initiated in . . ." He paused, and Lin realised that Teodor had let his tongue run away with him. "Those who are not invited by . . ."

"The Brotherhood of Frost and Flame?"

Lin turned to Rufus, eyebrows high. With that, Rufus had revealed that at least one of them had visited Teodor's turret. But Rufus looked so smug and the old fox so utterly shocked that she couldn't help but smile.

It took Teodor several moments to replace the slack jaw with narrow-eyed suspicion. "Indeed. And you two are not invited. So please explain how you got here. It ought to be impossible, unless you know the rowan path."

"We followed our own tracks," Rufus said. "It wasn't very hard at all."

"Ah. I suspected you might try that. Though after your panicked flight this afternoon, I did not think you would be brave enough. But what I really want to know is how did you find the clearing the first time? These woods are enchanted to lead all trespassers back to the Caravan Road."

"Well, we didn't trespass. We arrived by sled," Rufus said. "We raced down from the scargate hill to save time. It wasn't our fault we ended up here."

Teodor's lids made thin slits now. "By sled. I did not see a sled when you arrived here earlier today. Where is it now, this sled of yours?"

Rufus shrugged. "It's gone. We thought the Winn . . . That is, we thought you took it."

They all turned their attention to the parallel tracks that ended in the snowdrift by the well. They were barbed by sticks and twigs, but there were no footprints around it. "Maybe it was a gatherer," Rufus offered. "A Beak that took the reins and flew away."

Teodor made an annoyed clicking sound in his throat. "A Beak can't carry anything that heavy. Well, I surmise that the Twistrose requires patching up again. You had better come inside."

"I don't like it," Rufus hissed as they followed the old fox up on the porch.

"We don't have much choice," Lin whispered back, holding up her bleeding wrist. "That salve he used on my foot worked wonders."

"Fine." Rufus put on a fierce face. But when Teodor opened the door for them, Rufus forgot to be grim. "How is this possible," he cried. "Where's the miserable shed?"

The walls of the cottage were hung with bookcases and tapestries, and the ceiling painted with myriads of golden stars. A fire was lit in the black unicorn stove, filling the little house with sweet heat.

"If you know about the Brotherhood," Teodor said, "it shouldn't be too taxing for you to figure out."

"Magic." Rufus grinned. "The best kind!"

"A cloak rune." In the rough wood of the floor, an

elaborate three-tongue mark had been carved. A lilting humming drifted from it, full of words too subtle to hear. The music that filled these entire woods.

"Trespassers or no," Teodor said. "Welcome to the Hearth of Flame." The music stopped.

Lindelin Rosenquist.

Lin felt her name spoken behind her, the faintest whisper. She turned and found a curling twine of wood peeling from one of the timber logs of the doorway. An invisible chisel was carving her name into the beam. *Rufocanus of Rosenquist* sounded next, and Rufus's name appeared below hers.

The entire doorway was riddled with names.

"It's a safety measure," Teodor said. "If anyone has learned the secret of the Hearth, their names will be here for the Brotherhood to find."

"Figenskar!" Rufus exclaimed, and sure enough, three names above Lin's, there was the chief observer's name. The cuts were yellowed and blunt, made some time ago. "Figenskar has been here?"

"The night he arrived," Teodor replied. "I found him by the river, drenched and stiff with cold and fear, the most pitiful fresher I have seen. I had no choice but to get him warm quickly, so I brought him here."

"That's why he's always telling the Winnower legend," Rufus said. "He can't find his way back here, and it's killing him!"

"I have rued it many a time. That cat always had a fickle, angry heart. For all his pleading and grovelling, I didn't want him in the Brotherhood, and I didn't want him in the House. But the previous chief observer was free to choose her own successor, and somehow Figenskar managed to sweet-talk his way into her heart. Margaret was Canine. A kind one with a soft spot for strays."

"You can't mean you regret saving Figenskar's life," Lin said.

"No, but in hindsight, I'm fairly certain he would have made it into town." Teodor squinted toward the windows and the dark woods beyond. "No matter. He can't defeat the cloak rune." He pointed at the table, where several half-empty jars and tins were lined up, their lids unscrewed. "Sit."

He disappeared into the next room, letting out a smell of herbs and ointments. Lin sat down at the table, but Rufus paced along the walls, admiring the tapestries.

They resembled the falcon curtain in the Observatory with their rich jewel colours. One showed a Feline running through a forest of apple trees, her basket spilled on the ground behind her. Another depicted a seagull wheeling over a windswept island, clutching a human newborn by the umbilical cord.

Rufus stopped in front of a scene with a ship that fired its cannons at some obscure menace on shore, while peg-legged rats swarmed across the deck. "These are all places on the other side of the mountains. Lin, we have to go there!"

"We will." Lin fingered the jars and tins. The ones that weren't empty contained a seed or weed of some sort, grains of wheat, pumpkin seeds, and dried bladder wrack snipped into pieces. There were even a few grubby acorns.

Teodor returned from the other chamber, carrying a box of bandages, tinctures, and salves. But as he shoved aside the jars to make room for his medicine kit, he froze, scrutinising Lin as if she were a rare specimen, and he an expert taxidermist. "What *have* you been up to?"

Lin's heart pounded. For a moment she was convinced the old fox really could read her mind, that he knew not only about the visit in the turret, but also that she had found the briefcase and the blueprints for the Brain Tapper that Mrs. Zarka had drawn for him. It took her a moment to realise that Teodor was holding out his paw. Her wrist. He was talking about her wrist.

She gave him her hand, and he unravelled the bandage. Doctor Kott's spider-leg stitches were torn, and blood seeped out between the edges. "How did you get this cut?" Teodor asked.

"An accident."

"What a most unfortunate girl you are. But we can't have our Twistrose running around without the use of her arm." He rinsed the cut with willow drop and began to pluck the stitches out. "Firedrake salve alone will not be enough for this. I have a trick or two up my sleeve, but first I should like to know why you were mucking about in my well."

Lin turned to Rufus. It was the same dilemma: They didn't trust Teodor, but if anyone knew how to open the Winterfyrst Well, he was probably sitting across the table from her. Rufus swished his tail hotly, and Lin agreed. She closed her mouth.

Teodor sent Rufus a quick glance while he dripped the wound with a blue tincture. "Very well. Then perhaps you will tell me how you got the water to melt."

Lin shifted on her chair. "I didn't mean to. I just touched the carving at the bottom. It flared up, and the ice disappeared."

"I see." Teodor pushed his chair back and shuffled over to the black stove. A cooking pot sat on top of it, and now he touched it briefly, bringing forth a quick glint under his paw. Immediately a most delicious smell of dinner wafted through the room. "I am quite fond of this little cooking rune. Emperor morels from Legenwald, ready and hot when the need arises." He ladled stew into three bowls. "It will take a moment for the bleeding to quell. You may as well eat in the meantime."

Sceptical or no, Lin's growling belly insisted, and even Rufus came to the table. The stew was thick with barley and golden mushrooms like coins, and it tasted like bonfires and clear October skies. Teodor studied them as they ate. "How goes the search? Any news of our Winterfyrst?" He smiled faintly. "And did you find the *item* you had lost, young Rufocanus?"

"What item?" Lin asked, then remembered what Rufus had said: *Teodor doesn't need to know everything,* and *I've got it covered.*

Rufus gave Teodor a morose look, if such a thing is possible while stuffing one's face with stew. "We have some leads."

Teodor straightened his sleeves with crisp movements, but he didn't press the matter. When they had emptied their bowls, he pulled out a flat case from his coat pocket and opened it to reveal a quill pen. The tip was faceted like a diamond, cut in the shape of a talon. "Since you won't be sharing your secrets and you've already ferreted out mine, I might as well show you what a healing rune can do." Teodor placed a scrap of leather over Lin's wrist wound and let the talon quill hover over it. "Now stay very still."

Rufus bounded to his feet. His bowl clattered to the floor. "Don't!" he cried. "Don't touch her with that thing!"

Teodor turned to him. "I beg your pardon?"

"I said, don't touch her. And don't try that confused face with me. I'm not fooled by your concerned uncle act and your perfect stew. We know about your plans with Mrs. Zarka. We know about the Brain Tapper!"

Teodor's mouth worked in wordless anger, and Lin expected an acid retort. But then the old fox's face fell, and he put the talon pen down. "You found my brief-case. I knew I would regret running out on it."

"That's right." Rufus bared his teeth. "How could you even think about using that horrible thing on a poor, in-nocent boy?"

"I never asked Mrs. Zarka to make that thing!" Teodor rose, too. "Somehow, she had found a letter I wrote to my colleagues about Isvan and the Winterfyrst plight. The audacious fool thought it was for her."

A letter about Isvan and the Winterfyrst plight? Lin lifted her chin. "You're talking about the letter we found in Isvan's room! The one where you complain about Isvan's behaviour. The one you two argued about!"

"I wouldn't call it an argument," Teodor muttered. "But yes. That's the one. I have no idea how it came into Mrs. Zarka's claws."

"Then you don't consider her a colleague?"

"I despise her vile Technocraft and everything about it." Teodor snarled. "Those devices can be used by anyone, and they lend themselves to rash actions and uses that were not in the original blueprints. Technocraft has trans-formed Wichtiburg from the pride of the Realms to a nest of power-hungry predators."

"You mean the kind who would prey on the innocent?" Rufus's fur bristled with anger. "The kind who would stick thorns into someone's *brain* just to get information out of it?"

"I only kept those plans because I wanted to present them to the House elders. I've been trying to convince them to shut down the Machine. But then Isvan disappeared, and I turned all my attention to finding him." Teodor sank back into his seat. "Isvan is very dear to me. I would never harm him. This I swear to you, and by the Flame may you believe me."

Lin was not convinced. "But you stopped visiting him."

"He wouldn't let me in. He even locked the gate to the Hall of Winter."

"Locked the gate," Rufus scoffed. "You abandoned him."

"I left messages. I thought he was just coming of age. That if I gave it some time he would come back to me . . ."

"You thought wrong," Lin said. "You were one of the reasons Isvan left. He was scared of you, and he was terrified of Mrs. Zarka. I think he may have found the Brain Tapper plans."

Teodor rubbed his forehead. "My briefcase. Someone entered my house and opened it, that's why I kept it under guard these past few weeks. But I never suspected Isvan did it." His voice became a weary little croak. "He left? To go where?"

Lin hesitated. But then she felt Rufus's hand on her shoulder, pinching her three times. Go further. Look harder. There's something there. She brought out the page that Isvan had torn from *The Book of Frost and Flame*.

Teodor stared at the illustration as if it depicted a poisonous snake, and not a beautiful ice axe.

"Isvan went to great lengths to get this," Lin said. "It was stolen the night before he disappeared."

For the second time that evening, Teodor seemed not worried, not shocked, but afraid.

"Frostfang unlocks the Winterfyrst Well," Lin continued. "That's why we were 'mucking about' down there. So if you're telling the truth about your love for Isvan, you will help us get in."

"He went to the *Winterfyrst Well*?" Teodor picked up one of the empty jars and set it down again. "Stupid," he muttered. "Unprepared!"

"Unprepared for what?" Rufus asked.

"The well outside this house is carved with a melt rune, but it is still a simple hole in the ground. The Winterfyrst Well is no such thing. It is a secret glacial cathedral, and no one but the Winterfyrsts themselves know where it is hidden. But I knew Isvan's mother, and she told me one thing."

"What?" Rufus's eyes were already shining.

"The Well is outside the Palisade of Thorns."

Chapter Twenty-four

The Caravan Road wound up the mountain in sharp, steep turns.

Lin buried her fingers deep in Ursa Minor's fur. She had ridden Uncle Anders's horse up the trail to Buttertop a few times, but sitting bareback on a huge, brown bear was a different matter altogether. The great back lurched and swayed, and she had to shift her weight for every step. Behind her, Rufus had one arm around her waist, one hand grasping Minor's coat, and his tail looped around one of the bear's hind legs. "There's really no need for that," Minor said. "I won't let the little human girl fall, and not you, either."

"So you say, but Rodent bones are brittle. I'm just making sure you keep your word."

"An Ursa always keeps his word," Minor rumbled, but the swaying lessened some.

They had found Minor waiting for them by the Caravan Road, sharing a bag of caramel oats with Teodor's Hoof friend, Fabian. It turned out they had met the Ursa on their way out of Sylveros and brought him along. "For protection," Teodor had muttered, but he wouldn't say why.

The Flamewatcher sat lost in thought in Fabian's painted saddle, eyes trained on the twin spires of Whitepass. After the healing rune, he had not spoken much. Lin wriggled her wrist. The rune had closed the wound and removed all pain. There wasn't even a scar.

She had braced herself for the magic, expecting her magic ears to hurt and bleed. But except for the scratching of the diamond talon pen against the leather, the only sound she had heard was a faint singsong hum. "Teodor?" Lin smiled uncertainly. "Can I ask you something?"

The old fox didn't turn, but he swung an ear toward her. "Your healing rune didn't hurt at all, but Mrs. Zarka's Machine made my ears bleed. Why?"

"Technocraft is crude. It rips and shreds, leaving loose ends and ugly holes. For those with magical otopathy, the strain of it can be dangerous."

"I'll make sure I stay away from the Machine Vault," Lin said.

"And the Observatory," Rufus added. "That's not Technocraft, but your ears bled there, too."

Teodor whipped around. "The Observatory? Ah, I should have thought of that. You were in the mirrors."

Lin raised her brows. "How did you know?"

"To answer that question," Teodor said, "I need to tell you the story of the Observatory."

"Here comes another history lesson," Rufus muttered, but he settled down to listen.

"A thousand years ago, in a frozen, lonely valley far to the north, a travelling Flamewatcher discovered an underground cage. Inside it lay the remains of a giant Starfalcon."

Teriko's cage, Lin thought. Marvin had said something about it having once trapped a Starfalcon.

"The Flamewatcher knew she would never get the colossal skeleton out, so she created a chimney and burned the bones. As she watched the smoke rise, she had a compelling idea. She would make a bond between this world and Earth in the form of six great mirrors. One would be for remembrance, and the other five for children in need. And she used the Starfalcon's ashes to create the Observatory."

"That's how Sylver was founded?" Lin asked. "Because of the Observatory?"

"Just so. When the Petlings of the Realms heard of the magical mirrors, they flocked to the snowy valley to settle down. And so the Sylverings began their long vigil. They named the mirrors after the gifts the Observatory could offer: Strength, Courage, Luck, Comfort, and Hope, and when a child appeared there, the Sylverings wrote it down on a special index card. We believe the gifts noted there will somehow find their way to the child."

Lin sincerely hoped this was true. She remembered the girl in the Courage mirror, the one with the menacing blotch on her nightgown.

"But tonight," Teodor continued, "something unforeseen came to pass at the Observatory. A human child came visiting, and for some reason, while she was inside the building, she appeared in one of the mirrors." He narrowed his eyes. "Or perhaps even several mirrors?"

"Four," Lin whispered. "They said I was in dire need."

Teodor made a soft crowing sound in his throat. "The Observatory answered by granting you those gifts – all four of them – immediately." He reached out a bent, old claw and touched her hand quickly, as if it were charged with electricity. "And that is why you set off the melt rune in the well. Lindelin Rosenquist, you are brimming with magic."

Rufus's grip around her waist tightened. "So you're saying Lin is filled up with magic? Won't that be dangerous for her otopa-thing?"

"Otopathy." Teodor frowned at him. "It may aggravate it, yes. But as she spends the magic, the danger should lessen. Besides, it's not all bad. She may need those gifts tonight."

"How do I use them?" Lin asked. The thought that she might have magic in her blood had her belly tickling, dangerous or no.

"I don't think you can, by choice," Teodor replied. "The gifts – whatever they are – will choose their own moment. Some may already have done so."

"At least one," Lin said, disappointed. She should have known something was wrong when she had the strength to climb the chain in the cage.

They scaled the crest of the hill and found themselves at the mouth of a gorge, sunk into the shoulder between two mountaintops. An icy gale sprang up to meet them, whipping up Teodor's coat flaps. "We are here."

Halfway into the pass, where two great cliffs leaned in to form a bottleneck, a great shadow barred the gorge. The Palisade of Thorns.

As they rode closer, Lin realised that the Palisade matched her street in Oldtown for length, and Mrs. Ichalar's house for height. Its shadow closed around them, broken up here and there by starlight that filtered through, dappling the ground in patterns of leaves and thorns. For the Palisade was not a wall or a stockade, but a giant, living hedge.

The wind ripped itself to shreds on the thorns, and on the tatters, there was a long, ululating scream. Fabian shied some steps to the side, and even Ursa Minor's great scruff rose. Lin had heard a scream like that before, on the hilltop when she had just passed through the scargate from Mrs. Ichalar's cellar. "What is that?" Rufus cried.

"Something nasty come to sniff at the border." Teodor

scanned the top of the hedge. "You two fleet-feet, follow me."

They left Fabian and Ursa Minor on the ground and climbed a series of wobbly ladders and platforms until they reached a ledge at the top of the Palisade. Treacherous gusts tore through the branches, and Lin kept reaching out to steady herself. But she daren't risk being cut by the curved thorns, which were the size of sabres. Rufus, however, gripped the thorns as if they were life buoys, edging sideways on the ledge.

On the Nightmare side of the border, the snow had been scraped away by the cruel winds. At first Lin saw only a bleak landscape of moss and ferns between towering walls and jagged summits in the distance. But then she noticed it: an occasional scuttling out in the pass, like cockroaches darting over a closet floor.

Teodor shot her a sideways glance.

"Do you recognise them?"

Lin shook her head. Her pulse raced and her skin crawled, and it was not just because of the scuttlers. The air seemed different across the border. Brooding and shifting, full of unseen horrors.

Teodor grunted. "Remember I told you that the dreams and thoughts of children shape this world? Well, not all dreams are pleasant. These mountains are home to your secret fears. That is how they got their name."

"Nightmares!" Rufus held on to a thorn with both

hands. "I never knew there were so many of them this close to the border. What are they doing?"

"I do not know," Teodor said. "They usually shun the Palisade. But tonight, more and more of them enter the Whitepass by the hour. Something draws them here, the Wanderer perhaps, or some instinct, or . . . this."

He led them to a patch of hedge where the leaves and thorns had been cleared away, exposing a massive, writhing branch. It carried three-tongued marks within three-tongue marks, all filled with the Flamewatcher signs of lines and dots. The largest and most elaborate rune they had seen so far. Surrounding it was a circle of deep, ugly bite marks that split the wood right through the rune.

"Those marks look exactly like the ones in Isvan's mansion," Lin said. "What are they?"

"That I should very much like to know," Teodor said. "Because they are doing the impossible. They are killing Sylver's guard runes."

"That's a guard rune?" Rufus's voice broke into a squeak. "Aren't they what keep the Nightmares out?"

"Yes. The Palisade is strong, but it can only do so much to protect us. Without the guard runes the Nightmares would eventually swarm the border. Tell me. When you visited my turret tonight, did you perchance notice the runes on the wall?"

Lin tore herself away from the bite marks. Like the holes

in the floor of Isvan's mansion, they sounded like discordant fiddle strings. "The ones under the round windows?"

"Yes. My warning runes. They were made to fire if something happened to the guard runes. Did they seem burned to you?"

Lin tried to remember. She had been so preoccupied with *The Book of Frost and Flame*. But of course, she hadn't known that the carvings were runes, or that they were important. "I think two of them were smudged by soot."

"But not the third."

"No."

Teodor nodded. "Then we can hope that the last guard rune still lives. The rune in the Hall of Winter was killed over a month ago, not long before Isvan disappeared. I thought perhaps it was an accident. After all, ice is an unstable substance. But tonight the Palisade rune was destroyed, too. You heard it, Lin. Its warning rune fired while you were there."

So that was the scratch and the stink from the turret! That was why he had shoved them out the door and galloped up the Caravan Road!

"The guard runes are old, created generations ago, and far beyond my capacity to re-create. I would protect the third and final rune, except I do not know where it is located. I only know that it is carved somewhere to the north of Peppersnap Nook."

"Could the Nightmares be behind it?" Rufus's knuckles had turned white from clinging to the hedge.

"No," Teodor answered. "As long as the final rune lives, they cannot cross the border. And though Nightmares are lethal, their minds drift easily, like the dreams they came from. They do not deal in plots or plans."

Lin stared out into the pass. Had Isvan really come here all alone? Left the safety of the Palisade behind without anyone to guard his back? Now that she had seen the Nightmare Mountains, she doubted he would have gone out there just because he was afraid of Teodor and Mrs. Zarka. *Nothing* could be more terrifying than this shifting darkness full of howls and things that moved.

Teodor tensed beside her. Lin saw it, too. By a formation of low rocks near the end of the pass: a flash of light. Another.

She drew a sharp breath. The jars in the House of Flame! The grains and nuts and seeds!

Blink, blink.

Danger. Trolls nearby.

CHAPTER TWENTY-FIVE

L in's legs felt watery as they climbed down from the Palisade, fox, girl, and vole. Every few breaths a new, shivering howl rose from the Nightmares out in the pass. She still couldn't believe it. Nightmares were creatures made from the secret fears of children, and some of those fears were her own.

"Those are really trolls out there?"

"Snow trolls," Teodor said. "Our local tribe. Dumb brutes, but deadly."

"But that was a troll-hunter signal by those rocks!" Rufus said, edging his way across a platform. "Who else is out there?"

"I don't know, Rufocanus!" Teodor barked. "If I had every answer to every question, I would not have to deal with the likes of you!" He forgot all about his old man's bones and jumped the final ladder to the ground.

"Fabian," he called, stalking over toward the little horse and Ursa Minor, who stood huddled behind a big branch. "You must prepare yourself. We are going through the gate."

Fabian's nostrils flared with fear. "But there must be dozens of trolls out there! No one can last against a whole pack of Nightmares. Not in the open. Not at night."

"I know," Teodor said. "Yet we have no choice. If the Twistrose believes that Isvan is out there, then that's where we must go."

"We have pulled many wild stunts, but this . . ." There was resignation in Fabian's voice. As if he had no hope that they would make it. He scraped a shoe against the frozen earth. "It shall be as you say, old friend. But hooves are not much use against trolls."

Which was true. There was only one weapon that could kill a troll outright, and Lin didn't have any. Bane.

"Teodor," she said. "What is the bane of snow trolls?"

"Silvercone seeds." He fished a small lozenge box from his pocket. It was half full of pearly grains. "This is the reason I returned to the Hearth of Flame – we keep our stores there. But this year, somehow the silver firs did not yield any cones. These are all we have left."

He tossed the lozenge box to Lin.

"You're giving all of them to me?" she said.

Teodor inclined his head. "When the *Rosa torquata*

brought the Twistrose Key to you, it knew you are not only a riddle-cracker of some skill. You're an expert troll hunter, too. In this, we will follow your lead."

They all watched her. Fabian with his serious, sad eyes; Ursa Minor with his close-set gaze; Teodor with a sly glint. And Rufus, whose eyes were bright with pride. All four of them were ready to follow her into the Nightmare realm. Lin swallowed. She was an expert, all right, an expert at making the trolls terrible and dangerous, because that made the hunt more thrilling. She had never imagined that she would actually encounter them. And until now, she hadn't truly understood Teodor's words: *Tonight, young Rosenquist, you will find that some games are real.*

"First of all," she said slowly, trying her best to appear collected and calm, "we can't just go blindly into enemy territory. We have to know where we are headed."

Teodor grunted. "I've witnessed Clariselyn Winterfyrst leave for the Well and return within two hours. The Well has to be near the Cracklemoor. Yet I have never seen any well-like formations in these parts, let alone glacial cathedrals." He clicked his tongue. "I wish I'd had the foresight to bring a map."

Rufus looked from one to the other. "Oh, fine," he muttered, picking a roll of paper out from one of his scarf pockets. His "Comprehensive Chart of Sylveros and All Its Lands". They unrolled the map between them. At the end of the Sylver Vale, there was a bit of map that

Rufus hadn't revealed until now: The Whitepass and the Cracklemoor.

"Where did you get this?" Teodor said.

Rufus gave a pursed-lip shrug.

"You have been in the Cartography Chamber." Teodor shook his head in disgust. "I suppose it takes courage of some sort to trespass and steal right under the nose of your superior."

It did, Lin thought, but it took even more courage to own up to it. She leaned close and whispered, "One point to Rufus of Rosenquist."

The Cracklemoor was a wide, shallow basin, like a sheet tethered between mountain peaks. The Caravan Road cut a brave line straight eastward, toward a range of craggy peaks called the Shatterjaws. To the north lay the tall Towerhorns, from which the Crackle Creek flowed across the moor to the Grieve Cleft.

"I remember something Lass the gatherer said. She found Frostfang in a rimedeer carcass near the spring of the Crackle Creek. Which should be here." Lin pointed to the northernmost end of the stream. "It's no guarantee the Winterfyrst Well is in the Towerhorns, but it's the best lead we have."

"If we want to go there, the Crackle Creek is our only hope," Fabian offered. "It runs through a dell of shrubs and trees. Snow trolls don't have much of a sense of smell, so if they can't see us, we might stand a slim chance."

"Good idea," Lin said. She drew a line from the pass to the stream. "Once we're out on the moor, we'll head for the Crackle Creek dell and keep our heads down. But that won't work in the pass. In the pass we have to outrun them."

Outside the Palisade a new wave of howls rose, setting everyone's fur on end. Fabian nickered, and Lin could see the white at the edges of his eyes. Teodor frowned at the moaning, swaying, slicing hedge. "Something is not right here," the old fox said. "Snow trolls are loners. They have been known to attack one another on sight. Yet here they are, crammed together in the Whitepass, thick as lice. And that signal we saw – I cannot think of any other explanation than that the trolls sent it."

Rufus snorted. "Trolls making troll-hunter signals? That doesn't seem very likely, unless they're trying to lure us out through the gate. I thought you said Nightmares don't deal in plots or plans."

"Wait," Lin said. She heard a wheezing, grating voice in her head, clipped into pieces and deadened by static, but still as clear as ice. *On Wanderer's Eve, I shall have the Nightmares ready.*

Rufus smiled. "The quizzy face! Lin, do you have a theory?"

"What do you know?" Teodor's eyes blazed with impatience. "For the love of the Flame, Twistrose, our lives are at stake here! I cannot help you if you keep me in the dark!"

"I think the trolls are being *controlled*." Lin picked the falcon cylinder out of her boot and pried out the letter. "'The Margrave's Song' is not about a star, it's about a person. We found a second verse in Figenskar's office. He stole it from a falcon messenger."

Teodor snatched the song out of Lin's hands. "This message is for me! *I* am Vulpes of Lucke."

"You are?" Rufus gathered his whiskers in suspicion. "How convenient."

"My last name is Lucke, and *Vulpes* means 'fox'. Something for you to ponder, Rufocanus."

Rufus glared at him, but Fabian nipped gently at Rufus's scarf. "It's not intended as an insult," the horse said. "Merely as a reminder. Right, Teodor?"

Teodor didn't reply. He had his grizzled snout in the Queen of Soothsinger's letter, as if bringing it close would help him decipher the words. "A new lord on Wanderer's Eve. A powerful lord. A Blood Lord." He clicked his claws against the parchment. "*Margrave* means 'lord of the border'. And the border is under attack from the Nightmares. Nightmares that do not behave as Nightmares."

"That's what I was thinking about," Lin said. "I found something else in Figenskar's office. A recorded message from the Margrave. He said he would have the Nightmares ready, for Wanderer's Eve. That they were set for some plan they call Operation Corvelie. We don't know exactly what it is, but they're covering their . . ."

"*Corvelie?*" Teodor interrupted. "Corvelie, you say? But that means . . ."

The old fox licked his lips. "Oh dear. I have been looking at this puzzle from the wrong side. Yes, *Margrave* means 'border lord', but it is also another name for the Wanderer. For someone who is a long way from home. A very long way."

He turned abruptly and climbed onto Fabian's back, wheeling him around. "Lin. Rufocanus. May the Flame forgive me, but you will have to brave the Cracklemoor alone."

"Alone? You're not coming with us?" Rufus cried.

"I cannot." Teodor had the decency to look ashamed. "I do not know how you will fare out there alone, but I have no choice but to leave you. Remember, Lin. We trust in your gifts, and so must you." He whispered something into Fabian's ear, and the Hoof threw himself into a run.

"At least tell us where you are going!" Lin called after their whipping tails.

"The final guard rune!" Teodor cried. "I must find and protect the final guard rune!"

Chapter Twenty-six

"On the upside," Rufus said between his teeth, "we don't have to wonder if we can trust Teodor or not."

Rufus and Lin sat astride Ursa Minor. Lin held on to the fur between Minor's shoulders, and Rufus held on to Lin, and in their free hands, both riders clutched a small pile of twenty-six silvercone seeds.

All they had to do was touch the Gate Thorn, and the Palisade would let them through. Lin wished they could stay within the safety of Sylver's border. But Isvan had come this way. He was out there, *silenced and caught in the secret cold*. And a troll hunter did not back away from danger.

"I am ready when you are, small ones," Ursa Minor said. They had tried telling him that he didn't have to come, but the great bear had insisted. "I want to help find the little boy," he had said, shaking his massive head. "He was leaving, and I didn't understand. Maybe if I had, he wouldn't be out there with the howlers."

Lin took a deep breath. "Rufus."

Rufus leaned out and put his hand against the Gate Thorn, a white sickle covered with runes, like a carved and sharpened elephant's tusk. A thrum went through the Palisade. The branches stirred before them, unhooking, untangling, ungrasping, until a tall, pointed opening had formed in the hedge.

Ursa Minor walked through it. The frozen dirt of the Caravan Road crunched under his paws. Immediately, the brooding air enveloped them. It felt sluggish and full of foreboding and malice, like the very moment you shift into a bad dream. Rufus twisted back and forth behind Lin. "Where the rats are they?"

"Shhh," Lin hissed. The scuttlers had been over by the mountain walls, at least three hundred yards away from the gate on both sides. She had a small hope that they could slip through the pass unnoticed, that they would be out on the Cracklemoor before the trolls even knew the gate had opened. Behind them, the hedge whispered shut, braiding branch with branch, until the Palisade was whole again. In the silver and black of the mountain gorge, nothing stirred, save the wind that tore at their breath clouds.

Minor took a silent step forward.

A pair of green eyes lit up in the darkness, pale and big

like jellyfish. But they weren't over by the mountain wall. They were ten yards away.

The troll unfurled from its crouch, joint by joint. It became two metres tall. Three metres tall. It had a long neck and a matted, white pelt. And teeth. Many, many teeth.

A howl came tearing out of its maw and sunk into Lin's heart. "Go!" she cried. "Run!"

Minor's great muscles bunched up, and he threw himself into a wild gallop. And as he did so, hundreds of pale green eyes lit up in the pass, two by two, like shipwreck lanterns. They were everywhere.

The bane! Lin clenched her fist tight as she clung to the Ursa's tilting, lurching back, trying to find her balance so she could get a decent shot when the snow trolls came at them.

And come they did, scurrying out of the night, so fast their legs blurred against the ground. But Ursa Minor ran fast, too. The trolls gained on them, but whenever they came almost close enough, they fell back a few steps, howling with their nasty maws instead of attacking. Lin cast a confused look over her shoulder. The trolls were so fast. Why were they just chasing after them?

The answer appeared at the end of the pass. A whole wall of green eyes lit up, a barricade stretching from one mountainside to the other, like a mirror palisade. Only this one had teeth and claws instead of thorns. The trolls stood shoulder to shoulder, rows and rows deep, waiting for them.

It was a trap.

"Minor!" Rufus cried.

"I see them," Minor growled. "Hold on, small ones!" He veered left, running along the gnashing wall at a fifteen-yard distance. It bought them some time, but not much. The mountain wall was approaching rapidly.

Lin clutched her precious little handful of silvercone seeds. The trolls of the barricade didn't react to their change of course. They stayed put like toy soldiers lined up for battle. But to stand a chance of hitting the trolls with the bane, Lin and Rufus would need to move within the monsters' reach. And even if they threw all of the seeds at once, Lin doubted it would be enough to blast a hole in the wall. Her pulse thumped in her ears. Never, in all her years of troll hunting, had she imagined a situation this desperate.

"Troll hunter!" Minor roared, and it was both a warning and a question. Twenty more bounds, and they would have to choose between crashing into the mountainside or turning back toward the Palisade, straight into the claws of their pursuers.

A group of rocks rose out of the ground on their side. The stone formation where they had seen the mysterious troll-hunter signal! The troll wall curled along it, but the jellyfish eyes looked more sparse, only two trolls deep against the stones.

"Right!" Lin screamed. "Over the rocks!"

She felt Rufus's grip around her waist slip an inch as Minor turned again, lurching hard under them. His bounds grew hard and fast as he raced for the troll barricade. And when the first trolls reached for them, he leaped for the sky.

Lin held on with one hand and let a few seeds go with the other. Around her, bursts of silver, and some of the green eyes winked out as those trolls collapsed, shrinking, shrieking, in a distorted knot of melting flesh.

But not all the bane hit home. And the trolls that remained lunged at them. Claws sliced at their legs as Minor found purchase against the rocks and clambered up, pebbles skittering under his paws. Lin felt something sharp clawing at her foot, but she kicked and it missed. But behind her, Rufus cried out, and his arm let go of her.

"Rufus!" Lin screamed, wrenching around. One of the trolls had Rufus by the tail, and her friend's eyes bulged in pain and panic. Another gripped Minor's hind leg, opening its maw of splintered icicle teeth, ready to sink them in.

Lin felt a rush of electricity sting through her body. *She could save them.* She flung every single silvercone seed back at their attackers and grabbed Rufus by the scruff, hauling him onto Minor's back. And as the bane found the enemy, the troll wall finally let them through.

Minor landed on the other side of the stone formation with a great thud, and they shot out between the shoulders of the Whitepass, turning northeast over the open heath.

The hisses and screams from the trolls haunted them through the night, but they were not pursued.

CHAPTER TWENTY-SEVEN

On the Cracklemoor, every blade of grass wore a cover of thick rime. But it was not the crisp and sheltered cold of the Sylver Valley. A sour wind came howling over the bleak land, gnawing at their fingers.

Huddled down against Minor's back, Lin tried to hide inside the chaperon hood, regretting that she had turned down the offer of a parka. The unbroken row of glowing troll eyes came unbidden every time she closed her lids, as did the horror of the bane's work. She had never pictured it quite so *loud*.

In her right pocket, her bane pocket, her hand curled around Teodor's lozenge box. Nearly empty.

She had let all the seeds go in those frantic moments by the rocks, and Rufus had lost all his when the troll caught him. Lin pressed her lips together. She should have been more careful when she divvied up the seeds, kept more for later, for the way back. Now their only chance was to avoid any more skirmishes.

The moor looked empty as far as she could see, but Lin knew better now than to trust her eyes. Any moment a Nightmare could come looming out of the dark. She wanted to ask Minor if he thought the Crackle Creek dell was far, but even with the moaning wind, she didn't want to raise her voice. Minor seemed to know this, for he loped smoothly over tufts and tussocks, and his footfalls blended with the moor's own creaks.

The bear was so agile here in the wild, when he had ice and snow under his paws and not a scrubbed floor. Teodor had seen it, too, on their way up to the Whitepass. "Petlings may be better at town life and finicky finger work," he had said, "but we Wilders have feral hearts and true instincts, and the more we use them, the stronger they grow." Arching his brows at Lin and Rufus, he had added quietly, "Not for nothing are most Frostriders of our kind."

Minor changed his rhythm, slowing down enough to slide into a deep dell with a black, frozen stream at the bottom. The Crackle Creek, at last, and at last some good cover. Thickets of junipers and dwarf birches lined the banks, and there were even some white trees, which formed sheltering pavilions with their wintertrue leaves that sounded like bat wings when they flapped in the wind. "Cold oaks! They grow in the Winterwoods, too," Minor said. "Their bark is great for scratching."

Those were the first words anyone had spoken since the pass. Lin and Rufus couldn't help but laugh. The shifty nightmare feeling of the moor seemed less oppressive here, less menacing.

"You weren't kidding about the troll's bane," Rufus said. "That stuff works!"

"Are you hurt?" Lin asked. "That troll had you by the tail. . . ."

"It's nothing." Rufus lifted his tail forward so Lin could see, but it was not his usual dashing arc. Near the tip there were two deep scissor slices.

"Doesn't look like nothing to me," Lin said. "Maybe I should drag you off to see the doctor."

"You can drag me off to see whomever you like, as long as you keep saving my fur like that." Rufus's voice was light, but he hugged her fiercely.

They pressed on along the icy creek until the dell broadened into a stretch of shallows with banks and beaches of white pebbles. There, Ursa Minor stopped under a tree, bending his big head this way and that, snorting deeply. "I don't like to scare you, small ones. But there's death on the wind."

He turned his snout toward the western bank. "There."

Under the thick frost they had not seen it. But on the beach lay a lifeless shape under a white cloak. Whistling through his teeth, Rufus slid down from Minor's back and approached the shape on nimble feet. He pushed at the cloak. It creaked as it shifted. "Oh, no."

Lin feared the worst. "Is it Isvan?"

"No. It's a falcon messenger."

The cloak was not a cloak after all, but a frozen wing. The falcon lay pinned to the ground with a black thorn the size of a sabre through his heart. He had suffered the death of a sparrow.

"This thorn is from the Palisade," Rufus said. "Nightmares don't touch the Palisade."

They both knew what that meant. This was done by a Sylvering, or at the very least, the weapon had been provided by one. Lin climbed down from Minor's back, too, to examine the bandolier strapped across the falcon's chest. The loops were empty, but Lin recognised the falcon mark burned into the leather. It matched the one on the cylinder she had found in Figenskar's office.

"Lin." Rufus had lifted the messenger's other wing and uncovered a set of footprints that seemed to appear out of nowhere: deep ones, with sharp heels. Boot prints.

"Then he has taken the life of another," Rufus said softly. "He has broken the pact. To speak ill of the rules is one thing, but to kill . . ."

But Lin had heard the nervous strain on Figenskar's voice when he spoke of his "master". "I think the Margrave has a stronger sway over Figenskar than the Sylver Pact."

"But if he's scared of him, why help him?"

"It does seem strange," Lin said. "The Margrave must have offered him something big in return. Something Figenskar couldn't resist."

"Here's a pretty thing!" Minor said, sniffing at the falcon's feet. He stuck his muzzle into the frozen gravel and pulled something out of the ground. It was another letter cylinder. Before he was murdered, the falcon must have managed to trample it into the ground with his talons. Lin unstoppered the tube and read aloud.

> Twistrose,
>
> All the pieces are falling into place. The foot lifts, ready to crush. The wings soar, ready to strike. The heart beats, ready to rip and rend should you fail.
>
> Do not fail.
>
> Trust the Lights and the Gifts you have gathered. The Blood Lord is waking.
>
> Raymonda, Queen of Soothsingers

Rufus made a harsh sound in his throat. "Trust the Lights and the Gifts you have gathered? What is that supposed to mean? How could she know that you would be here?"

"I don't know. I don't know what any of this means." Lin bent down to stroke the falcon's neck feathers. "Poor falcon messenger!"

On the eastern moor sounded the sad bellow of a rimedeer in the distance. Lin rose quickly, frowning at the shallows and the tangled birches. The nightmare terror hooked its claws into her again, because she had seen something. Along the frozen stream where they had just passed: two flashes.

Their mystery signaller was back.

"We have to hide," she breathed. "Now!"

"Up the tree," Rufus said. Of course. Trolls were sure of foot on boulders and mountainsides, but they preferred to keep their soles on the ground for fear the wood wouldn't bear their weight.

They skimmed up the cracked-leather trunk, high enough to conceal themselves among the white, rustling leaves.

Rufus wrapped his arms and legs hard around a sturdy limb of the tree, spreading his whiskers askance at her. Lin hoped she had done the right thing by trusting the warning. Her hand shook slightly as she opened Teodor's lozenge box. Only six grains left.

That very moment, there came a stomping along the creek. Snow trolls, creeping toward the shallows. Lin put a finger over her mouth, and even Minor understood that particular sign. None of them dared move.

Fabian had said snow trolls didn't have much of an olfactory sense, yet Lin could have sworn there were shivering sniffs whenever the footsteps halted. Pale lights appeared below the tree, green and jellied. Three pairs for three trolls.

In the grunts and rumbles, there were words.

"Called we are," said one of the trolls.

"Called to the stabbing hedge," said another.

"Called by the master," the third agreed. "But *this one* calls us more."

Master? This one? What did that mean? And weren't snow trolls supposed to be dumb?

Lin scooped the remaining silverseeds out of the box. They should be enough, if she aimed well. She waited until the trolls were gathered close around the great trunk, took her time aiming, and let the seeds go, all but one. They fell toward their targets, straight and true. Lin waited for the howls.

None came.

Could she have missed so fatally? Their only hope now was that killing one would scare the others off. Her heart pounded as she leaned far out and dropped the final seed. This time she saw it land on the back of one of the trolls, but it just bounced off the white ferns it had plastered to its back. Lin blinked. This should not be possible. A direct hit should mean death for any troll. Unless . . .

Tonight, young Rosenquist, you will find that some games are real.

"Smell her," the first troll hissed, curling its long tongue around the words.

"Smell the girl enemy," the second said.

In the branches above, the girl enemy sat and held her breath. These were not snow trolls. They were Summerhill trolls. And the monsters she and Niklas had invented were not dimwitted brutes at all.

"Smell her in the tree," said the third troll, and lifted the huge weapon it carried. An axe.

The first blow fell, making the leaves flap, and there was no longer any need to whisper. Rufus squeezed Lin's arm. "Are those . . ."

"Yes!"

Rufus nodded toward the rim of the dell as the second blow shook the tree. "We could make a run for it!"

But Summerhill trolls were fast. They could catch and they could hunt. Lin had made sure of that with her stupid game. She shook her head. No running. They wouldn't even make it out of the dell.

"Then, troll hunter . . ." Rufus paused for the third blow. "I hope you have a better idea."

Lin put her hand in the right pocket of her cardigan. No bane. Why hadn't she brought some from her troll-hunting casket? Or taken some from that tin in the Hearth of Flame? Think, she told herself. Bring your brain to the party!

Cold oak. Minor had called these trees cold oak!

She looked up. Above the next branch there was a squirrel hole. She leaped to her feet and stuck her hand in the hole. Her fingers twinged with some sort of electricity. They came out again clutching a fistful of white-capped nuts.

Not caring if she hurt herself, she dropped hard along the trunk, and when no more branches blocked her way, she threw the acorns down on the trolls. The jellied eyes grew red and winked out, and the dell filled with sizzles and wet gurgles as the troll's bane did its damage.

When the cries had died out, Rufus climbed carefully down to the branch next to her. "Not bad, troll hunter! How did you know they were coming?"

Lin squinted back toward the river bend, where she had seen the flashes. Who had sent them? A Frostrider that Teodor didn't know about? But if so, why didn't he reveal himself? She pressed her lips tight. If not for the signal, they would never have had time to climb the tree.

"Because I did what the Soothsinger told me. I trusted the lights."

CHAPTER TWENTY-EIGHT

They continued north, meandering across the moor, with their pockets loaded with cold oak acorns. But they neither saw nor heard more trolls. With every bend of the river, the Towerhorns grew taller and the dell grew shallower, until the banks barely reached above their necks. And at last the Crackle Creek went where they could not follow: underground.

"Where to now?" Rufus asked.

"I don't know. This must be the Crackle Creek spring, where Lass found Frostfang. It's as far as our plan goes."

"Well, then we had better find . . ." Rufus fell silent. Out on the slopes there had been another flash, at the edge of the sparse forest that grew along the skirts of the mountains. "Minor," he whispered. "Our mystery guide is over there by the trees. Can you pick up his scent?"

Minor sniffed. "The wind is right, but no. All I smell is wood. Maybe some kind of metal. But no beast or creature."

Lin gave Rufus the triple pinch. They would be exposed out there in the open, but they had no better idea. Ducking low, they crept from shrub to shrub until they reached the thicket. Among the roots, there were patches of snow that the wind hadn't swept away, and by a big juniper bush, Rufus found a set of very odd tracks. Deep puncture wounds in the ground.

"If it's a troll, then it's on stilts," Rufus said, scratching his ear. "I can't picture a troll on stilts. Can you?"

Lin could not. But Teodor had said the Nightmare Mountains were home to the secret fears of children. Who knew what creatures lived out here, and what legs they had?

The puncture marks wandered up the mountainside for a brief stretch, always in the cover of bushes or crags, until they ended at a steep ridge overgrown with bilberry bushes. Lin thought their guide must be an excellent mountaineer to avoid being seen on the bare slopes. But where had he gone from here?

"I can feel a draft," Ursa Minor grumbled. He pawed at the bilberry bushes, and to everyone's astonishment, they could be pulled aside like a curtain. Behind it was the mouth of a ravine that cut into the mountain like an axe blow, barely wide enough for them to squeeze into. A perfect hiding place, and, if you hid in the brambles along the edge, a perfect spot for an ambush.

"Shhh." Rufus bent his head. "I'll try to hear his breathing."

They waited for a long while in the brown scent of slumbering roots in winter. Even Ursa Minor tried to keep his big, hot snorts quiet. It was the first real silence for some time, and perhaps that was all Lin needed. Just as Rufus lifted his head in defeat, Lin heard something. But it wasn't breathing. It was music.

Or rather, music was too tame a description of the curious sound that hooted in her ears, a haunting, wild voice that Lin could not properly name.

"I don't hear anything, little girl," Minor said.

"Me neither," said Rufus. "You're sure?"

Lin nodded. "It's coming from the ravine. I think I'm hearing it with my magic ears."

"All right," Rufus said brightly, though his back was straight and tight. "As Teodor put it: Then that's where we must go."

Under the trailing roots, they saw no more tracks or flashes. The walls leaned closer and closer until they touched overhead, and the ravine became a tunnel. Silvery veins wove through the rock, surrounding them in an exhausted light as they moved deeper into the mountain.

"This place is funny," Minor muttered. "A cave like

this should smell like dung and old bones, but the air gets fresher the deeper we go."

"No wonder," Rufus said, spreading his whiskers. "There's an opening up ahead."

They all felt it now, a cold, sweet breeze that blew in to greet them. And as they reached the end of the tunnel, all three stopped to watch in wonder.

They were standing on the bottom of a deep, sheltered valley, enclosed by mountains curled up like a fist. A hundred feet up the mountainside, the lip of a glacier jutted out, green and opaque. Below it hung a majestic frozen waterfall that caught the light from the Wanderer, filling the tiny valley with blue, wavering light.

More than anything, the valley resembled a well.

"This must be it!" Rufus said. "The Winterfyrst Well! And in here, the Nightmares don't rule at all!"

It was true. Within the Well, Lin could shake off the sluggish heaviness of the moor. No troll could climb down those mountainsides, she knew, and all around, the music swirled and whistled, lulling her calm.

"Look!"

Rufus had found a lonely set of footprints that crossed the snowy valley floor, headed for the waterfall. They weren't punctures or boot tracks, but the smooth, five-pebbled marks of bare feet that appeared human, except no human could walk barefoot through a frozen wilderness.

"You go on, small ones," Ursa Minor said, frowning up at the masses of ice. "I will guard the tunnel opening so no dream beast can follow."

They entered the Well, Rufus with his tail held high, troll wound forgotten for now. Far above, the wind gnawed at the rim of the valley, blowing a veil of snow crystals over the edge. The stars winked, momentarily erased by wisps of clouds, and the Wanderer could not be seen.

When Rufus whooped with joy, it felt like he was shouting in a place of worship. He sat beside a shining cairn at the foot of the waterfall. A snow light, with silver milk and golden white beaming out through the holes. Inside they glimpsed not a candle, but a glowing ball of glass, with a tiny shadow fluttering at its heart. It could only be Isvan's snow globe.

Lin fell down on her knees to pick it up, but instead she cried out in pain. The cold that radiated from the globe was so severe, her fingers instantly turned blue.

Rufus pulled her back a step. "Isvan didn't have his Ice Mask, remember," he said in a great cloud of breath.

Lin nodded slowly. Her lips had stiffened. "I'm not sure it's right to touch someone's soul anyway. We should leave it here until we find him."

The wind stirred her hair, and she heard a whisper behind her.

Find him.

She turned around, expecting to see someone standing

among the ice pillars of the waterfall, but there was no one, not on the valley floor, and not on the mountain walls. "Did you hear that?"

"Hear what?" Rufus said. "More music?"

"No. Voices."

The icicles of the waterfall twisted and wound around each other, sometimes thick as pillars, sometimes gossamer frail. Near the ground, two pillars joined in a tall archway. Lin took a step toward it.

Another soft moan came rustling, and this time she didn't hear the words, she *felt* them in her spine. "They're saying he's here."

Rufus grasped her hand, and there was no need for the triple pinch. Without another word they walked into the waterfall.

Dark ice covered the ground like glass; frozen drops lay scattered like pearls. This felt right, Lin thought. This felt like the Winterfyrst mansion. The doorways and arches seemed wilder, though, less like grand architecture and more like living roots that creaked and sighed and didn't want to let them through. Rufus spread his whiskers as he pressed between two icicles. "Isvan? Are you here? Don't be afraid. We're here to help!"

"Help, help, help," the waterfall echoed.

They weaved their way to the back of the waterfall, where the ice slanted away from the rock, creating a tall chamber. "You're right," Rufus said. "He definitely came this way." Lodged in the floor was an ice axe with a carved shaft and a transparent head bearing the Winterfyrst snow crystal. The magical axe that was also a key.

Frostfang.

Rufus grasped the slim handle. "Don't mind if we do!" He pulled hard, but the axe didn't budge. "I can't get it out," he said, annoyed. "Here. You try."

But Lin wasn't looking at the axe, she was looking up the mountainside. Out of the darkness dangled something she had not expected. Someone had struck bolts into the rock and threaded a red climbing rope between them, and there were more bolts on the ground. Far above, she could make out the mouth of a cave, enclosing the top of the waterfall. But the rope only reached two-thirds up the wall, and there it ended in a loose coil.

"Isvan!" Lin called. "Are you here?"

"Here, here, here," came the echoes, and it seemed to Lin that there were too many of them, and that they sounded too sad.

Rope. Bolts. Loose coil. The puzzle pieces came together with a painful click. Lin turned around, still gazing up, wishing very hard that she was wrong.

She was not. Inside the thickest frozen pillar, a falling boy hung suspended. Through the ice he resembled a porcelain figure with his raven hair and pale skin. A desperate porcelain figure grasping at nothing.

They had found Isvan Winterfyrst.

"Is he . . ." Rufus cleared his throat. "Do you think he's dead?"

"Dead, dead, dead," the waterfall sighed.

Lin bit her lip to stop it from quivering. He couldn't be. After all those lonely hours sitting in his windowsill or outside the Waffleheart, he couldn't end like this. She was supposed to save him. She was supposed to get him home. "No," she said, shaking her head stubbornly. "His snow globe was alive. That has to mean there is still hope."

Rufus hunched with relief. "Then my next question is: How are we going to get him down?"

Lin shook her head again. She really didn't know. Isvan must have fallen where the rope ended, but he had fallen far enough that they couldn't reach him from the mountain wall.

Rufus twirled his whiskers. "This may sound crazy, but . . . Remember how you set off Teodor's melt rune? He said you were charged with magic from the Observatory. I don't know if there's any of it left after our stunts on the Cracklemoor, but . . ." He nudged her toward the ice axe. "If the melt rune worked for you, then maybe a magical axe would work, too? And Frostfang is supposed to let the bearer control ice. You could ask it to bring him down."

It was worth a try. She *had* set off that melt rune, and maybe even the gramophone in Figenskar's office had sparked into life at her touch. But since the frantic skirmish in the Whitepass, she had felt lighter somehow, and she knew some of the magic had passed out of her when she found those cold oak acorns. Maybe there were no more Observatory gifts left.

Lin closed her hands around the shaft, preparing to use all her strength to pull it out. But Frostfang slid out of the ice as if it were butter. "You know, I think your theory might be right," Lin said. She couldn't quite smile with Isvan frozen right above her head, but the cool handle of the axe still felt wonderful in her hands; it flowed, creating strands of music as it cut the air.

She put the edge against the root of Isvan's pillar. It made a thin, white scar. "Let him go," she said.

"Go, go, go," the ice whispered back to her. Frostfang trembled in her hands.

Crack.

"It's working!" Rufus peered up along the pillar, now split in half by a fissure. If Lin hit it again, there was a good chance it might break off and tumble down on them. But they had to get Isvan down, and if this was the only way . . .

"Rufus," she said. "I think you had better get to safety."

"What?" Rufus snapped back to look at her. "What about you?"

"I said, you should run!" And Lin buried the axe deep in the ice, yelling, "Set him free!"

This time, there was no echo, but a thunder that shook not just Isvan's pillar, but the entire waterfall. From the deep notch where Frostfang had bit, fractures spread out, marbling the floor, racing up the pillars.

"Rats," Rufus cried.

"Rats, rats, rats," the waterfall moaned, and then the voice drowned in a host of cracks.

Lin's last waking view was of icicles colliding, crumbling like the bones of an ancient temple, raining ruins down on her.

CHAPTER TWENTY-NINE

"L in!"

The voice sounded woollen. Her head felt woollen, too. She was lying on her back, and her face almost touched the ceiling. She was very cold. Where was she?

"Lin!"

Whoever kept calling seemed distressed, for there were tears in the cries, mingled with the occasional thud and crunch. "Little one, where are you?"

Little one! Rufus! And everything came crashing back into her head: Sylver, Isvan, the waterfall. She must be trapped under the avalanche. She tried turning over on her side. Her feet and hands moved feebly against the ice. Something heavy lay across her chest and thighs, and she couldn't shift. Well, at least she wasn't dead, or paralysed.

One point to Miss Rosenquist.

"Be quiet, Rufus!" said a deep voice. Ursa Minor. "We won't be able to hear her."

The thuds and crashes stopped, and Lin knew they were listening for her. She wanted to call out, but she couldn't draw her breath properly. Instead, she scraped at the ice with the tip of her boot.

"Here!" came an urgent squeal. A beam of light fell on her face. "It's her!" A wild-eyed Rufus appeared among the ice blocks. "Are you hurt? Are you in pain?"

"Can't . . . move . . ." Lin wheezed.

Rufus began scratching at the ice. The shavings swirled down to land on Lin's cheeks.

"Let me." Big, brown paws ripped away ice block after ice block, replacing the ceiling with stars.

"Careful, Minor!" Rufus said. "Don't drop anything on her! She's not a teapot."

"Oh, I'm careful," Ursa Minor said. "Mustn't crush the little girl." Ever so gently, he removed the block that pinned Lin down. She drew a blissful breath and lifted her head. Frostfang stood upright next to her, blade lodged in the ground. It had carried some of the weight of the block. Quite possibly it had saved her from being crushed.

She got to her feet, gaping at the mess around her. Nothing was left of the waterfall but a row of splintered stubbles where the glacier and mountain met, and a chaos of shattered beams and rubble on the valley floor.

"I'm going to lift you out now," Minor said, closing his

paws around her waist. A soft hug later, she was standing next to Rufus. She felt fine, except for a bruise or two and the thousands of bony Rodent fingers that poked at her back and neck and legs, prodding for injuries. "Does this hurt? How about this?"

"How about you?" she countered. "You weren't hurt either?"

"I tried to get you out, but there was just too much falling stuff. I ran." Rufus's shoulders were hunched with shame. "I'm sorry. We weren't supposed to leave each other."

"No, of course you did," Lin said. "I told you to get to safety. It was the right thing to do. The *only* thing to do."

"No. The whole stupid Frostfang idea was mine. And when we go on our adventures, we have to be able to trust . . ."

A shout from Minor interrupted him. The bear was wrestling with a thick pillar that poked out of the debris. "The little boy! The little boy!"

Isvan!

Lin and Rufus clambered over broken chunks and gravel. Together, the three of them pulled the heavy log out of the pile. Minor rolled it over so it faced the right way and used his paws to brush away the crystals that powdered the surface.

It was a stroke of incredible luck.

Two feet below and one foot above Isvan's body, the

icicle had been smashed to dust. But the part that encased him was whole. He stared out through the glassy ice with eyes of sapphire blue that shone with fear. Lin felt that he was looking at her.

"What are you waiting for," Rufus said. "No waterfall will crash down on you this time. Finish it."

Lin hefted Frostfang. No waterfall would crash down. But she couldn't shake an uncomfortable feeling that nagged at her, like a chill splinter moving through her body, worming its way toward her heart. She was forgetting something. Something important.

"Wait," she said. "Do you think the avalanche could be heard out on the Cracklemoor?"

"Maybe." Rufus frowned at the now unguarded tunnel. "I don't know how deep into the mountains we are."

That must be it, Lin thought. "Maybe you should go back and watch the entrance," she said to Minor. "Just in case."

The Wilder nodded, grim of face. "They won't get past me."

As Minor shuffled off to work his way through the ice, Lin turned back to Isvan. It was the first human face she had seen all night. But none of the Sylverings had reminded her more of the taxidermied animals in Mrs. Ichalar's cellar.

"Can he see us, do you think?" she said.

"I don't know. To me he seems . . ." Rufus shrugged

uncomfortably. "I guess we won't know until we get him out."

Lin touched Frostfang to the end of the log, as far away from Isvan's face as possible, and whispered, "Release him."

Crack.

Isvan's prison burst into a million tiny shards. They flew away like smoke, settling on his body like ashes.

Lin crouched down beside him, making sure she didn't get too close. It felt like sitting by a reverse fire. The cold beat at her skin, freezing her nose on the inside. She shook her head to clear it. No, the trolls were not it. There was something else, something she was supposed to be doing . . .

She blew at the Winterfyrst's face, and the ice caught in his lashes. They were stirring.

"We did it! He's waking up!" Rufus's voice echoed all through the Well as he did a little victory jig. "Who would have thought he could survive all those weeks inside the ice!" He bent down to hug Lin, laughing in her ear. "I guess there are times when it actually helps to carry your soul outside your body!"

Isvan blinked. His blue stare passed over Rufus to Lin and widened in recognition. A shy smile tugged at the corner of his mouth.

The splinter reached Lin's heart. She bolted to her feet.

From across the valley came a small crunch.

Isvan's chest heaved once, and a faint wind escaped his lips. Then his eyes released Lin's and slid shut.

"Isvan?" Rufus sounded completely bewildered. "Lin? What's wrong?"

Lin already knew. There was a sound missing in the Well, the beautiful whispering voice that had sung to her since the ravine, and that had come from Isvan's snow globe. Now it was gone.

Instead there came a long, terrible, grief-stricken howl from the great, brown snout of Ursa Minor.

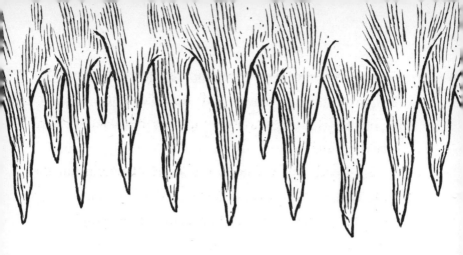

CHAPTER THIRTY

M inor shuddered hopelessly with every sob.

"Please," Lin said. "Don't cry anymore."

"The little boy!" The wail that came out of Minor was so thin, so helpless. But there was nothing Lin could say to comfort him. She wanted to cry herself.

The foot lifts, ready to crush, the falcon message had said. Lin clutched the sleeves of her cardigan. Why couldn't Raymonda just have told her to make sure no one stepped on Isvan's soul? Instead she had told her "Do not fail." So of course, Lin had done just that.

Isvan lay lifeless in the snow. His hair was messed up from Minor's attempts at shaking him awake. Ice crystals were creeping across his brow and cheeks, already claiming him back.

She understood now, how Minor and Lass had mistaken her for the Winterfyrst. Isvan could be her brother.

Even their clothes were the same, white and blue. Only Lin's garments were sturdy and warm, and Isvan's were thin, like funeral silks.

"Is there really nothing we can do?" Rufus switched restlessly between chewing the tassels of his scarf and licking the wound on his tail.

"I don't think so." Lin looked down on the shards she had picked out of the trampled snow light. Seven in all. She had hoped beyond hope that the Observatory magic could bring back the silver and gold light. But the only thing she had accomplished was to nick her finger on the jagged edges and smudge them with blood. She heard no song from the shattered orb, and her spine didn't tingle when she touched it. It was just glass, like any broken fishbowl.

"We should think of getting back. Teodor knows more magic than anyone in Sylver. Maybe he can help."

"If we make it back across the moor," Rufus said.

Lin nodded. They had some cold oak acorns, but no more silvercone seeds. To stand a chance at all, they needed Minor, but he was in no shape to carry them. "Dry your tears, now, Minor," she said gently. "Everyone understands that it was an accident. We'll think of something, you'll see."

Minor lifted his head. The fur on his face was all wet, but not frozen, since Isvan no longer radiated cold. "Do you really think so?"

"I do," Lin said, trying to sound confident.

Minor smiled tremulously. "You have to come with me

now," he said, lifting Isvan up in his arms as if he weighed exactly nothing. The boy's head lolled to the side, and his arm fell down, exposing the left pocket of his coat. Something white poked out from the thin fabric.

"What's this now? Another letter to inform us we've failed?" Rufus picked the paper out and handed it to Lin. "You do it. I'm sick of prophecies."

Lin opened it. It was a crumpled letter, yes, but the Queen of Soothsingers hadn't written it.

"I'm going to read it aloud," Lin said. "Because I think this is the letter he wrote for you, Minor."

"The one I couldn't read." Minor drew a shivering breath, but he bent his head to listen.

> Last night I dreamed of my mother again. And this time she spoke to me.
>
> I have to go to the Winterfyrst Well and try to free her. The path will be dangerous, but Sylver is no longer safe for me anyway. And I have a feeling I might meet her there, the scared girl from my dream, the one surrounded by shattered ice.
>
> Lass the gatherer will be very angry with me. If I don't come back, tell her I am sorry. If Teodor asks, don't tell him anything. I don't know who to trust, except you, my dear, wild friend.

Fresh tears flecked the snow with grey as Minor hugged Isvan close. "And I'm the one who killed him! After he made it all the way past those trolls and everything."

"We all forgot about the snow globe," Lin said. Isvan had been dreaming of her. Of the moment of his death. That's what the girl in Minor's portrait was: Lin Rosenquist the failed Twistrose. Favoured murder weapon: stupidity. "I'm as much to blame as you."

"Wait a moment," Rufus said. "He came here to free his mother? But don't you see? That means . . ."

He turned and frowned up at the red line of the climbing rope. Around the stubbles of the waterfall, the cave mouth between the rock and the glacier was exposed now. That was where Isvan had been trying to go when he fell. And if he had been right, if Clariselyn Winterfyrst was alive somewhere in that cave, she could make the Wandersnow and save them all.

Almost all.

By way of apology, Lin touched Isvan's hand. It felt so very cold.

"It means we have to finish what he started."

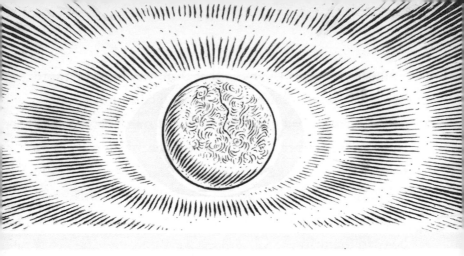

CHAPTER THIRTY-ONE

The green slab of the glacier gate fit seamlessly into the mountain. White scrollwork obscured whatever secrets lay behind it, but Lin and Rufus had the key.

Lin lifted Frostfang uncertainly. She had used the axe twice now, and both times, the ice had more or less exploded around her. But she didn't know how to control its force better. She might as well get it over with.

"Could you move aside, Rufus?"

Rufus stood with his back pressed against the gate, eyeing the crushed ice on the valley floor. Ursa Minor was like a small cub down there, with an even smaller porcelain doll in his arms. As they had climbed the rope up the mountain wall, Rufus had not said a word.

Lin knew he had developed a fear of heights, so she had told him he could stay on the ground if he wanted.

Rufus had refused, claiming that there would be no more "leaving behind" of any sort. But it had cost him. The cave at the top of the waterfall was really not much more than a ledge full of slippery pebbles, and Rufus was too terrified to move.

"Rufus," Lin said. "You know how Teodor said Minor's natural skills and instincts would grow stronger the more he used them?"

"Mmmh," Rufus said between his teeth.

"Well, one thing I know about you voles is that you're good climbers."

He looked up. There were white sickles at the edges of his eyes. "We are?"

"You are. You climbed everywhere on my cardigan, re-member?"

"But I fell." Rufus screwed his face up. "My tail was numb and useless, just like . . . just like now."

"You fell once, and only because you were getting old. But you were never happier than when you rode on my shoulder. You can do this, if you try to remember that feeling. And you can hold my hand so you don't need your tail."

She reached out for him. Rufus stared at her hand, and at her cardigan, and Lin almost thought he would refuse. Instead he began to take proper breaths in place of shallow gasps. Carefully, very carefully, and keeping his back to the rock, he stepped aside. "Hurry."

Lin buried Frostfang in the middle of the slab, between two whorls in the pattern. "Open!"

In place of another thunderstorm of breaking ice, there came a hush and a crackle. Like the branches of the Palisade, the ice pulled away, creating a doorway. A blue shimmer came pouring out, along with a faint chorus of music.

Rufus took two trembling steps and darted through the gate. Lin heard him take a few relieved gulps of air, and then he fell still. "Lin," he whispered. "You have to see this." Lin left Frostfang in the ice and stepped inside, too.

The glacial cathedral.

The room was a great chamber, where the stars shone through the cut-glass facets of the roof. Scattered snowflakes danced and whirled under the ceiling, never settling on the ground. The walls were carved with the same white scrollwork that covered the gate and the handle of Frostfang. Now and then it gave way to three-dimensional mosaics of gems and blue glass sunk into the ice, showing Winterfyrsts with globes of giant pearls.

In a corner sat a shrivelled, rime-covered snow troll. It had been preserved in the intense cold, but Lin guessed it had been dead for a long time. How had it found its way up here?

The snow troll was not alone in the chamber. On a bier in the middle of the floor lay Clariselyn Winterfyrst, clasping her snow globe with slender, white fingers.

She might be sleeping, but her chest didn't rise and fall under her pearled dress, and her skin was waxy. "She looks just like Isvan," Rufus said, and Lin knew he didn't mean the raven hair.

"Her snow globe should give us the answer," she replied, crossing the floor to examine the glass ball.

There was a small flaw in the glass, no longer than a spider's leg, but it splintered the light. Lin could hear it, a sour note in the Winterfyrst music. But in the centre a little speck glimmered bravely, silver milk and golden white.

"She's alive! We have to find a way to wake her." Lin reached out to touch Clariselyn's arm.

"Don't!" Rufus cried. "You'll freeze your fingers off."

"I won't," Lin said. "Clariselyn has her Ice Mask. If she can live among the warm-blooded, she can't be dangerous to come in contact with. Besides, I'm only going to touch her dress." Here goes nothing, she thought, and shook the Winterfyrst's sleeve.

Ice Mask or no, her fingers still smarted. Without thinking, Lin snatched her hand away, but she immediately realised her mistake. The ice pearls woven into the fabric of the dress stuck to Lin's skin, hard enough that she pulled Clariselyn's arm with her.

Clinking against the ice pearls, the snow globe slipped and began to roll off her bodice.

Lin had no choice but to catch it. In the split moment

before she could push it safely back onto Clariselyn, a wave of nausea flowed through her body, and she could feel a rush of electricity pass through her fingertips. Even as a streak of blood dripped down her chin, she could breathe easier.

"That was the last of it," she said. "The last Observatory gift."

Rufus caught her raw hands between his. "What was it?"

"I think it was Hope."

Fresh roses bloomed on Clariselyn's cheeks, as if she had just returned from a brisk walk in the snow. She opened her eyes, and they glowed like sapphires. Confusion leaked into them when she saw who had woken her up – a redback vole and a human girl.

"Who are you?" Her voice was low and melodious.

"My name is Rufus of Rosenquist," Rufus said. "And this is Lin Rosenquist, my human girl."

"A Twistrose." Clariselyn rose from her bier. "How long have I been lying here?"

"You have been missing for seven years," Lin said. "It's Wanderer's Eve. The time is nearing midnight."

"Midnight on Wanderer's Eve. And you are a Twistrose, here to save us in a time of desperate need." For a moment, Clariselyn's face contorted. "You . . . You have come because you need me to create the Wandersnow."

"And to free you," Rufus added quickly. "Seven years is a long time to spend inside a glacier." He widened his whiskers toward the shrunken remains of the snow troll. "Especially trapped in with a Nightmare."

The Winterfyrst's hands trembled as she regarded her snow globe. Whatever she was searching for in the light, she didn't seem to find it. Her shoulders slumped. "I came here to carve the ice for my son's Ice Mask. But a pack of snow trolls must have found the entrance to the ravine. They sneaked up behind me and caught me by surprise. In the fray that followed, one of them pulled Frostfang out of the ice."

"The gate closed!" Lin said. "And no one knew where to find you, because no one knew the location of the Well."

"In my anger, I called the fury of winter down on the north. But my rage cost me dearly. It only served to conceal what tracks I had left behind." Clariselyn stepped onto the cathedral floor in a rustle of silk. "Seven years lost because I was not clever enough to watch my back. I believed snow trolls did not climb, but these had learned to trust stairs. I will not underestimate them again."

"I second that," Rufus muttered, curling his tail gingerly. "There are other tribes than snow trolls on the moor. We met three of Lin's old acquaintances from her home woods."

"Wood troll kin? On the Cracklemoor? Then the Realms have truly changed while I sat here." She lifted her snow globe to examine the crack. "My son was my only window to the world. His snow globe and mine are attuned to one another. I knew how to look into his, to see what he saw. For years I tried to reach him in his dreams to tell him where I was. But he heard nothing but the echoes of my voice." Clariselyn shook her head. "Then one day I witnessed a terrible scene in his globe. That dreadful Observatory Feline . . ."

"Figenskar," Lin said.

"Figenskar, yes. He ambushed my son in our home. Isvan barely escaped through the hidden stairwell, and he did not see the face of his attacker. I knew he and Teodor were estranged, and there was no one else who could keep him safe. So I lay down on the bier and spent all my remaining power, risking my snow globe to finally reach him, to show him the way here. Perhaps . . ." She searched their faces. "Perhaps he did not hear? Since you have come and he has not?"

Rufus scrutinised his toes, biting his fast tongue. Lin would have to try and find the right words, only she had no idea how.

But Clariselyn bent her head and whispered to her globe. "You do not need to answer, for I already know. Take me to him."

At the gate, Clariselyn freed Frostfang from the ice, and it sprang eagerly into her hands, as if to greet an old friend.

The glacier grew back, scrollwork and all. Then the Winterfyrst touched the axe to the stubs of the broken waterfall and said simply, "stairs".

Creaking and groaning, the waterfall grew back, icicle by icicle, except this time there was a winding staircase among the pillars.

"I don't think Isvan knew about that particular feature," Rufus muttered.

Clariselyn led the way down the transparent steps. Her bare feet made no sound against the ice. "Unlike the Sylver Valley, the Nightmare Mountains have true seasons. Sometimes thaw reigns in the Well, though never in the cathedral. And when the waterfall is not frozen, Frostfang will conjure the steps for its bearer."

"That must be how Isvan was trapped in the ice," Lin said. "He fell backward into the waterfall, and it froze around him. And Frostfang couldn't help him."

"There were so many things I never had time to teach my son," Clariselyn said sadly. "But it grieved me the most that he didn't have his Ice Mask. He was always alone, even among the kind Sylverings." She shook her head. "There were more of our people, once, more who could keep the treasure of knowing. But the power of glaciers is waning, in this world and the other."

Ursa Minor was waiting for them when they reached the bottom. He held out Isvan's limp body without a word. A broken sigh passed Clariselyn's lips. Her hand hovered over Isvan's brow for a moment. The pearls of her sleeve tinkled. She smoothed down his hair with light fingers. "Such a grown young man."

The expression on her face made Lin's belly turn. It reminded her of something she could not quite recall, some unnamed grief she had pushed away. Rufus shifted beside her. "We were going to take Isvan to Teodor," he said. "We thought maybe he could do something."

Clariselyn turned away, toward the tunnel out to the Cracklemoor. "Perhaps. In any case, we need to leave the Well. I will try to create an ice horse for Isvan, but the ravine would only spook it."

"I wonder if he's still out there," Rufus whispered to Lin as they passed through the dark gulley. Already the weight of the Cracklemoor tugged at her, head and hand, and Rufus had to remind her. "Our mystery guide."

They hadn't seen any sign of him since they discovered the ravine, and they felt sure he hadn't entered the Winterfyrst Well. As they emerged from behind the bilberry curtain and out on the Towerhorn slopes, they watched for his tracks. But there were no fresh puncture marks.

Clariselyn gazed into her snow globe. The crack had crept another inch along the surface. "I had hoped that when Isvan found me, he could use his snow globe to heal mine," she said. "Now I do not even know if it is strong enough for the simplest of winter spells. But I will try."

She lifted the globe toward the sky and sang. A cloud of ice leaped off the ground, shining and shimmering, growing slowly into the shape of a horse.

To Lin's magic ears, the Winterfyrst spell resembled neither the whispered commands of carved runes nor the brutal whining of Technocraft. The music of the snow globes and of the gathering horse flowed gentle and mysterious, like light from a horned moon.

All through the evening, Rufus had never once failed to pay attention when magic took place. But now he stood with his back turned to the ice horse, staring out on the moor, chewing the tassels on his scarf. Lin stole over to him. She could see no movement on the windswept field, but she knew as well as Rufus that the trolls were out there. "What's going on?"

"Hmmm? I just thought I smelled something. It was here a moment ago, but now . . ." He sniffed so hard his whiskers trembled. "It's so faint. I can't quite place it."

"Smells like frozen heath to me."

"No. It's something else, something familiar. Something unpleasant . . ."

Lin turned to ask for Minor's opinion, but the Wilder stood rocking Isvan in his arms, watching Clariselyn struggle. The horse would not fill in, it seemed. Already the crack had snaked another inch across the snow globe, and now the glow of silver milk and golden white dimmed, as if a shadow had fallen upon it.

Lin frowned. The dimness moved with the wind. She looked up, behind them.

A shadow *had* fallen on the snow globe, and it was the shadow of the creature that came swooping down the mountainside, faster than Lin could draw her breath. What was *he* doing here?

And before Lin could cry out, before Clariselyn could finish her magic, and before Rufus could remember where he had smelled that smell before, the creature reached its target.

It was a perfect attack.

He only had a fraction of a moment, but his sharp talons closed precisely around the snow globe and ripped it out of the Winterfyrst's outstretched hands. With a triumphant caw he beat his wings and flew off, with Clariselyn's soul and all of Sylver's hope in his claws.

Clariselyn looked like she had been punched in the face. Her song ended in a croak, and she tottered two steps to the side. The ice horse dissolved into a wisp that blew away.

"Teriko!" Lin finally managed, but of course it was too late. Figenskar's lieutenant was already nothing more than a scudding shadow that made the stars wink above the Cracklemoor. He aimed straight for the Whitepass.

"Well," Rufus said darkly, "I recognised the smell at last. Parrot dung."

CHAPTER THIRTY-TWO

*A*ll the pieces are falling into place. The foot lifts, ready to crush. The wings soar, ready to strike. Lin clutched the falcon message from the Queen of Soothsingers in her fist. Now the only missing bit was a ripped and rent heart, and her score sheet would be perfect.

Above the Cracklemoor, the Wanderer blazed strong. She had lost all sense of its position now that they could no longer use the Sylver Fang to measure it by, but she didn't doubt that they were running out of time.

"Why did he take the snow globe?" Lin said. "Why didn't he take me?"

Rufus spat in the snow. "I'm sure he would have if he could, but you're too heavy for him. He wants us to follow." He tugged at his scarf. "I'm guessing there won't be any Wandersnow without your globe, Clariselyn?"

Clariselyn gazed down at the shards of Isvan's snow

globe, at the red fingerprints Lin had left there when she tried to piece them together. "No, I . . . No."

"Then we have to try and catch him. Except I don't see how."

"I can carry you," Minor said. "I can run really fast."

"I know you can," Lin said. "But with four passengers on your back and the Whitepass crawling with trolls? We don't have any silvercone seeds left. This time we will be coming from the open. We won't even have the element of surprise on our side."

Minor didn't answer. Instead there came a snapping of twigs and rustling of branches from the woods.

Lin's pulse picked up. Just what they needed. More trolls.

"Get back into the ravine!" she hissed, filling her hand with acorns from her pocket.

"Wait!" Rufus took a step forward. "There! Between the junipers!"

A small, but bright light. The signaller!

"Hello?" Lin called. "Is someone there?"

"Please!" Rufus cried. "We want to thank you for saving us. Come out!"

And it did, crashing out through the bushes, picking its way over tufts and stones on long, black legs that punctured the ground with every step. For a sickening moment, Lin thought it was some sort of giant spider. But then she saw that its body was made of flat burnished wood and that the limbs were solid cast iron, except for the fourth leg, which ended in a stiffer bit of grey steel. Like a peg leg. Or a spare part!

"It's our sled," she murmured to Rufus. "Our hilltop sled!"

For the last few yards, as if to prove that Lin was right, the sled stretched out its legs and curled them up in elaborate spirals at the ends, until they became runners. It skidded to a stop right in front of Rufus. He stared at it, wide-eyed. *"This* is our mystery guide? A sled?"

The sled shook its small lantern, and the dim light flashed bright.

"Well, this explains how it vanished from the Winnower's clearing, and why it doesn't smell like a creature." Rufus scratched his ear. "What does it want? No, I take that back. A better question is how can it want something? It's a sled!"

"That isn't just a sled, young Rufus." Clariselyn spoke in a hushed tone, as if in the presence of a dangerous animal. "It's a caravan sled. And it just might save our hides. There is no faster creature on this side of the wall."

"It travels with the caravans?" Rufus's ears pricked up.

"It *is* the caravans. Without it and the others of its kind, there would be no trade across the Nightmare Mountains. They are just too dangerous. But a caravan sled can climb any mountain and race down any hill, and it can fight off Nightmares as well as any Frostrider. It is fiercely loyal and very picky about the company it keeps. I believe this one has set its heart on you two."

"It has?"

"I would say so, or it would not have aided you. You must have done something to impress it somewhere along the way."

"The spare part!" A delighted grin spread on Rufus's face. "The sled was broken, but I thought it was so beautiful, so I had someone make a new runner tip and brought it up on the hill."

Clariselyn nodded. "That would win its favour, and rightly so. But I will also say this: Caravan sleds have magical otopathy. They can tell when someone has the potential for powerful magic." She clutched the shards of Isvan's snow globe to her chest. "I do not know how this one came to be separated from its caravan, but we must be thankful for the hand of fortune. Ask it if it will help you catch the Beak."

"Caravan sled," Rufus said, "I know you've already helped us tonight. Without you we would never have found Teodor at the Hearth of Flame, and we would never have found the weak spot in the troll barricade or escaped those trolls in the Crackle Creek dell, and we would never have found the entrance to the Winterfyrst Well. But now we need to ask for your help once more. Will you take us back to Sylveros?"

The sled edged forward, and the reins fell from its back

and landed at Rufus's feet. They were a snarled, midnight blue mess. He lifted them up, picking at the knots with quick fingers. "How do I do this?"

"Ask it, Rufocanus," Clariselyn said. "Caravan sleds can speak with their riders."

Rufus climbed onto the seat. His eyes widened. "It *does* talk to me," he said. "Not words exactly, just images and feelings, but . . ." He drew a startled breath. "It's so old! And there are bergfolk children in there! A witch trapped them in the wood and cut down the tree, and oh, no! Its caravan was swarmed by trolls! It was the only one who escaped, but it was so tired it crashed into a mountain and broke . . ."

Rufus's mouth hung open and his eyes were glazing over. Lin grabbed his leg. "Maybe you should just come down from there."

He snapped to. "No, it's fine. It says you should come up, Lin. It wants to help us. But . . ." He turned to Clariselyn and Ursa Minor. "But it says it can't carry all of us. Not with a bad leg. Not if we're to catch Teriko."

"No." Lin shook her head. "Out of the question. We can't leave anyone behind out here on this hellish moor."

"I will carry you, my lady," Ursa Minor said. "I will carry both you and the little boy home to Sylveros."

Clariselyn tightened her grip on Frostfang. "The caravan sled is right." Her voice sounded like hardening ice. "Go.

Catch the parrot and take back my soul. Minor and I have Frostfang. We will bring Isvan home."

"No," Lin said dully, but she knew they were right. Either someone went after Teriko, or no one did. She put her forehead against Minor's flank. "I'm so sorry we brought you into this." To the broken boy in his arms she said nothing, but she hoped he understood. *I'm so sorry for not saving you.*

"I will get him home," Minor rumbled. "And an Ursa always keeps his word."

Rufus pulled Lin up, and she settled in behind him, arms gripping tight around his flanks. Immediately, the sled unrolled its runners into legs and began clawing its way along the mountain slope. Lin looked back uneasily at the bear and at Clariselyn Winterfyrst, now the last of her people. "Do you think they'll make it to the Palisade?"

"Did you see that dead troll inside the glacier?" Rufus answered. "I don't think Clariselyn should be underestimated, either. The sled has great respect for her."

"I hope you're right." Lin rested her head against Rufus's back. Since she had spent the final dose of the Observatory magic, the jittery thrumming in her arms and legs had stopped and she felt strangely quiet inside. "Rufus?" she mumbled. "I don't think the *Rosa torquata* chose right when it gave me the key. Everything breaks all around me. I don't care that the name of Twistrose never lies."

"And I don't care what you say, little one. The night is not over. They'll make a statue of you yet."

"But Rufus?" She reached up to scratch the fur behind his ear. "I've been thinking about that thing Fabian said at the Palisade. That *Rufocanus* is meant as a reminder? Well, *Rufocanus* means redback vole, just like *Vulpes* means fox. You lived your whole life in a human house, but that's not where you belonged. You're not just a Petling, Rufus. You're a Wilder, too. I think that's what Teodor is trying to tell you."

Rufus didn't reply. But he leaned against her hand.

They hurtled through the brush. Lin hid her face in her hands to avoid the whipping branches. She had expected the sled to strike across the moor, but instead it kept climbing upward through the woods. "Shouldn't we be going the other way?"

"I may be holding the reins, but I'm not in charge here," Rufus said. "The sled goes where it wants to."

Halfway up the mountainside, the sled turned. The legs curled up into runners.

"Oh, rats," Rufus mumbled.

The sled set off down the rime-covered moss, rattling and creaking with every rock and root, while the wind howled in their ears.

Lin closed her eyes. Suddenly her belly pressed down on her legs, and the rattling from the sled softened. When she dared to look the moor was a sea of frost, not in front of them, but below them. The caravan sled could not only crawl like a spider and glide like a sled. It could also fly!

But only barely. They could feel how much it struggled as they climbed into the sky on treacherous currents. Rufus hunched down, clinging hard to the reins. He must be very frightened, but he didn't complain.

Not until he spotted the Nightmares. Then neither of them could keep from crying out.

All over the Cracklemoor snow trolls were marching in ragged bands. They weren't alone. Lin saw wood trolls with bark-and-sap armour, river trolls on many-jointed legs, and sand trolls with glass carapaces. There were other shapes, too, tall, thin marionettes with scythes for arms, red sleep-walkers with flapping robes, and insect-filled man clouds that changed and shifted with the wind.

Down on the dark ice of the Crackle Creek, Clarise-lyn made a small, white speck on Ursa Minor's back. No Nightmares had discovered them yet, and as long as they kept to the dell, Lin thought they might be safe enough. She had given them all the acorns they had taken from the cold oak. But bane or no, Lin feared they might never get through the Whitepass.

Between the steep walls of the pass, the Nightmares had gathered in squares. They lined up before the enormous hedge, blocking the Caravan Road.

"They're getting ready to attack!" Lin cried above the

wind as the sled crossed the border, high above the Palisade.

"I think you're right," Rufus yelled. "If this Blood Lord is controlling them, he must have a plan."

Operation Corvelie. For the first time since they had gone through the Palisade gate, Lin's thoughts turned to the Margrave, and Teodor's desperate departure to protect the final guard rune. It was the word *Corvelie* that had set him off. What was it? What did it mean?

They cleared the Whitepeaks, and the Sylver Valley fell away below them. It seemed so peaceful and innocent, with Sylveros as a sparkling necklace by the lake. The sled struggled hard now, and turned its nose downward, diving for the river. Right before they dipped below the treetops Rufus called, "Lin! There!" He pointed toward Sylveros.

Far away, so far it was like a drop of ink on a clean sheet, Lin glimpsed a soaring, blue figure outlined against a white dome.

Teriko had arrived at the Observatory.

CHAPTER THIRTY-THREE

L in Rosenquist found herself standing at the broad Observatory steps. In the star shade behind the columns towered a fortified door with bronze falcon heads. Rufus clutched her hand.

"You shouldn't be here."

Lin turned to him. "What?"

"We know they're only trying to lure you here, back into Figenskar's claws. And what if you turn up in the mirrors again? What if the magic is too much for you?" Rufus prodded the wound on the tip of his tail. "I should go in alone."

"No." Lin squeezed his hand three times. "No more leaving each other. What's to keep Figenskar from attacking me out here while you're inside? And what kind of Twistrose would I be if I didn't show up for my final test? We go in together."

Rufus flashed his cleft-lipped grin. "I knew there was a

reason I wanted you for my travel companion." He planted his heel in the door. It gave a shuddering boom, but though the sound must have rolled through the corridors and galleries, no one came to remove the bolt.

"The workers must have gone down to the Great Square," Lin said. Since they had no time to run around for support, she had hoped to bring the news of the falcon messenger's murder and win at least some of the workers over to their side. But they were on their own. Even the caravan sled had left them, to go back and help Clariselyn and Minor.

"I don't care about the workers. I want Figenskar, and I just know he's still in there." Rufus swished his tail. "Let's try his private entrance."

They sneaked around to the back, to the low, square wing that housed the chief observer's office. They didn't even have time to try the handle before they heard a noise on the other side of the door. A scraping, jangling noise.

"He's coming!"

Rufus spat in the snow. "Let him!"

A familiar shape appeared in the doorway, holding a great key chain. Not Figenskar, but a portly guinea pig with a vest and wild bangs that had overcome the pomade once and for all. Marvin placed a rounded claw over his mouth.

"Hush or he'll hear!"

The chief observer's office was lit only by the embers in the fireplace. Marvin's horn-rimmed glasses reflected the wavering glow as he ushered them inside. "You have no idea how glad I am to see you." The Rodent's voice kept rising into squeaks, and he was constantly running his fingers over the key chain. "Here I was, wishing desperately for someone to come to my aid, and who should knock on the door but a Twistrose and her Sylvering?"

"Calm down, Marvin," Lin said. "We will help you if we can. What is going on?"

"It's the chief observer. I think he has lost his mind!"

Rufus steered Marvin over to Figenskar's desk chair and made him sit down on the red silk cushion. "Where is Figenskar?"

"In the hall, on the floor."

"And Teriko?"

"I haven't seen him. This is awful! I shouldn't say anything. He is my boss, I . . ."

Rufus caught Lin's glance and nodded at the door to the corridor. Lin hurried over to listen for footsteps.

"Just tell us what you saw!" Rufus said.

Marvin began picking at the sign on Figenskar's desk. "We were closing down, extinguishing all the mirrors. Apparently, it's not safe to stay in the hall on Wanderer's Eve. We've been having fluctuations in the mirror magic all night. Something to do with the celebration?" The last he said to Rufus, rushing through the words.

Rufus shrugged. "I don't know."

"Oh. I was the last one here, and I was making a final

round of the gallery, when suddenly all the mirrors rekindled around me. Soon after, the chief observer entered the hall with some sort of glowing object."

Lin and Rufus exchanged looks over Marvin's fat neck. The snow globe.

"Figenskar sat down on the floor, and began to hum and chant an old song. He seemed quite disturbed. Confused, even."

"What sort of song?" Rufus said.

"I didn't know it. Something about a grave. Or Margrave? Yes, I think that was it. Margrave."

Lin and Rufus frowned at each other again. What was Figenskar up to?

"I retreated as quietly as I could," Marvin finished. "Thank goodness he didn't hear me."

Rufus wrinkled his snout. "Why didn't you just leave?"

"I was about to! But my key only fits the front door, which I couldn't get to without passing through the hall, so I needed Figenskar's master key chain. I had just found it when you arrived." He looked up, lips trembling. "Do you have any idea what has got into the chief observer?"

"Not really," Rufus said. "But we do know what that shining object is. We'll just have to find a way to take it from him."

Marvin sprang to his feet. "Wait! I mean, you can't just march into the hall! I told you, the chief observer isn't himself. He could be dangerous!"

"We're two against one, and that's the best odds we've seen all evening," Rufus said. "Even if Teriko shows up, I think we have a fair chance."

"You must promise me to be careful," Marvin said. "You still have Lin's index card, I hope?"

"We do." Rufus patted one of the pockets of his scarf.

"Thank goodness for that," Marvin sighed with relief. He shuffled over to Lin and gave her a stiff and awkward hug. His fur scratched her cheek. "Good luck, Lin Rosenquist. You are a very courageous human child."

He turned to Rufus.

"And you, Rufus. I'll never forget how you stood up to Mr. Figenskar up on the Memory balcony." He squeezed Rufus tight. Rufus patted his shoulder, rather embarrassed.

"Not to worry, Marvin. Lin and I know what we're doing. We'll be fine."

Reluctantly, Marvin let go. He fished a handkerchief out of his vest pocket and dabbed at his eyes.

"I daren't come with you. Please forgive me! I'm not a true hero like you."

Rufus grew a little taller. "Don't say that. You've been a great help. If you want to do more, it couldn't hurt to let the right people know what's happening here. Find Teodor at the House or in Peppersnap Nook, and if you can't, try Doctor Kott."

Marvin nodded, too choked up to speak.

"All right." Rufus flung the ends of his scarf over his shoulders and turned the doorknob. "Ready?"

Lin attempted a deep breath. "Ready."

They stepped into the corridor. The lamps were out, but an indigo blur seeped through the glass windows at the end.

"Farewell," Marvin croaked as he closed the door behind them, glasses shining blue.

"Poor guy," Rufus said. "He seemed quite disturbed himself."

They sidled along the corridor, trailing long, undulating shadows. Lin could feel the magic from the Observatory hall like humming high voltage wires. At the double doors, they tried in vain to peer through the buckled glass. But they could hear Figenskar screeching above the sighing rush of the mirrors.

"Thorns of gold through flesh and marrow! Thorns of gold through flesh and marrow!"

Rufus pushed at the doors. But they moved only half an inch before hitting something large and heavy on the other side. Lin couldn't get as much as a hand through the crack.

"Now what," she whispered.

"I don't know. If only we could see what is going on in there. . . ." Rufus tried the handle to the gallery entrance. It opened without a sound. "Come on, let's do what a cartographer would do. Let's get an overview."

In the pitch-black stairwell, Lin's back itched and tingled. It was as if someone hovered behind her, waiting for the perfect moment to attack. Rufus must have felt it, too, because he kept turning around, tickling Lin's face with his whiskers. The first balcony door – the one for Luck – stood ajar, inviting them into the flickering light.

As they crept to the edge of the balcony and spied out through the banisters, it became clear why the Observatory hall was tinted blue. The glass dome that had shone with such brilliance earlier in the evening was now dead, the Earth night sky gone. The only light came from the mirrors. They were empty, and so was the whole hall. Nobody soared under the dome, nobody scribbled names on cards. On the great stone floor, there was not a soul to be seen.

Except for one.

Figenskar sat crouched on the floor with his back turned and his tail in a coil. He rocked back and forth, gloating over something that Lin couldn't see, and all the while he cackled and yowled: "Thorns of gold through flesh and marrow!"

Rufus rose silently to watch through the telescope, then sat back down to whisper into Lin's ear.

"It's Clariselyn's snow globe all right. We have to get down there."

Lin glanced around the hall. The double doors were

blocked by one of the counters, that's why they wouldn't open. But the curtains on the Memory balcony were sturdy. Maybe they could tie them together to make a rope?

Suddenly the door to the Strength balcony slammed and Teriko hopped out. Lin ducked, sure that they were discovered. But the parrot didn't even turn an eye in their direction. He jumped up on the banister, spread his wings, and cawed at the dome: "Ready! Everything is ready!"

Figenskar stopped singing. His tail uncoiled. In one fluid motion he straightened his back and rose, and when he turned toward them, there was neither madness nor weakness in his face, only menace. In his hands he held the snow globe.

"Excellent," Figenskar said. "Tonight, lieutenant, you have truly earned your treat."

"Treat!" Teriko screamed.

The snow globe sparkled bravely, golden white and silver milk, but its light all but drowned in the blue mirror radiance.

"I hear rumours that Isvan Winterfyrst is dead," Figenskar drawled. "Dead and lost on the Cracklemoor! That suits me rather poorly, I will admit. But what is killed is dead, hmmm, Teriko? We will just have to trap another sparrow. And this time it won't slip through our claws!"

Figenskar tossed the globe lightly into the air, catching it with one paw. "Since Isvan is no more, this is the only remaining Winterfyrst snow globe. Of course, it has not escaped my notice that a certain pair of Rosenquists have desperately sought a Winterfyrst tonight. It must be important, or the Brotherhood would never have called a Twistrose. So they need this snow globe."

He paused to scrape his claw against the fragile glass. "Which is why they have no choice but to come here, to Figenskar in his own den. They have shown a remarkable talent for worming in and out of places that are forbidden to them, so I assume that they have found a way. Hmmm?"

He gazed around the hall. Was Lin imagining it, or did he linger on their balcony for a heartbeat? He raised an arm toward the gallery.

"Well? What are you waiting for? This is your cue!"

To Lin's surprise, he was neither pointing at them, nor at Teriko. He was pointing at the Memory balcony, where a face emerged from the shadows. "I . . . I'm right here, Mr. Chief Observer."

Marvin.

He looked like he was about to throw up, but instead he turned on the projector. In his hand he held a small, grey square. He fed it to the machine. It whirred. It clicked. A bright, dust-speckled ray streamed across the hall.

Rufus turned to her. There were sickles of white at the edges of his eyes.

"What is it?" Lin breathed. Rufus didn't answer. He grasped at his scarf, rummaging desperately through the secret pockets. In the Memory mirror, a blue image was rising out of the murk.

"Ladies and gentlemen," Figenskar cried. "The time has come for a final game of cat and mouse! I give you . . . Lindelin Rosenquist!"

Rufus seized her by the hood and hauled her away from the railing, as if that could save her.

It could not. For all the mirrors of all the six walls of the Observatory hall filled with the same scene: Lin Rosenquist, age eleven and in dire need, struggling to her feet with dark lines of blood creeping out of her ears.

CHAPTER THIRTY-FOUR

R ufus of Rosenquist was furious.

Never had he walked so witlessly into a trap. Mouldy lost his mind. Mouldy hug. Mouldy hero! Well, maybe they still had a chance. Two against three were less pretty numbers, but they should still be able to run.

If Lin could manage. The little one was shaking, and she was bleeding from her head again. That ratty magical otopathy! Rufus wanted to chuck it all the way to the Cracklemoor. And this time it was *all the mirrors*. He had to get her out of this building.

"Lin. We need to leave. Can you make it downstairs?"

Lin nodded, but she didn't fool Rufus. Her irises looked like they had been dipped in milk, and her neck was ropy. Too vulnerable. Snap, crack, no problem for a cat.

A loud flapping disturbed the sighing waves under the

glass dome. Teriko was flying straight for their balcony, claws and beak open, one eye fixed on Lin.

No problem for a parrot, either. Rufus pushed Lin toward the balcony door. "Run! Down and out through Figenskar's office! I'll be right behind you!"

He rushed back to the railing and peeked down. Oh yes, plenty high enough to crush a brittle bone or many. No matter. If that dolled-up chicken wanted Lin, he would have to fly through one seriously angry Rodent first. Rufus climbed onto the railing, balancing on his hind feet.

Teriko squawked at the sight of him, flapping his wings, treading the air. But Rufus had timed it well. It was too late for Teriko to change his course. Vole and parrot slammed together in an explosion of blue feathers. Teriko grabbed on to Rufus, and Rufus held on to Teriko. They swayed and tilted, and then they fell.

To Rufus's eternal relief they fell inward, filling the balcony with thrashing limbs, claws, and teeth. Rufus kicked and scratched as hard as he could, but Teriko was just nastier. Soon the parrot had him trapped under a horned foot.

"Treat!" he screamed. "Treat!"

The hook of his beak glittered as he drew his head back to strike. Rufus lifted his hands to at least protect his snout and kicked with his hind legs one more time. He braced himself. Waited three heartbeats, ten.

But Teriko didn't strike. Instead he collapsed over Rufus with a dull squeak and made no effort to get back up.

Rufus craned his neck to see who had come to his rescue. He whistled through his teeth. Not who. What. The narrow end of the telescope dripped with blood. It must have hit Teriko in the head when he kicked him.

Lucky.

Not so lucky, though, that he was stuck under Teriko's lifeless body. His bird bones were hollow, so he wasn't very heavy. But he was tall, ten feet from his beak to the tip of his tail, and his wingspan was huge. The entire balcony was so full of mouldy parrot that Rufus couldn't get free. He had to settle for wiggling under the horned claws until he could peer out between the banisters.

Lin's footfall was lost in the depths of the Observatory, but the mirrors showed her every step. Just now, the little one was reeling from door to door in the hallway. None of them would let her in.

A chill prickled at Rufus's scruff. Predator. He looked down.

Figenskar was standing on the Observatory floor. He had stuffed the snow globe back into a black bag, but other than that, he hadn't moved. A blue feather swirled past his face and landed at his boots, but the chief observer didn't even glance at it. He just stared up at the mirrors as patiently as, well, a cat outside a mouse hole.

This was not right. Figenskar had been chasing Lin all night. He had lured her in his trap, had her caught in a corridor, even. Why was he just watching?

In the mirrors, Lin had made her way to Figenskar's office. She stumbled to the back door, but it was no longer open, and there was no key. That pile of dung Marvin must have locked up before he came to the hall to betray them.

Rufus's nose twitched. A great many mistakes could have been avoided tonight if he had only had the sense to trust his mouldy snout. The parrot dung on the slopes of the Towerhorns, yes. But before that, the odd smell in the Hall of Winter, left by Figenskar's secret accomplice, waiting to catch Isvan if he should come back. He knew it now, of course; he excelled at seeing how the jigsaw pieces fit once they had been puzzled together by someone else. Pomade. Sticky, stinking pomade. It made him sick just to think about it. And those dainty little tracks in the garden. Marvin all along.

Rufus turned to the Memory balcony, intending to skewer Marvin's straggly, fat face with his stare. The guinea pig deserved to know how vile he was, how spineless and cowardly. But he wasn't there.

A smug snarl sounded down on the floor. Figenskar's pointy teeth were all bared in triumph. Lin had pulled the tapestry with the Starfalcon aside and was crawling into the hole in the wall. She had taken the only way left. And, Rufus realised, the only way Figenskar didn't know about.

So that's what he was waiting for. For some reason, Figenskar needed to know how Lin had escaped from the cage. And now that he did . . .

Mould and twice.

Figenskar swung his bag over his shoulder and headed for the double door with long, purposeful strides.

Rufus let all his Wilder fury out. This time he wasn't going to let Lin down. This time he was going to save her. "Stay away from her!" he screamed, pushing and wrenching Teriko's wings, not caring if they cracked and broke, until he managed to flip over and gather his legs. He leaped for the balcony door. It was locked. He kicked and clawed, but the *mouldy* door wouldn't open.

Figenskar had pushed aside the counter and was leaving through the double door. The cat had a big key in his paw, and even though the mirrors still hissed and murmured, Rufus heard it turn in the lock on the other side.

"Marvin!" Rufus roared. "Marvin, you giant heap of rat's dung, are you there? Open the door!"

But there was no reply. Rufus sank down on his haunches. He didn't want to watch what was happening to Lin, but he couldn't bear to turn away, either.

The mirrors were nearly dark now, except for a pair of trembling hands groping at a ladder inside a narrow shaft. The hands halted for a moment. Then they raced down at a terrible speed, missing and catching every other rung.

Lin emerged from the shaft into a brooding, red light,

legs kicking. Her face was wild as she let go of the ladder and flung herself at the nearest perch. She landed on her feet, but slipped immediately and smashed belly first onto the grime-covered beam. Blood trickled out of her nose and ears.

Behind her, in the corner of the image, a shadow was gathering. Lin crawled along the perch, but the shadow was quick and sure. It reached out a clawed hand, but before it could catch her, Lin threw herself from the perch to the chain. She slipped again, rushing down in cruel jerks, until she hit the top of Teriko's mirror. There she stayed with her legs twined around the knot that tied the mirror to the chain, while the metal frame danced back and forth. The little one was breathing hard.

"Keep going, Lin!" Rufus said through his teeth. "You have to try!"

But Lin didn't try, and when the image widened to show more of the scene, Rufus understood why. The door was closed, the heavy padlock in place. Lin had nowhere to go.

Behind Lin's skinny shape, a deeper darkness slid down the cage bars. Soon Figenskar stepped into the circle of torch light, twenty feet beneath the mirror frame. He held his paws out and spoke. Lin didn't stir. The torches reflected in her face.

The cat shrugged. He opened his bag and brought out a

small, twinkling star that filled the cave with golden white and silver milk. Placing the snow globe on the cage floor, Figenskar rested the heel of his boot on top of it. One step and Clariselyn's soul would be crushed forever.

"Mould," Rufus whispered.

A tear found its way down Lin's cheek. She looked up the chain, toward the cave ceiling and the end of the shaft. But no one came to save the little one. Lin lowered her head and let herself fall into Figenskar's waiting claws.

CHAPTER THIRTY-FIVE

Lin's mouth tasted of metal, and her thoughts were scattered birds in a storm of a headache. It took her several gulps of dank, reeking air to remember where she was, and why she couldn't move her arms.

Cage. Trapped. Figenskar.

He had tied her hands back and propped her against the cage bars. Something chafed at her throat – one of his burlap sacks, pulled up over her body and bound tightly at the neck.

Figenskar was hanging from the chain, upside down, using his teeth on the knot that held Teriko's mirror. Clariselyn's snow globe lay in the muck next to a black bag and a red velvet pouch, not far from Lin. And in the padlock on the cage door sat a small hope: the key. She tried to get up, but this time, Figenskar had been thorough. He had bound her legs as well. With a small thud she slumped back against the cage wall. A tiny sound, but it was enough for Figenskar. He twisted around and grinned down at her with a mouthful of needles.

"Good girl, hmmm? Sit tight for Figenskar. It will soon be over, little Twistrose!"

He had untied the knot now and was lowering the mirror frame, all the way down, until it dangled two feet above the floor with its front turned toward Lin.

The mirror was full of shards.

Someone had picked the broken glass out of the parrot dung, wiped the pieces thoroughly, and placed them back into the frame.

Figenskar landed softly and sauntered over to Lin.

"I must confess that I am curious. Did you break the mirror on purpose, or was it dumb luck?"

Lin blinked. What was he talking about?

"Come, it won't change anything if you tell me. Indulge a poor, curious cat. Did you do it on purpose?"

"I . . . I wanted to cut the rope." Lin's tongue felt sticky and numb.

Figenskar laughed. "I knew it! For a while I thought I was exposed. That it was some ingenious Twistrose plot to stop me. But you only wanted to cut the rope!"

He picked the velvet pouch up from the ground.

"I suppose it was just luck that inspired you to steal this as well," he said, taking a small, glittering object out of the pouch. A sliver of glass.

It was the shard Lin had plucked out of her wrist up in the secret tunnel. One end was still black with dried blood. Figenskar licked the tip of his tail and used it to polish the shard clean.

"I knew you must have hidden it somewhere in the Observatory, because you didn't have it when I frisked you on the Memory balcony. I had my clerks search everywhere you could possibly have set your pasty little feet, behind every door that was unlocked while you were on the loose. Finally I realised that it had to be concealed where you escaped from the cage. And nobody knew where that was except you and that disgusting Rodent of yours."

Figenskar squinted up toward the ceiling. From the floor, it was impossible to make out the entrance to the shaft, but the topmost perch formed a grainy line in the darkness. Where was Rufus? Why hadn't he come?

"It was stupid of me, I'll admit, that I never suspected you had found a way out through the ceiling. I was convinced you had wriggled out when Marvin unlocked the door. But I couldn't find my missing piece. That's why I had to trick you into showing me where it was. And you did. You walked into trap after trap."

Lin blinked again. What did he mean? He had put on that whole show up in the Observatory hall only to get that small piece of glass?

"Of course," Figenskar purred. "In my hunt for you this evening, the shard was only a minor detail. But a vital one. No point in possessing a juicy little Twistrose without this!"

Ever so gently he eased the final shard into place. The splinter of worry was back in Lin's chest, worming its way toward her heart. What was it about the parrot mirror? What was she missing?

Figenskar inspected the mirror, pressing at the lines until the glass was even. "It's a shame you look like something the cat dragged in. But I'm sure my master will be pleased. After all, you are a Twistrose, and you are in dire need. Every single mirror of the hall, all filled with Rosenquist." He snickered. "That terrified little heart of yours must be dripping with magic gifts, hmmm?"

With the heel of his boot, he began scraping away the layers of dirt from the cage floor. As he cleared the grime, a pattern emerged, hewn into the rock: three tongues of flame filled with strange letters of slanted lines and dots. Now that the muck didn't smother it, Lin could hear its whispered chant quite clearly.

A rune, a powerful one.

"Do you know, I think this is my favourite part of the plan. Only the chief observers know the location of this rune. As a balance against the Brotherhood's *mighty power.*" Figenskar lifted the large, black bag and brought out a steel device that he held up for her to see, as if he were presenting a loaded weapon of particular deadliness. It resembled an arm ripped from its socket, with wires coiling along its length like exposed muscles and ligaments. But in place of a hand, it had a mouth full of shark-like teeth.

A swell of magic flushed through Lin, pushing at her eardrums. She knew this feeling: sickening, screaming, *wrong*.

Technocraft.

Figenskar petted the device. "My Runemaw. It's quite something, hmmm? My cooperation with Mrs. Zarka has proved most useful. No more begging and pleading with those pompous fools of Frost and Flame. I no longer need their permission to wield magic." He pushed a button that poked out between the coils. "And it makes it all the sweeter that I can use my magic to take away theirs." The device gaped wider, unhinging its jaw like a snake. The teeth looked impossibly sharp, and Lin had no doubt they matched the bite marks in the floor of the Hall of Winter and in the branch of the Palisade of Thorns.

"Sylver's third and final guard rune," Figenskar said, almost solemnly. "They carved it here because of the Starfalcon's magic. And like the falcon, Sylver's famous magical protection will now be history." He plunged the device into the floor. There was a metallic wail like a knife being sharpened, followed by a loud *crack* and silence.

Through the stabbing headache, Lin thought of Teodor's turret, and the warning rune that must be smoking there at this very moment. Was the old fox there? Would he come and find her? But those weren't the right questions at all. The right question was *why* Figenskar had destroyed the runes.

The cat regarded her in the mirror. One of the cracks tore his grin in half. "So, the guard rune is cracked, the mirror is mended, and the little Twistrose trussed in her sack. I do believe the stage is set."

He touched the back side of the frame.

Hundreds of red lights awoke around him. They switched on and off, chasing each other in sharp, angular patterns. Lin's headache tightened its grip. The mirror was another Technocraft device.

Figenskar wasn't cursed with magic ears, because he seemed quite at ease as he took a small bottle out of his bag. It was filled with a dark liquid that left oily marks on the glass when he shook it.

"Thorndrip. Or as I like to call it: sparrow juice." He jammed the bottle in a hole in the side of the frame. It chugged thickly.

"That Soothsinger ditty was really not too hard to decipher, hmmm? Thorns of gold through flesh and marrow? Coupled with the death of a sparrow?" Figenskar flicked another switch. "What else could it be?"

The mirror frame buzzed and clicked while the red lights flashed quicker and quicker. Brown, sweet exhaust coiled up from the back. The glass wavered, like scorching air, and one by one the cracks disappeared.

The pain was so severe that Lin had to squeeze her lids

shut until the frame stopped humming. When she opened her eyes, white spots danced across her vision.

The mirror image had changed. Figenskar's excited face was gone. The entire cave was gone. Instead the mirror showed a new scene: a great chamber of grey stone, with a gigantic mosaic of a red crow on the floor. The hall had a single window. It overlooked jagged summits in the distance, and a wide, shallow mountain vale whose shape Lin recognised. The Cracklemoor.

Before the window stood a figure with his back turned.

He was tall and clad in a black cloak, and his head was hidden behind a stiff collar. But Lin didn't need to see his face to be afraid. His back sucked in all life and all hope. All her instincts howled at her to run.

"Smile, little Rosenquist." Figenskar took off his hat and dropped to one knee without caring that his fur sank into the parrot dung. "Smile for the Margrave."

The tall figure turned around and looked at them.

The Wanderer was his namesake, as well it should be, for set against the night black collar, the Margrave's face shone white like the star. His slicked hair was pale and translucent, and so was his skin. For the Margrave was neither Petling nor Wilder, but a human.

Swiftly he crossed the floor, and as he neared the mirror, Lin saw that the skin around his mouth was strangely grey and withered. Leaning close, the Margrave breathed on the glass. Lin caught a glimpse of his teeth of pewter colour, set in inky gums. With one long, pale finger, he wrote three words in the fog: "Child of Ice."

Figenskar rose, and with a whipping tail, he shook his head. The Margrave bared his teeth in fury, and Figenskar's tail fell to the ground, but the cat didn't step back. Instead he breathed another cloud on the glass and wrote his answer: "Twistrose."

Lin's throat constricted, shutting out all air, shutting in all sound. He was offering up her instead of Isvan.

The Margrave unstoppered a vial with a slim spout and sucked at the black fluid inside.

"That's right, master, *think*," Figenskar muttered. "A Child of Ice is potent, yes, but not even a Winterfyrst could surpass a Twistrose, hmmm? A Twistrose filled to the bursting with Sylver magic!"

He lifted up the burlap sack for his master to behold. Lin dangled helplessly before the mirror while the Margrave considered her from under hooded lids.

She *knew* him.

It was hard to see in that haggard, grown-up face, but she recognised the heavy eyes, the pinched nose, the forward-leaning posture. The boy in the shadows. The hidden Twistrose statue with the dead crow at his feet. The Margrave was Edvard Uriarte.

"What happened to him?" she croaked.

"The Margrave's mouth is withered from drinking Thorndrip. It helps him control the Nightmares, but it poisons him." Figenskar cocked his head. "That will change tonight. Tonight, on Wanderer's Eve, the Margrave will become the most powerful lord in all the Realms, a Blood Lord, with all the magic he could wish for. It says so in the prophecy. It says so in the song."

"No!" Lin struggled, but Figenskar's grip did not ease one bit.

"Oh yes. All the Margrave needs to do is drink his special draught, and he will become stronger than death itself."

Behind the Margrave, mounted on a wheeled hospital rack, hung another Technocraft contraption. A metal ring with three slim thorns of gold, and pots and tubes hooked up to the thorns, and a great glass vial to cook liquid down to the right thickness.

A Thorndripper.

"You see, my little Twistrose," Figenskar murmured, "the blood of sparrows cannot make a lord. But the blood of a child . . ."

At last the splinter of worry hit home. She understood. It was she, Lindelin Rosenquist, who would suffer the death of a sparrow. *The heart beats, ready to rip and rend.* A scream built in her chest, but all that escaped was a tiny mewling.

"Poor little girl," Figenskar hissed. "Trapped in the sack, can't run, can't breathe, can't do anything about it."

The Margrave watched Lin struggle. He opened his

mouth to breathe on the mirror, and in the grey-tinged fog he wrote, YES.

"No!" Lin cried. "Rufus will never let you take me. He will come. He will stop you before you can even cross the Sylver Bridge!"

Figenskar laughed his squint-eyed laugh. "Silly child! I will not cross the Sylveros Bridge at all, and neither will you. For Operation Corvelie there is no need."

He searched along the bottom of the mirror frame until his paw found a small lever. He pushed it. All the red lights flared, and once more, the frame began to creak and buzz and shake.

Another violent surge of Technocraft tore through Lin's body, and she let out a pained, terrified gasp. For with the surge of magic, the mirror glass had melted away. The frame was no longer a window.

It was a doorway.

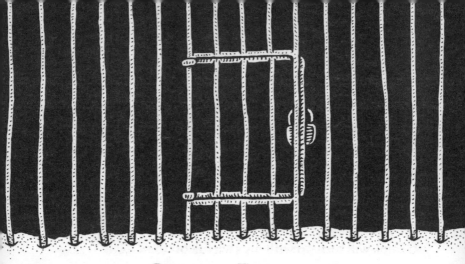

Chapter Thirty-six

The chief observer of Sylver bowed low for the Margrave. "Excellent decision, my lord of Nightmares," Figenskar said in his silkiest, smoothest voice. "And now for the second part of our plan."

The Margrave sucked at the Thorndrip and lifted his arm, like an officer on a battlefield, or a puppet master of very long strings. And into the mountain hall they came creeping, rank by hulking rank, lining up on the red tiled floor until the crow mosaic was lost under their claws.

Trolls.

Snow trolls with teeth like broken icicles, river trolls on many-jointed legs, and even a few Summerhill trolls that eyed Lin with hot malice. All of them carried burning torches, and all of them waited for the Margrave's command. He controlled them, as he had controlled the army at the Whitepass.

"Do you know, I've changed my mind?" Figenskar could not stop himself from gloating into Lin's ear. "*This* is my favourite part of Operation Corvelie. I deliver a magical child for the Margrave's draught, and he delivers Sylver into my hands. You see, the trolls will slice through the good people of Sylveros like claws through butter. And when the brave, the stupid, and the unfortunate have been killed, who do you think will turn up with his sack full of troll's bane to save the rest?"

He let go of Lin momentarily to scoop his red velvet pouch off the floor. "Crammed full of acorns and silvercone seeds and round, white river pebbles. All the treasures that the gatherers have failed to find in the Winterwoods this year, and there's more in the casket upstairs."

"That's why you're working with the Margrave?" Lin cried. "To have a troll invasion so you can *pretend* to save Sylver?"

"Just a modest troll invasion. I do want to make sure I can handle it." Figenskar chuckled. "After tonight, the Sylverings will bring flowers to *my* statue, not yours. Except mine won't be in Eversnow Square. It will be in the Great Square, right in front of my palace."

On the Nightmare side of the portal, two of the Summerhill trolls had stepped forward to seize Lin when she came through. Their long fingers twitched, and their jellyfish eyes glowed with hatred. Over by the Thorndripper, the Margrave made an impatient sound in his dead, withered mouth. "The child," he wheezed, as if every word pained him. "The Wanderer is setting. Send her through now."

"Certainly, my lord." Figenskar slid his claws into the burlap sack. Chill air poured through the opening, tearing at Lin's hair, and the Summerhill trolls slavered as Figenskar pulled her closer to the doorway. She struggled with all the strength she had left, bending and tossing her head. "Help me! Please! Help!"

"Nobody can hear you," Figenskar said. "Nobody's coming. Time to go, little Rosenquist!"

"Don't do this!" Lin pleaded. "Figenskar, think of your human child! I know you loved a child once, you must have!"

Figenskar growled. "I loved her, yes. She loved me, too, even if she poked me cruelly. One time only I bit her back, and then her father went and drowned me in the river. So spare yourself the snivelling, Lin, because inside a burlap sack, love and pleading mean nothing. Nothing at all."

He lifted the sack off the cage floor. Tears streamed down Lin's face. "Please," she whimpered. "Let me go."

A voice cut the air above their heads.

"That's right, Figenskar! Let her go!"

Lin's eyes rose on a wave of delicious hope. Clinging to the end of the chain was Rufus. In his hand he gripped a little pocketknife, blade against the rope that held the mirror.

"Let her go, or this whole Technocraft piece of mould goes to ground!"

Figenskar froze. "Rufus," he said, and there was such hatred in that one word that Lin's scalp prickled.

"Surprised, Figenskar?" Rufus said. "You shouldn't be. Doors can't keep me out. I am, after all, a Rosenquist."

"How?" Figenskar hissed.

Rufus snorted. "Oh, Marvin had the key. I just had to make him understand what his boss had planned for poor Isvan."

The grip around Lin's neck tightened. The tips of Figenskar's claws were razors against her skin. "I'll break her neck."

"No, you won't," Rufus said, clipped and cool. "This Margrave of yours seems to want a magical child for his draught, and you've already lost one tonight. I bet he wouldn't like it if you lost another. *Hmmm?*"

Figenskar snarled. His claws slid in and out of his paws as he considered. In, out, in, out.

In.

He flung Lin to the floor and dove away from the mirror. With a smooth tumble he was back on his feet, clutching Clariselyn's snow globe.

"Fine! But this I'll crush with pleasure."

Rufus bared his teeth. Only now did Lin notice that the pocketknife trembled against the rope, and that his injured tail hung limp beside him. "Give me the snow globe, and I'll give you the pocketknife," he said.

"Give me the pocketknife, and I'll give you the snow globe," Figenskar countered, edging closer to the mirror again. Rufus started sawing at the rope. The mirror danced and squeaked, the portal shimmered.

"Wait," Figenskar cried, holding the snow globe out from his body. "I'll throw it to you if you throw down the knife."

Rufus stopped sawing and nodded curtly.

"On three," he said. Lin held her breath.

"One." Figenskar's tail lashed.

"Two." Rufus removed the blade from the rope. A few fibres had been cut, but nowhere near enough to sever the rope. The icy wind from the portal ruffled Lin's hair. She heard grunting and scraping from the Margrave's hall.

"Three!"

And chaos erupted.

Rufus dropped the pocketknife. It sank into the parrot muck. Figenskar tossed the snow globe, but he threw it wide, so Rufus had to let go of the chain with everything but his tail to catch it. He hung upside down from the end of the chain, hugging the globe to his chest, bleeding from his wound.

Figenskar lunged toward Lin. She bucked and fought to get away, biting at his paws, and at last she could *scream*.

In the Margrave's hall, all the trolls screamed in answer.

And so Figenskar never noticed the squeak squeak of danger until it was too late. Suddenly, a clear sound rang through the cave, clean and true in the rasping churn of troll voices, like a guitar string breaking.

The rope had snapped.

The mirror hit the ground with a great clunk, sinking a foot into the parrot dung. Groaning and creaking, it remained standing. The frame sparked. The red lights flashed. A few of the shards winked back into existence, showing not the mountain hall, but the cave.

On the other side, the Margrave gave a terrible roar, so wild with rage his withered lips split.

Ever so slowly, the mirror frame began to tip backward, tilting the Margrave's face more and more toward the ceiling until he was lost from Lin's view.

There was a choked whine from Figenskar. Tail quivering with dread, he leaped forward in an attempt to keep the mirror from toppling.

Lin had no time to consider. Twisting around, she threw her bound legs into the air and slammed them into Figenskar's back, shoving him forward and into the mirror.

He howled and flailed, but to no avail. The sputtering portal swallowed his front paws. His hat and shoulders disappeared. His back sank into the shower of sparks. And when the whole Technocraft piece of mould thundered to the cage floor, Figenskar's howl was sliced to silence.

Glass exploded everywhere. Lin curled into a ball,

trying to hide her face with no hands to cover it. Shards rained all around her like arrows, piercing the muck, some only inches from her head. But by an incredible stroke of luck, not a single one of them hit her.

When everything grew quiet, she raised her head. The mirror lay flat on the ground. Tiny spirals of smoke still seeped out of the frame, but the red lights were gone.

Rufus had made his way down from the rope and came skipping through the broken glass, throwing himself down in the muck next to Lin.

"Little one! Are you all right?"

"Yes!" Lin said, and it was true. The relief that rushed through her was so strong it swept away both the dizziness and the metallic taste in her mouth. Rufus sniffed at her, whiskers taut with worry. "Oh, your poor ears . . ."

But Lin stared at him in wonder. "How did you get the mirror down? You threw down your knife!"

"So I did. And knives are well and good for whittling crosses and such. But you're forgetting something. Something Figenskar, too, forgot. Not only am I a Rosenquist and a Wilder. I am also a pesky Rodent!"

And with that Rufus leaned forward and gnawed through the ropes that bound Lin in the wink of an eye. As he freed her from the burlap, Lin couldn't help but laugh.

"What's that?" Rufus grinned. "One point to Rufus of

Rosenquist? Let's make it two points, for both of us. We just saved Sylver from an invasion of Nightmares."

"For now. But actually, let's make it three. Because now we have this." Lin lifted the snow globe in the air. Grimy and dirty, it shone brighter than ever, silver milk and golden white. "That is, if we can find Clariselyn in time."

Rufus turned the key in the padlock. "I sent Marvin ahead to find Teodor. And you know, this time I think he did as I told him." He pushed the door open.

Lin turned and looked back on the parrot cage. The Starfalcon cage, she corrected herself, and she ached for the great white bird that had once been trapped here. What a terrible place to lose all hope. For a moment she thought she felt a stone cold draft on her face.

But the mirror remained on the cage floor, broken, the glass spread in the muck like a red halo. In the middle of the empty frame lay something bloody and limp and striped.

Half a cat's tail.

CHAPTER THIRTY-SEVEN

T he Rosenquists raced down Observatory Hill toward the heart of the city. The streets and alleys were deserted. Nothing moved but lacquered signs that swung gently in the breeze, and the torn flap of a poster of the pretty Wanderer's Eve sky that said "See you in the Square!". In the real sky, only a thin strip of black remained between the Sylver Fang and the churning, shining Wanderer.

Pressed against the fur on Rufus's chest, Clariselyn's snow globe shone, too. He had to carry it, because Lin's feet were not to be trusted. Sometimes they barely touched the ground, other times they felt like lead, sinking through the frozen layer on the snow. The Observatory had done this to her, she knew that. Once more she had been in dire need inside its bowels, and once more, the Starfalcon's gifts had flooded her. She felt the magic chasing through her, untamed and fickle, pushing bile up into her throat.

As they scaled the final hill before the Great Square, a gigantic thunderclap broke over the city and blasted past them, deep and hard. Rufus caught Lin's arm to steady her. "There's a storm coming. We have to find her fast."

"We do," Lin answered. "But that was not thunder. Didn't you feel the tremors? I think something just exploded. Something involving massive powers."

"Oh, mould. You're right. Look."

The Great Square was packed with people. Their bodies were a black mass that concealed the ground completely, and they were not in a festive mood. The orchestras had stopped playing. The popcorn stands had been abandoned. The Sylverings stood completely still, facing toward the belfry and the great main door beneath it, as if they were listening to a speech. Except the door was closed and the steps empty.

But Rufus wasn't pointing at the ominous gathering. He was pointing at a fat, brown chimney of smoke that rose from one of the red storage barns behind the House.

The Machine Vault.

"Come on. Let's go round the back," Rufus said. "I was going to suggest it anyway. We can't risk going through that crowd."

They backed down from the hilltop unseen and slipped into the alleys of Heartworth. On the street outside the Machine Vault they found an unlikely pair: Clariselyn

Winterfyrst, leaning on the storage barn bridge, and Nit, the calculation clerk, fretting beside her. The cracks in the barn's foundation had spread several yards out from the stairwell, and dirty smoke oozed up from the entrance to the Machine Vault.

"Clariselyn!" Rufus ran toward her. "We have it! We took your snow globe back!"

But the Winterfyrst stared right through him. Her dress was smeared with soot and brown liquid, and the pallor had returned to her face. When Rufus tried to give her the globe back, she made no move to accept. "Where is Isvan?" Rufus asked. "And Teodor? Could he help?"

"You . . . You're a Twistrose!" Nit's tall forehead was all wrinkles and wonder. "A real Twistrose! No wonder you stood up for me!"

"Hello, Nit," Lin said, somehow finding a smile for the little Rodent. She was glad he had made it out of the vault.

"I think the Winterfyrst is in shock," Nit said in his high-pitched, too-soft voice. "She won't move or speak. Even when I've told her she should get away from the Thornvapour."

Lin winced at the fat smoke that gushed up under the cogwheel. "What happened down there?"

"Mrs. Zarka saw them when they arrived at the House," Nit said. "With Isvan and the broken snow globe. She saw it as an opportunity to prove her craft, to convince the House that whatever Rufus might tell them about the dangers of the Machine, it was too valuable to forbid. She felt confident she could reconstruct the globe using the shards as the base. So she sent me to the House to invite Teodor to the vault." He darted a glance at Clariselyn. "But Teodor wasn't in his chambers, and when I learned that she was Isvan's mother, I asked her instead. I hope . . . I hope I didn't do anything wrong."

"You tried to use the Machine to reconstruct Isvan's soul?" Lin said. "That machine was dangerous enough making buttons and shoes!"

"I'm sorry . . . But Mrs. Zarka insisted, and the calculations actually added up, and Clariselyn seemed most eager, so . . ."

"I had to let Mrs. Zarka try." Clariselyn's voice was no longer melodic and rich, but a hoarse whisper. She held on to the barn railing, knuckles all blue. "I am a Frostrider, ever bound, ever sworn to protect the balance of the Realms. To give my life if need be. But not the life of my child." She glanced at her snow globe as if it disgusted her. "Using Technocraft in this way would be wrong, I knew that, but . . . Not using it would be worse. I had to let her try."

"But she failed," Rufus said.

Nit cleared his throat. "I suppose the Machine was still unstable after we changed so many parts earlier. Everything started shaking and the walls were coming down. I tried to get everyone out, but Mrs. Zarka wouldn't leave the Machine . . . I . . . I should go back and find her."

"You can't." Lin shook her head. "The whole barn might collapse on your head, and that smoke . . ."

"Thornvapour," Nit repeated, wringing his hands.

"Whatever it's called, it might kill you."

Clariselyn let go of the railing. "Isvan's snow globe. Everything. Everyone. Lost."

Lin searched for words that would make the Winterfyrst feel better. But she couldn't think of any. The lines on Clariselyn's face cut into Lin's heart, too. She was supposed to save him. She was supposed to save Isvan. "I'm sorry," she whispered.

Rufus looked from one to the other, whiskers drooping. "But we still have your snow globe. And the Wanderer still shines on Sylver." He proffered Clariselyn her snow globe once more. "Here. Take it."

The Winterfyrst let her hands fall and considered the globe. They all did. The crack in the glass had lengthened until it reached from pole to pole, and a thin band of red leaked from it, tinting the light pink. The music had turned sour.

"You saw what happened when I tried to make an ice horse," Clariselyn said. "And that was a simple song, one we learn when we are very young. The Wandersnow is the most powerful and complex magic a Winterfyrst can perform. My globe is not strong enough. Not with that flaw."

Rufus tried to swish his tail, but his troll wound wouldn't let him. "Are you saying that even if we have a snow globe, and a Winterfyrst, and a wandering star in the sky, we still can't make the Wandersnow?"

"I . . ." Clariselyn fell silent. Someone was watching them from the street corner. His tweed coat had come unbuttoned and his pupils showed purple in the dark. And when he moved toward them, hunched and fast, Lin thought he no longer carried himself like an old man, but like a fox hunting in the woods, choosing his moment.

Teodor gave Lin and Rufus a look, but it was Clariselyn he greeted. "My sister of Frost. I am delighted that Sylver is no longer without a Winterfyrst. I will not ask you where you have been. We shall have time for old friendships once the Wandersnow is conjured. Will you come with me to the belfry? There is work for you." He held out his arm for her to take.

"She can't."

Teodor turned to Rufus. "I beg your pardon?"

In reply, Rufus simply held out the snow globe.

Teodor stared at the crack. "How . . . ?"

"Isvan is dead. His snow globe is destroyed," Clariselyn husked. "I laid him out in your chambers at the House."

Teodor's tail hung very limp, but he straightened his sleeves. "I will do what I can." Clariselyn searched for answers in her old friend's face, and when he offered her his arm once more, she took it. They hurried down the street, like a stately queen kindly supporting a crippled old man, though Lin knew it was the other way around. "We had better keep up," she said, taking Rufus's hand.

Nit was left alone under the cogwheel that looked so much like Mrs. Zarka's monocle. His eyes watered in the Thornvapour, and he whispered to himself, "A Twistrose."

Chapter Thirty-eight

They entered the House through one of the back entrances and passed through what seemed like an endless succession of dark offices and waiting rooms. The candles were all blown out and the lamps extinguished, and the Petlings that watched them from gold-framed portraits were painted in shadow.

"Where is everybody?" Rufus said.

"They are all gathered in the Square," Teodor replied.

"Even the House assistants? I thought for certain they would be busy trying to come up with a solution."

"I have not informed them of our predicament. And what solution could there be, except the one that walks by my side?" He regarded Clariselyn, who had withdrawn into her own thoughts and did not seem to be listening. "How did she break her snow globe? Did you find her in the Winterfyrst Well?"

They told Teodor what had happened outside the Palisade, and about the Technocraft mirror in the cage, and Figenskar and the Margrave and their evil Operation Corvelie.

"We don't know how Clariselyn and Ursa Minor got Isvan through the Palisade, but maybe the caravan sled had something to do with it." Rufus peeked out into the House courtyard. "I wonder where it is. It said it would meet us here if it could."

Teodor stopped abruptly. "Right now we have more important things to worry about," he huffed. "Take Clariselyn into my chambers. I will return shortly." And he doubled back and disappeared down a different corridor.

In the hallway outside Teodor's chambers, they found Ursa Minor, standing guard. He had a nasty gash across his chest, and one of his ears had been mangled.

"Minor!" Lin hugged him, taking care not to come near his injuries. "I'm so glad you made it!"

The great bear's eyes shone. "It was easier when the caravan sled arrived, but we would have fought our way through anyway, wouldn't we, my lady? Didn't you say so? That we fought like Frostriders?"

Clariselyn didn't acknowledge him, and Minor shook his head sadly. "Maybe she should sit and rest?"

They helped Clariselyn into the chief chronicler's office, a large study populated by books and quills and maps weighed down by magnifying stones. Wax candles waited cold in great chandeliers, and the ashes in the fire-place were dead.

But from the innermost chamber spilled a white glow, from snowflakes that danced under the ceiling with a light of their own, always tumbling, never settling, like in the glacial cathedral.

The room was furnished only by a narrow bunk and a small nightstand. But the bed had been encased in twisting layers of ice, and on top of this silver nest lay Isvan. His face was covered in a thin glaze that reflected the snowshine, and his arms were crossed on his chest, stitched with frost.

Clariselyn stood at his feet. "Leave us."

"Here's your snow globe." Rufus held it gently against the Winterfyrst's belly, and to their relief she took it. "Minor is right. You should sit and rest," he said. "The crack will only get worse if you . . ."

Clariselyn sighed, and the very sound of it coated the walls in a fresh layer of rime. Lin and Rufus found it best to retreat into the study.

The candles in the chandeliers blazed up, and the fire sprang to life. Teodor came in, carrying a steaming cup that clattered and spilled with every hurried step. He walked right past Lin and Rufus, into the makeshift tomb. The door was frozen stuck, and so the old fox could not shut Lin and Rufus out. But he spoke softly, and Lin couldn't decipher his words, not until desperation leaked into his voice.

"But you know what will follow if the Wandergate does not open! The falling Palisade and the failing pact. The slow winding down. The creeping sluggishness. Until every speck of magic is spent and gone and Sylver is no more!"

"My strength is broken," Clariselyn replied. "I cannot perform the simplest of tricks, let alone make the Wandersnow. And even if by some wondrous stroke of Luck I do succeed, my soul would shatter in the process, and the Winterfyrsts would be no more. In ninety-four years, when the Wanderer next appears, the world would still end."

A heavy silence filled the room, broken only by crackles from the hearth. Lin held her breath. Finally Teodor spoke. "Ever bound, ever sworn. But only you can make this decision."

The old fox came out of the bedchamber, still carrying the cup which now contained frozen tea. He shuffled over to the nearest desk, unwrapped his rune quill, and sat down to carve a melt rune into the milky lump of ice. Rufus leaned over the table. His entire fur stood on end. "You're not even going to *try* and heal Isvan?"

Teodor didn't look up. "No healing rune can bring someone back from the dead."

"Then what did you mean 'Sylver is no more' and 'The world would still end'?"

"Ah," Teodor said, cocking his head as he drew the three tongues of flame. "I suppose I might as well tell you why the Wandergate must open. It makes no difference anymore." He began to fill the leaping tongues with letters. "That storm of wild joy from the Wandersnow is the stuff – the material – our world is made from. Over the years, the thoughts and dreams and games of all the children of Earth continue to shape the Realms. But without the raw material of the Wandersnow joy, Sylver and all the rest of this world will slowly but surely die. Ponderous magic like the Palisade of Thorns will be the first to crumble."

Rufus slammed his fists into the desk. The teacup rattled. "Why the *rats* have you not told us this before?"

Teodor finally raised his muzzle, and his golden eyes were murky. "Would you have done things differently if you knew, Rufocanus? Would you have tried harder to save Isvan or Clariselyn? Or would you have faltered, lamed by the possible consequences of your actions? No. It was better that you did your best, unfettered by fear." He put down the diamond talon quill. "A pity you failed."

"That," Rufus said, and he was shaking now, "is not fair. Lin and I have done everything you asked of us. We found Isvan. We even found Clariselyn. We uncovered a traitor in our midst, and we stopped an invasion of trolls into the heart of Sylver. And you're saying we're failures? That we've done nothing good?"

"Don't be silly. I *expect* the good. If you were not half acceptable half of the time, do you think I would have chosen you?"

"Chosen me?" Rufus stomped his foot. "Chosen me for what? Your chopping block?"

"No, you twice-chewed idiot. My apprentice in the Brotherhood of Frost and Flame."

For a long moment, Rufus stared at Teodor. "Me. Your apprentice. To be a Flamewatcher."

Teodor sighed, wrapping his rune pen in its leather. "Perhaps you have figured out by now that you are a Wilder as well as a Petling. Therefore, you ought to have the potential of both, bravery and true instincts as well as diligence and finger skills. Doctor Kott has pestered me about your talents from the day you arrived, and now you have gone and charmed a caravan sled into supporting you. I find myself outnumbered."

"Oh." For once Rufus couldn't seem to come up with a clever retort.

"And tonight, you have even proved you are ready to give your life for others. Though how you would ever muster the patience and skill to draw a rune, the Flame only knows."

"No need to worry about that!" Lin brought out Rufus's map and unrolled it beside the teacup. "Rufus drew all of this, including the legends."

The old fox frowned at the "Comprehensive Chart of Sylveros and All Its Lands." "It's not half bad." He pushed the teacup to the side. "But it does not matter now. The Wandergate will not open. Sylver's guard runes are all destroyed. There's an army of Nightmares in the White-pass, and the Palisade will wither this night. Rufus won't have time for the simplest of carving lessons before our world falls to pieces." He lowered his voice. "Unless you two have some Twistrose miracle up your sleeve."

The great bells in the belfry tolled, twelve heavy strikes that boomed through the House, set the inkwells on the desk to tinkling, and curled around Lin's spine.

Midnight.

Outside on the Great Square, a groan rose from the crowd. Lin peered out behind the curtains. She couldn't see much, but she heard angry shouts and breaking glass. In the sky, the Sylver Fang obscured nearly half of the Wanderer. In nine more minutes, it would be gone. She drew a deep breath and turned back to the others. She had no idea what she was going to say or do.

Do not fail.

The door to the chamber flew up, and a small Petling came stumbling through, coughing hard.

"Nit!" Lin cried. "Are you okay?"

"Yes, I . . ." A racking bout of coughing shook the mouse, making him double over. "Sorry. I . . . The Thornvapour . . ."

Lin sat him down on a chair and patted his back.

"You have been to the vault?" Clariselyn had emerged from the chamber of ice, and her voice wavered.

Nit smiled radiantly at Lin. "Yes . . . I wanted to be worthy of your help . . . I wanted to be worthy of the

Twistrose!" His smile slipped and he coughed some more. "I heard what you said about Isvan's globe, and I wanted to bring the shards out. The Thornvapour let up a little, so I went down there. Mrs. Zarka is . . ." He shook his head. "I couldn't help her. I couldn't get the hatches open either, and there was a switch that seemed to be jammed, and the Machine woke up, and . . ." He lifted his arms in a feeble gesture that might mean "huge". "And afterward, I found this."

He straightened out to reveal a small ball of glass in his hands. "I'm afraid it didn't come out right."

Isvan's snow globe lay whole and perfect in Nit's hand. But instead of silver milk and golden white, it was filled with something dark. Something that sloshed and lapped when the mouse's hand trembled, not brown like Thorn-drip, but deep crimson of colour.

"It's *blood*!" Lin said.

Nit yelped and shoved the globe into her hands so quickly it was more a toss.

Lin caught it. It felt cool and heavy against her skin. The blood left muddy, weeping marks on the inside of the glass. Was that . . . Did she just feel something move in there?

She felt their eyes on her, Teodor's golden and Clarise-lyn's sapphire and Rufus's black.

Start with what you know.

She knew the Observatory gifts gave her power to

ignite magic. And she knew the gifts worked. Strength and Comfort, Courage and Luck, and Hope. All the things that Isvan had needed so badly for his journey, and even more for those long, lonely hours in the windowsill of the Hall of Winter. She only had to give it to him.

Lin closed her eyes.

Suddenly a rush of electricity made her back arch. Her ears throbbed and her palms glowed as the Observatory magic rushed out of her in one wild torrent. Isvan's globe grew hotter and hotter, until it burned her fingers.

Finally someone pried it out of her hands. Lin took a long, gasping breath, the first since she caught the snow globe. A lovely calm flooded her limbs.

Rufus caught her as she sank to the floor, and his grey face was the first thing she saw when she blinked away the tears. The second was Clariselyn, staring into the globe of blood. The third made Lin lift her chin.

On the threshold to the chamber a boy stood shivering. His hair was tangled with rime and broken icicles, and Lin recognised the small tug at the corner of his lips that told of a whistlewind coming. But his eyes were no longer sapphires. They were brown, like peppernuts. Like Lin's.

He opened his mouth.

"Mother. I'm cold."

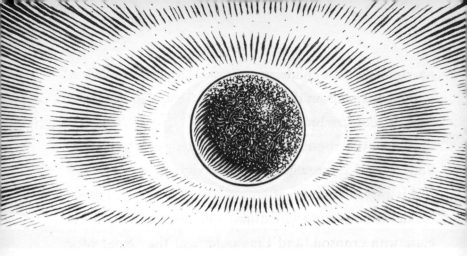

CHAPTER THIRTY-NINE

Clariselyn placed the globe of blood gently in Isvan's hands. With a sigh, she fell down on her knees before him, wrapping him in her arms. Isvan smiled, and for the first time he resembled the boy in the photo in the Hall of Winter. But as they hugged, Isvan's skin grew pale and paler, and then blue.

"I'm cold," he said again. His teeth were rattling. Clariselyn released him. She rose, nodding slowly to herself, and took a step back.

"I heard your dream, Mother. I tried to find you."

"I know. All will be well."

"No, it won't." Isvan frowned at his mother. She handled her snow globe carefully, stiffly, like a wounded limb. "You're hurt."

Clariselyn smiled the sort of brittle smile parents put

on, thinking their children won't see through it. "We don't have to worry about that. Let's get you warm instead. Perhaps Teodor can bring you some tea."

Across the room, Teodor flinched into action, shuffling toward Isvan with the clattering cup in its saucer. But Isvan paid him no attention. He raised his red globe. Inside it the blood swirled momentarily, covering all the glass with crimson, and Lin could hear the sound of it. Not music. Not words. A heart.

A flexing heart that made Lin's own skip a beat. And the crack in Clariselyn's globe paled and closed, until it showed as the thinnest of scars. The Winterfyrst music rang pure once more.

Clariselyn gasped, reaching out to steady herself, and Teodor was there to catch her. "You're healed!" the old fox said. "He healed you! But how? Could it . . ."

His golden eyes darted around the room and found the timid Rodent hovering by the door. "Nit," he said. "Am I right that Mrs. Zarka put the shards of Isvan's snow globe into the Machine without cleaning them first?"

Nit's tall forehead wrinkled. "Yes, Mr. Teodor. I believe she did. They were a little smudged, but she felt time was of the essence . . ."

Teodor threw his head back and barked a laugh. "What a fool I have been! I thought Lin must be the clumsiest Twistrose in history with all the cuts she managed to inflict upon herself." He stroked his cheek fur, still chuckling. "We should be grateful that you at last received a wound I was not around to patch up."

"I don't understand," Lin said.

"The shards were smudged because *you* cut your finger on them." He pointed a bent claw toward Isvan's new globe. "Lindelin Rosenquist, that soul is made from your blood. A machine could never create life. But the blood of a child . . ."

". . . can make a lord," Lin finished breathlessly.

Gold doesn't always mean gold.

At last, the prophecy of "The Margrave's Song" had drifted into place, but they had all got it wrong.

The Blood Lord had awakened. But he wasn't the Margrave. He was the Child of Ice.

Isvan's gaze shifted from Teodor to Lin and back. He looked ready to flee.

"Don't be scared," Teodor said quickly, realising his mistake. "Your mother is right, all will be well. We will help you. And please forgive me, dear boy. I should have realised you shut me out because you were afraid. I swear it was a misunderstanding. I never asked Mrs. Zarka to make that abominable Brain Tapper."

The rune in the frozen lump of tea flared up. "You look terribly cold," the old fox said. "Won't you have some tea?"

Isvan let a soft breath out through his lips, but it no

longer sounded like the wind. With shivering hands, he accepted the now steaming cup and drank a long sip. "Thank you."

Teodor smiled like someone who feels the first warmth of spring. "A good cup of tea cures every ailment, particularly if there's milk in it. Or so we used to say where I come from."

Silently and straight-backed, Clariselyn watched her son, the Blood Lord, drink his tea. But when Isvan's cheeks began to heat and his hands stopped trembling, her shoulders sank and tiny ice pearls dropped down her face.

A different scene in a different place came unbidden to Lin's thoughts: Anne Rosenquist, standing with her back turned on the threshold of Lin's attic room. She was wearing her checkered dressing gown, the one she put on for cosy mornings of waffles and milk tea, and she held a breakfast tray. But her hands clenched white around the handles of the tray. That, Lin knew, was what her mother would look like if Lin was not in her bed by morning.

When she turned, she found that Rufus was watching her. His tail hung all heavy and his eyes were ink. Lin tried to smile, to think of something to say, but Rufus took a deep breath and opened one of the pockets in his scarf. Nestled inside it was an old, blackened key, as large as his hand and fashioned in the shape of a rose. The Twistrose Key.

"You have the key?" Teodor's growl looked more like a grin. "You never lost it at all, did you?"

But Rufus kept his gaze on Lin. "I wasn't going to keep it. I just wanted to make sure no one could force you to leave against your wishes. The gate won't let you through without it." He put the key gently in the palm of Lin's hand. "Clariselyn," he said, "if you don't mind making that Wandersnow, I think Lin would like to go home now."

CHAPTER FORTY

In the great reception hall under the belfry, Isvan sat wrapped in blankets by the fire. Lin crossed the marble floor and cleared her throat. "They said I had a minute. I just wanted to say good-bye."

He looked up at her with his peppernut eyes. "I wish you didn't have to leave so soon. I always dreamed of a sister. Of you, actually."

"You're not coming outside?"

Isvan shook his head. "I wanted to see everything from the belfry, but Mother and Teodor need me to gather my strength." He stretched his hands toward the leaping flames. "I never knew a fire could be so soothing."

The red glass globe flickered in his lap, and Lin couldn't help but wonder. What could it do? Was it even safe?

"Teodor wants me to help make a new guard rune for Sylver," Isvan said. "He thinks we won't need more than one. He thinks my magic is as strong as a Starfalcon's now."

"That's good," Lin said, trying to make her voice light. "Nightmares wouldn't do well in mead houses and shops. Does it feel very different? Your snow globe?"

"It's not a snow globe anymore." Isvan's fingers twitched against the glass. "I'm not sure what to call it. Red globe? Blood globe?"

"How about heart globe?" Lin said. "Sounds less . . . grisly."

He nodded. "And yes. It does feel different." He drew a shaky breath, and laughed it off. "Wild."

A strand of music came drifting down from the belfry. As soon as Clariselyn's song began in earnest, Lin would need to be in position. "I have to go now," she said. "I'm sorry we broke your globe. I'm sorry you can't be near your mother or live in the Hall of Winter."

He smiled at that, his crooked tug that Lin already liked so much. "For as long as I can remember, my mother has been trapped in the farthest corner of my dreams. What's a yard or two compared to that? And I won't miss that house. I just need my drawings and my telescope."

"The thing about telescopes," Lin said. "They only show things that are far away."

"True." Isvan's brown eyes glinted. "But you don't have to worry. I can't wait to try Pomeroy's waffles warm. Besides, the same can be said about maps."

Lin laughed. "True."

On the Great Square outside, a sigh swept the crowd. Clariselyn must be ready. Lin put her hand forward. "I really wish you could come troll hunting someday."

Isvan shook her hand solemnly, and his skin felt warm and dry. "Who says I won't?"

Lin waited at the edge of the Great Square, at the bottom of the first hill, as she had been instructed. Rufus was off doing some important errand for his new teacher, but he would meet her here. Lin craned her neck to find him in the crowd, but all she saw was silhouetted ears and hats and restless shuffling. The eerie silence had broken, and she heard laughter and talk and even the band had begun to play again. All that remained of the Wanderer was the edge of its iridescent disc and the wavering tail of white and green. Under the arches of the belfry danced Clariselyn Winterfyrst, and the clock below showed five minutes past midnight.

Rufus had wanted to bring Lin out on the House steps so the Sylverings could meet her and know what she had done for them tonight. But Teodor had told them there was no time for speeches and explanations and the usual feast in her name. Lin would have to leave as quietly as she had arrived.

"Do not worry, Twistrose," a voice said. Lin whipped around to see Teodor stepping from the shadows of the pavilion with a white bundle in his arms. His eyes shifted from mirrors to gold as he took up position next to her, gazing out over the Square. "You will not be forgotten."

"I'm not worried," Lin said, annoyed that he had caught her by surprise again. But at least she would be able to ask him something that had bothered her since his reappearance. "Teodor, why *did* you leave us at the Palisade?"

"I guessed the identity of the Margrave. And though I failed to find the guard rune in the end, I judged my strength would be better spent defending it." Teodor straightened his sleeves. "It was *Corvelie*, you see. Few outside the Brotherhood know her by that name. The legend calls her the burning bird. But she was once the Wilder of a Twistrose."

"Edvard Uriarte," Lin said. "The boy with the crow at his feet. You knew he had a way to get past the Palisade?"

"I knew he could control Nightmares. For his task all those years ago, young master Uriarte stopped a brood of red sleepwalkers that kept attacking caravans. He made them obey him. It seems he has enhanced that skill since 1919. And I knew that without the guard rune, Nightmares led by a clever, bitter mind would find their way into Sylver one way or another."

The dial on the belfry clock jerked. Six minutes past the hour. "How did he turn into the Margrave?" Lin asked. "Why is he bitter?"

"Not all Twistrose stories are of the pretty sort. On Earth, Edvard Uriarte's family were all gone, dead in a flu epidemic. He lived on the streets, he starved. So when the time came for him to go back through the Wandergate, he did not want to."

"Oh." Lin's voice came out very small. Her own hardships in Oldtown didn't sound quite so bad all of a sudden.

"In those days, the Sylver Flamewatcher was a peacock who enjoyed a good spectacle. She had made a set of rune-carved wings and a beak for Edvard, so he could fly up to the Wandergate looking like a Starfalcon. But instead Corvelie powdered her wings and painted her beak silver, and she took his place in the ceremony. Perhaps they figured the gate wouldn't work for her, that she could go through unharmed, as if it were any stretch of sky, shake the powder from her wings, and slip away. It was a daring plan, and it might have worked, except for one thing. Only two can pass through the gate, the Twistrose and the Key. Everything else *burns*."

Lin swallowed. "She caught fire?"

"She died before she hit the ground. Edvard tried to hide, but he was seized before the Wanderer set and sent home. Or so the records say. It appears they were wrong." He sighed. "The Brotherhood decided the truth would be too cruel for the Sylverings, and tried to keep the fate of Edvard and Corvelie out of the mead houses. But their story has, as stories will, found a way to trickle through. It became a scary tale. A legend of horror."

"But what about Edvard's statue? Why don't people wonder about it?"

"They do not see it." Teodor smiled sadly. "Like you, Edvard Uriarte was here in secret. He had completed his task, and the Brotherhood felt he could not be denied a statue. But they placed it in the shadows and carved it with a cloak rune. It is visible now only to the Brotherhood, and in rare cases, others with very powerful magical otopathy. We let it stand so the horror will not be forgotten by those who are tasked to remember."

"I understand why he wanted to stay. Rufus and I . . ." Lin corrected herself. She didn't want to get Rufus in trouble. "*I* wanted to stay, too."

"Of course you did. All Twistroses do, at first, when they are drunk on the joy of reunion. But you all change your mind in the end."

"At least there is the Memory balcony," Lin said. "I feel a little better knowing that Rufus will be watching me."

"So Rufus didn't tell you. Well. For that I cannot say I blame him." Teodor shook his head in pity. "The Observatory allows us to see our human children, but only for a time. One day, their index cards stop working. The projector simply cannot read them anymore. And from that moment our children are lost to us for good."

"You mean because they died?"

"No. Because they aren't children anymore."

Lin lifted her hands to her mouth. What did Sofie say? *One moment, everything is as it used to be, and the next . . .* She must have known her girl was about to change. And Rufus . . . No. Lin refused to cry in front of Teodor.

"It is the way of things," Teodor said, not unkindly. "In time, Rufocanus will be just fine, too." He shoved the white bundle into Lin's arms. "You must put these on. Since you were wearing them when you crossed the threshold, they will make it through the gate."

It was her pyjamas, dry and mended. Reluctantly, Lin shed the chaperon, the tunic, and the warm trousers, and put the pyjamas on. "Where will the gate open?"

"In the sky. You won't have a pair of rune-carved wings, but you will have someone to take you."

Teodor pointed: a drifting commotion in the crowd. Rufus. The vole was making his way toward them, and the Sylverings parted wide around him. From the way he struggled, Lin could tell he hauled something big with him across the Square, and then she caught a glimpse of cast-iron spirals. "The caravan sled."

"Just so," Teodor said. "It is a noble creature. When I explained the situation, it volunteered. And who knows? It might be fast enough to turn aside at just the right moment."

"What if it isn't?" Lin pulled her cardigan tight. "It has a spare part that hampers it. I can't let it risk itself like that!"

"You cannot stay here. I would think the case of Edvard Uriarte illustrates the point perfectly." Teodor cleared his throat. "You must return to your own world. The caravan sled knows. It is allowed this choice."

Rufus cleared the throng and came toward them, limping heavily. He tugged the sled to a stop, looped the reins neatly, and placed them on the seat. "For you."

A murmur washed over the Square. A white light had appeared under the arches of the belfry. Clariselyn Winterfyrst's dress billowed over the edge, and her snow globe shone in her hands. The clock showed seven past twelve.

"It has begun," Teodor said. "And in time, I do believe. Farewell, Lindelin Rosenquist." With a smug expression, he buttoned his tweed coat. But right before he left, as if it were an afterthought and mattered not at all, he added, "And Twistrose? If you ever meet a boy – or rather, a very old man – by the name of Balthasar Lucke, you could perhaps do me the favour of giving him my regards."

He walked away, stiff-legged and hunched, and the last Lin saw before the crowd swallowed him was the white tip of his fox's tail. She turned to Rufus. "Watch your back with that one."

Rufus snorted. "Finally you're beginning to talk sense. But don't worry. If all else fails, I can always steal his keys." He moved aside so Lin could climb onto the sled. "You should get ready."

"No." Lin struggled with the lump in her throat. "I don't want to."

"Yes," Rufus said. "You do."

She flung her arms around him and hugged him tight. He patted her back. "You know they're already discussing who gets to make your statue?"

Lin stepped back, blinking through her tears. "But I thought we agreed not to . . ."

"Marvin and Nit are spreading the word to any and all who will listen. You'll be a huge hit at the Burning Bird tonight." Rufus smiled. "I refuse to bring you flowers, though. Maybe some peppernuts or something, if I see in the Memory mirror that you've caught a troll."

He bent down to straighten the already perfect coil of roins.

"Oh, Rufus." Lin couldn't stop a single, lost sob. "I know about the index card. It will go blank soon. Were you going to send me off without telling me?"

When Rufus lifted his head, the fur on his face was slicked down. "I didn't want you to feel this sad, that's all."

"What if I just didn't change," Lin said, burying her fingers in his fur. "We can arrange a time. I can't hear you, but I can tell you things. Who knows, when you're a Flamewatcher, maybe you'll find a way to reach me back."

Rufus didn't answer, but he leaned against her hand.

"Please," Lin whispered. "I can't bear to say good-bye. Not for good."

He made that strange sound in the back of his throat, and as he hugged her again, he held on to her cardigan as if it could keep her there. "All right. Saturdays at seven."

"Good-bye, Rufocanus, Petling and Wilder of great talent."

"Good-bye, Lindelin, quizzy face and hero of your own song."

The sled turned its runners and began crawling up the slope. Lin held the Twistrose Key in one hand, carefully so the thorns didn't pierce her skin. With the other hand, she gripped the reins so hard her knuckles hurt. Every moment, she wanted to jump off and run back down the hill. Once, she turned and called, "I won't change! I promise!"

In the belfry, Clariselyn still sang, a whole choir of voices that swept from harmony to discord and back. Light spilled out through the seams of her dress and her mouth and fingertips. The Winterfyrst shook her snow globe lightly, and Lin found herself wondering where the snowstorm would begin. She had forgotten to ask.

Behind the Sylver Fang, the heavens kindled as the sliver of star flared up and its halo swirled faster. A single ray of light shot out from the Wanderer and struck the dome of the Observatory, which lit up in gold. Fine strands of silver and blue and green peeled off the beam, snowing down on the upturned faces of the Sylverings, winking out before they hit the ground, like fireworks.

The clock showed nine minutes past twelve, and the Twistrose Key thrummed against Lin's skin. She kicked off her boots and pulled at the reins to the caravan sled. "It's time," she whispered.

The cast-iron runners curled into spirals. Images flashed through her, cobalt mountains and black loam and dark faces, and seasons and years that grew and withered until they were a blurred stream, and Lin didn't think the sled was afraid. "Thank you," she said, patting the burnished wood. "And if you do make it back, take care of Rufus for me. He likes adventures best of all."

They raced down the hill, and before they reached the solitary figure at the bottom, the ground dropped away beneath them.

Rufus watched the sled grow smaller and smaller until it was only a speck in the sky. Already the beam was narrowing, thinning out as the Wanderer was lost from sight. As the light winked out, and the black of night filled in, he said softly, "Everyone changes sooner or later. Even you, my little one."

CHAPTER FORTY-ONE

When she woke, Lin Rosenquist heard a voice whisper in her ear, and at first she thought it was telling her secrets that she absolutely must not pass on.

But then she opened her eyes and saw the floorboards under her cheek and the ashen light that seeped up through the cracks, and she knew it was the river brushing past the poles beneath Mrs. Ichalar's house. Dawn had broken.

She stood up. In her hand she held not a key, but a twig of rosebush with three sharp, curved thorns. The rose roots still trailed down the back wall, but they seemed more frail now, brown and dry, and though Lin stepped close and whispered *"Rosa torquata"*, the roots did not stir and the twig did not change. The wall had mended, and of the cracks and the strange keyhole and the unnatural frost, there was no sign.

She lifted her finger. There was a puncture wound where the Twistrose Key had pricked her yesterday, but all the other cuts that she had suffered had left no mark on her skin. Shivering, she pulled her cardigan close.

The taxidermied animals looked weary in the milky dredges of the night. At the banister, she ran her fingers along the sleek line of the animal skull with its yellowed teeth and tilted sockets. She thought she knew it for a fox now.

The cellar key dangled from the hole where she had left it, and the wind still poked restlessly at the mail slot. Lin slipped up the stairs, treading lightly on the icy steps and skipping the ones that creaked.

On the attic landing waited a bowl of rice pudding and raspberry sauce. She wolfed it down before she opened the door to her room.

Someone had been in there, because the curtains, Grandma Alma's old cotton ones from Morello House, were drawn against the morning. She could see no sign of panic, though, no emptied-out drawers or riffled-through papers on her desk. No one had touched the closet, and her map of Oldtown lay undisturbed in the windowsill. Instead her bed was made with fresh sheets.

She pulled off her cardigan, hung it on her bedpost,

and crawled under the thick down comforter, not sure if she should be relieved or disappointed that they hadn't worried about her. As she sank back into her pillow, sleep was already blunting her thoughts. Frozen woods and dagger thorns and wandering stars faded into silver around a familiar silhouette. He was standing with his back turned and whiskers spread wide, tall and fierce with bristling neck fur she knew to be soft underneath, and he was waiting.

And though rain drummed on her windowpane, her dreams were all of snow.

She didn't wake until the tray clacked onto her desk and the smell of fresh sweet buns filled the room. From the glare behind the curtains, she could tell that it was late.

"I thought no school today," her mother said. She was standing at the window, peering out. "You seemed so tired yesterday, and I didn't want you to catch a cold."

Lin sat up, frowning at the sweet buns and the large cup of tea. She had been wrong. They had worried, and quite a lot, too. Not sure if she was in trouble, she said, "What's going on outside?"

"Come see."

Lin slipped out of bed, pulled aside the curtains, and found Oldtown quite transformed. Snow rested lightly on the steep roofs and crooked windowsills, tucking in the tired cobblestones and covering the gutters, and the river bridge was decked out for a winter ball with white cones on its red pillars.

Harald Rosenquist had slept in, too, it seemed. He stood in the middle of the street, wearing Anne's dressing gown over his pyjamas and slippers, facing the grey, woolly sky. Spiralling snowflakes landed on his glasses.

Lin laughed. "I bet he'll be poring over his meteorological books all day."

"I bet you're right," her mother said, laughing, too. "Well, come downstairs when you're done. I thought we might call the Summerhills and ask if Niklas wants to visit."

Lin stared at her. That was the most wonderful thing she had heard in a long time, at least in this world. Her mother put the plate and cup on the nightstand, gathered up the tray, and made to leave.

"Mum?"

Anne Rosenquist turned on the threshold. "Yes?"

"Thanks. For the sweet buns. They're my favourite."

"You're welcome." Her mother smiled as she closed the door. It was a little moment before she started down the stairs.

Lin opened the window, letting in the crisp air. The rosebush slept under a snowy veil, and the whittled cross was dressed in frost, and she thought they seemed peaceful. Taking a bite out of the still-warm sweet bun, she picked her cardigan off the bedpost and pulled it on. If her father could greet the first snow in his pyjamas, then so could she.

Out of old, sweet habit, Lin stuck her hand in her left pocket, and that's when she found it.

"Oh, very clever," she whispered. "One point to Rufus of Rosenquist."

In her palm, she held her cardigan drawstring, still damp from the snow, still tied into a twice-bound knot. The troll-hunter signal for "I am here".

Lin tucked it back into her pocket, smiling to herself. Whatever happened she would not be alone.

THE·MARGRAVE'S·SONG

The Mar-grave wan-dered in woods win-ter-wild.

Stole through a gate for the heart of a child.

The boy gave to them his heart to de-vo-ur.

A Win-ter Prince lost in the Wan-de-rer's ho-ur.

Ro-ses will wilt as the eve grows old.

Si-lenced and caught in the se-cret cold.

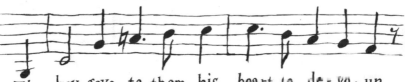

ACKNOWLEDGEMENTS

My deepest thanks are owed:

To my sister, Line Almhjell, for whom I glued the very first version of *The Twistrose Key* into a scrapbook, one page a day. You truly are the hero of this song, *søsterfnugg*.

To my brother, Eivind Almhjell, who wrote the music for "The Margrave's Song", and who frowned at and whooped over draft upon draft upon draft.

To my husband and love, Peter Brown, who kept me flying beyond reason and without coin, all the way to the second star.

To my agent, Jane Putch, for the incredible things you have done for me, and for taking a chance on someone on the other side of the world.

To Lauri Hornik and *everyone* at Dial who helped make *The Twistrose Key* real and so very beautiful. I am truly honoured to work with you.

To my editor, Jennifer Hunt, for teaching me how to make my story shine.

To Ian Schoenherr for the exquisite maps and illustrations.

To Laini Taylor, for everything. The pockets are yours, forever.

To Thomas Ingebrigtsen, who somehow sensed this book's potential and with usual impatience and flair pushed me headlong out into the world.

To Kristian Johnsen, André Wallin Sagvolden, Jonny Berg, Kjeld Helland-Hansen, Shanti Gylseth, and Jim DiBartolo, for all your enthusiasm, inspiration, and help. And to Michael Benskin, for always expecting the good.

To Heidi Reinholdt and Ina Vassbotten Steinman, for invaluable linguistic and moral support.

To my mother, Unni, for the ocean. To my late father, Harald, for the mountains and the elm tree. And to both, for the love.

To my sweet kids, Magnus and Martine, for the sticky kisses, and for being.

To all regulars and visitors at Moonglen Manor over the years, for the cheese stews and stories.

And last, but with so much love: To Maika, Mario, Lass, Claus, Josef, Gwen, Pillerill, Puskas, Pims, Balthasar, and all my other little ones. I will see you in the Square.